To Mom, with Love

Daria put down her brush and settled herself under her covers. couldn't anything in her life be easy? Plenty of women went on without their sons immediately pressing them for a new father. been mistaken in thinking she alone could be enough to s Nicholas's parental needs. But did her son have to pin his hopes o one man Daria could never give him?

And worse yet, why was she cursed with the desire to be with hi find out where things with them might lead if left to follow their course? She'd known from the beginning this date would lead to ter. Why hadn't she stuck to her guns and turned down Alonzo and his mystery date?

Tears formed at the corners of her eyes. She tried to blink them but it didn't help. She buried her face in her pillow and let the tea A good cry could sometimes clear the mind and cleanse the psyche

Oh hell. There wasn't any point to trying to rationalize her emd She hurt, ached somewhere way down deep, somewhere prim unchecked by logic. Somewhere where she feared she would ne less alone than she was at this moment, and it terrified her right d her bones.

To Mom, *with* Love

DEIRDRE SAVOY
JACQUELIN THOMAS
KAREN WHITE-OWENS

BET Publications, LLC
http://www.bet.com
http://www.arabesquebooks.com

ARABESQUE BOOKS are published by

BET Publications, LLC
c/o BET BOOKS
One BET Plaza
1900 W Place NE
Washington, DC 20018-1211

All Kensington Titles, Imprints, and Distributed Lines are available at special quantity discounts for bulk purchases for sales promotions, premiums, fund-raising, and educational or institutional use. Special book excerpts or customized printings can also be created to fit specific needs. For details, write or phone the office of the Kensington special sales manager: Kensington Publishing Corp., 850 Third Avenue, New York, NY 10022, attn: Special Sales Department, Phone: 1-800-221-2647.

ISBN: 1-58314-389-0

First Printing: April 2003
10   9   8   7   6   5   4   3   2   1

Printed in the United States of America

Contents

Fairy Godfather

Deirdre Savoy

Prologue

Alonzo Clark leaned back in his chair as Van Morrisson's "Moondance" began to play. Humming along to the music, grateful his listeners couldn't hear him, he crossed his arms behind his head. Life was good. He'd just signed another contract that would guarantee another two years of life for the *Alonzo Clark Morning Show* and a significant raise for himself, as well as more input into the show's format. Being the top on-air personality at WLIS had its privileges. Three years ago when he'd come to WLIS it had been an obscure easy-listening station. Now it ranked number four in the New York market, a near impossible transformation.

Taking credit for that transformation was no act of arrogance on Alonzo's part. Listeners had flocked to his brand of talk and music mixed with celebrity interviews made popular late nights on another station. The show had gone into syndication two years ago and now reached every major market in the nation. Now there were talks about a television show, which didn't interest him, and a book deal that did. But whether he wrote one word or not, life as he knew it was rosy.

A movement detected from the corner of his eye drew his attention—his morning show partner Vanessa Rios reentering the control room. The one thorn in his otherwise perfect bouquet, Vanessa had disappeared about twenty minutes ago to God only knew where. She'd probably returned now only because the show was over. The next crew might notice her missing in action. For some reason she believed they would report her to the powers that be but he wouldn't. She was mistaken.

She slid into her seat beside him in the small room. "What's happening, hot stuff? or should I say, *'Que pasa, Papi Chulo?'*"

If he had a choice, he'd have picked neither. He didn't know what Vanessa's problem was, but he was content to let her keep it to herself. In the four months she'd worked at the station, she'd joked she was hired as the token Latina. Yet he suspected if she worked at a station that played all salsa all the time, she'd find a way to be the token Latina, the token whatever, as long as the word *token* implied someone whose special circumstances explained why she couldn't do her damn job like everyone else. If she didn't watch it, she'd be the token fired Latina, and he wouldn't be sorry to see her go.

He ignored her comment, the first part of it being a line from an old movie she liked to repeat. He'd already cued up his "traveling music," a farewell song he played at the end of the show every morning, a technique he'd learned listening to Frankie Crocker on WBLS as a teenager. Crocker had his "There I Go." Alonzo preferred Satchmo's "What a Wonderful World."

He'd never explained his penchant for the song publicly, though he'd been asked on many occasions. He'd first heard the song at his mother's knee and appreciated its message of taking pleasure in the simple things in life. As the song began to play, he leaned forward and pressed the button that allowed his voice to reach his listeners. "That's it for me today," he said in his famous made-for-radio baritone voice. "Thanks for sharing your morning with me. Let's do it again tomorrow."

He released the button, leaned back in his chair, and pulled off his headphones. Not his most inspired bit of dialogue, but it did the job. He dropped the headphones to the desk and rose to stretch his back. Vanessa remained seated, but he felt her gaze on him. When he turned to leave she maneuvered her chair to block his exit.

"Where are you off to in such a hurry?"

"Meeting with the promotion department. Something about a contest for Mother's Day."

"Oh."

He heard the disappointment in her voice mixed with a touch of indignation at not being included. As much as he hated these meetings he'd gladly change places with her. Except the show bore his name and since listeners assumed he made every decision concerning the show he wanted to make sure they came up with something he could live with. He stepped around Vanessa.

"Wait up. I wanted to ask you something."

Sighing, Alonzo paused. He was tired and hungry and he wanted to go home. Unfortunately, neither the nap nor the meal he wanted would be forthcoming any time soon, nor did he have much patience for Vanessa's machinations.

Still, he turned to face her, mimicking her crossed-arm posture. "What can I do for you?"

"The NAC dinner is coming up in a few weeks. Are you going?"

Alonzo's eyebrows lifted. Only if someone hog-tied him and knocked him over the head. The National Arts Council dinner was an excuse to act stupid masquerading as a charity event. Between courses, the revelers could be counted on to indulge in the kind of antics that guaranteed them a spot on *Entertainment Tonight* or Page Six of the *New York Post*. "Why?"

"I already paid for my tickets. I wouldn't mind sharing one."

But he'd have a hard time accepting one. He knew Vanessa had no interest in him as a man or even a friend. She saw him as a means to advance her own career: success by association. Being seen with her off company time would appear to be an endorsement of her, or at the very least it might generate speculation about what, other than broadcasting, went on in the control booth of WLIS.

"Maybe some other time." Like if he had a prefrontal lobotomy. "Gotta go."

He let himself out the door as the next crew came in for the 10:00-to-2:00-P.M. slot. Let them deal with her.

Shaking his head, he headed down the hallway toward the receptionist's desk, the outer office door, and eventually to the candy machine by the elevator. The promotion meeting would start in less than fifteen minutes, which wouldn't even afford him a decent catnap. He'd settle for a sugar rush instead.

He wasn't completely surprised to find eleven-year-old Nicholas Johnson seated in his path on the floor beside the candy machine. His mother was the office manager for a small law firm that occupied space on the other end of the hall. She often brought her son to work on days when school was closed. Although the answer was obvious, he asked, "Hey, little man. What are you up to?"

Nicholas grinned up at him. "Hi, Mr. Clark." Nicholas began collecting the piles of bills. "I'm counting up my savings."

Alonzo inserted the necessary coins for the candy and pressed the appropriate buttons, watching Nicholas in the periphery of his vision. What did kids save up for nowadays? A lifetime ago, Alonzo had hoarded his money to get an eight-track tape player that went out of style almost as soon as it hit the market. "Saving up for a new video game?"

"No. A dress."

Alonzo bent to retrieve the candy from the slot, trying to hide his surprise. "A dress?"

"Not for me, for my mom." Nicholas began to collect the coins scattered on the floor. "Mother's Day is coming up."

Was that the only thought on everyone's mind these days? Even so, most kids Nicholas's age barely bothered to buy their mothers gifts, and if they did, they aspired to a more modest purchase. He wondered why Nicholas didn't.

"Why a dress?"

Nicholas pulled out a blue nylon wallet from his back pocket and began inserting money in the appropriate places. He shrugged. "My mom is always buying me things. She never gets anything for herself." Nicholas shrugged again. "I want her to look pretty."

Alonzo stifled a smile as an image of Nicholas's mother, Daria, formed in his mind. Earth-mother Daria. He didn't doubt that a pretty woman lurked somewhere under the no-nonsense persona she projected. In that regard, she reminded him of his own mother, who, like Daria, had raised her son without the benefit of a husband.

"How much have you saved so far?"

Nicholas frowned. "Only twenty-three dollars."

Alonzo nodded. Not nearly enough. He dipped his hand into his pocket and pulled out his money clip. "Can I make a contribution?"

Nicholas shook his head. He collected the last of the coins and put them in his wallet. "I want to do this myself." He stood. "Besides, my mom would kill me if she found out."

Alonzo returned his money to his pocket. He understood both the boy's need for self-sufficiency and the wisdom of his mother's caution. "Let me know if you change your mind." He tore the end off the M 'n' M bag and extended it toward the boy. "Want some?"

The boy gave him a droll look. "Even babies know you're not supposed to take candy from strangers."

And Alonzo supposed he should have known better than to offer without checking with his mother first. But he didn't really fit into the category of stranger, did he? Although he wouldn't exactly categorize them as friends, he'd known Daria for two years. Okay, so he'd passed her in the hallway for two years, but he certainly wasn't a stranger.

"So this is where you disappeared to."

Both Alonzo and Nicholas looked up to find Daria standing just outside her office's glass doors, hands on hips. She wore a long straight skirt topped off by a rose-colored sweater set that matched the floral pattern of her skirt. The outfit lent her a matronly air, though Alonzo doubted she was more than thirty-five years old.

Nicholas affected a sheepish scowl. "Sorry, Mom."

A smile lifted the corners of Alonzo's mouth. "It wasn't his fault. I kept him here talking to me."

Her skeptical look told him how likely she thought that was. "Come on, Nicholas." She held the door open for her son to pass through. "Thank you for keeping him company, Mr. Clark."

Not for the first time he prompted her to use his first name. "Alonzo."

With a smile that told him he could prompt all he liked, she turned and headed back into her office.

Sighing, Alonzo leaned his shoulder against the vending machine. He admired Nicholas's devotion to his mother. At eleven years old, it would never have occurred to him that his own mother might have wanted or needed anything he could possibly have provided. He'd been too immature and too self-absorbed to worry about anything save his mother providing for him.

To this day his mother claimed that she didn't regret a single sacrifice she'd made in raising him. Maybe he could atone a little for his youthful shortcomings by helping some other woman's son get his mother what she needed. Alonzo smiled as a plan began to coalesce in his mind.

What Daria Johnson needed was a fairy godmother, and he was just the man for the job.

One

The next Monday morning, Alonzo leaned back in his chair as his pre-recorded voice filled his headphones. "And now I have a special message for all the kids out there. Here at WLIS, we're holding a special Mother's Day contest. Five single moms in five cities will be selected to win a one-thousand-dollar shopping spree, a full-day makeover at a spa in their area, and a night on the town with an eligible bachelor in their own hometown.

"Kids, here's what I need you to do. Write to me and tell me in your own words why you think your mom deserves the makeover. Tell me what makes her such a great mom." He rattled off instructions for sending e-mail, faxes, and snail mail. "And, fellas, don't be shy about writing in to tell us why you deserve to be considered for a date with one of our fabulous single moms. Entries have to be received at the station by March fifteenth. The contest winners will be announced on April first."

He leaned back, letting the music wash over him, wondering if Daria's son had heard the announcement. Nicholas had confessed to him once that he listened to the show as he got dressed in the morning, even though his mother didn't. It stood to reason that Nicholas was listening. For the entire week before, the station had been running promos telling listeners the contest would be announced today. He could only wait and see if a letter from Nicholas Johnson found its way to WLIS. If not, he'd have to find some other way to help the boy do something special for his mother.

~

Daria leaned on the wrought-iron gate in front of her house on Grace Avenue in the Bronx and let out a sigh. Her neighbor Stella sat on the front porch pushing a fan in concert with the movement of her swing. Stella looked as wiped out as Daria felt. Although Stella had been Nicholas's baby-sitter since he was four years old, she wondered if her son wasn't getting to be too much for the older woman to handle.

Daria pushed the gate open. "Rough day?"

"That boy of yours had me skateboarding today. Doesn't he know I'm an old woman with brittle bones to worry about?"

"Don't you?" Smiling, Daria shook her head. "I suppose he tied you to the skateboard and pushed?"

Stella lifted her bony shoulders. "He implied I was too ancient to do a nollie."

"You are." Daria settled into the swing next to her neighbor.

"Well . . ." Grinning, Stella let her words hang.

Daria shook her head again. She knew Stella couldn't bear to disappoint Nicholas in any way. She indulged the boy as if he were her own grandson and Daria as if she were her own daughter. Since Stella had never had any children and Daria's mother had died before Nicholas was born, it was an arrangement that suited them all. Daria only wished Stella would accept some financial compensation for watching Nicholas, but Stella wouldn't hear of it.

"Speaking of Nicholas, where is he?"

"Marcus Brent took his girls down to the park for some ice cream."

Daria's eyebrows lifted. Her son was still at the age where being with girls—especially prissy little girls like the Brent twins—was less desirable than eating broccoli. "And Nicholas went with them?"

"Why does that surprise you so much?"

"Nick can't stand those girls."

Stella stopped fanning herself and the swing came to an abrupt stop. "Open your eyes, girl. Your son didn't leave out of here because of the twins but because of their daddy."

Daria's eyebrows lifted. "Excuse me?"

"Your child isn't a baby anymore, Daria. And one of these days, he's going to be a man. You may not realize that, but your son does. Who you know who's gonna teach him how to be the right kind of man?"

Daria stared back at the sober, stubborn expression on Stella's face. They'd had this conversation before, though Stella had always couched her opinions in general terms. What was wrong with the crop of young brothers coming up today? According to Stella, the lack of a good role model in the home was responsible for nine-tenths of what was wrong with black youth, male or female.

"What that boy needs is a father," Stella continued, nodding to reinforce her position.

"He has a father." One who had abdicated any role in his son's life save for providing court-directed child support. Every day Daria thanked the Lord that Connor Johnson couldn't spare any of his time or concern for his son. In Daria's mind, a bad role model was worse than none at all. She'd learned that lesson from her own father who did his family a world of good by dying at the untimely age of forty-seven. She wouldn't have wished the sort of childhood she'd been cursed with on an enemy—to live under the dominion of a controlling perfectionist who found fault with everything. Her maternal grandmother used to say that if Christ came down off the cross, her father would tell him he needed a haircut.

She supposed that's why she'd married a man who sought perfection in nothing, least of all himself. If they'd lived in California, Connor would have made the quintessential beach bum. Living a carefree existence had suited her—until she'd found out she was pregnant with their child. Any attempt to get Connor to settle down had met with complete resistance. He'd disappeared when Nicholas was four years old. Daria would have been lying to herself if she'd said she was sorry to see him go.

Stella sucked her teeth and set the swing back in motion. "He's got a sperm donor. You and I both know a father is more than the man who provides half your genetic makeup."

Daria couldn't argue with that. "Then he's got me."

Stella shook her head. "I'm not saying you haven't taught your son to be a good person, but you can't teach him how to be a good man. A boy needs a man for that. And your son hasn't even got an uncle to look up to. No wonder he's following behind every decent man in the neighborhood."

Daria sighed. Even if Stella was right, there was little she could do about it. She didn't even know any decent men, aside from those already snatched up by more enterprising women than she. Even seven years after her divorce she was still in male-avoidance mode. In all the time her separation from Connor had become legal, she hadn't had one date.

Daria sighed again, this time with a hint of longing. She did know one man who treated her with deference and seemed to harbor a real fondness for her son. She'd had two years to watch him, to interact with him, and she liked what she knew of him. He possessed a natural elegance and gentility that charmed her.

But his station was grooming him for stardom. His radio show reached every major broadcast market across the country, and quite a few not so major ones as well. Undoubtedly, he was going places. That's why, despite the secret schoolgirl crush she harbored, she always maintained a polite, distant demeanor with him.

Well, almost always. There was that one dance they'd shared at the WLIS

Christmas party last year. The band had struck up one of those songs you could take fast or slow depending on your inclination. He'd pulled her into the haven of his arms, the first time in a long time a man had put his hands on her. For a moment she'd allowed herself to melt against him, absorbing his warmth and masculinity before reestablishing a safer distance between them. After the dance ended, she'd gone home, half embarrassed and half furious with herself to find that being in a man's arms had been so alien and so alluring that she'd allowed herself to forget, even momentarily, about her resolve.

"Whatever planet you're on must have gorgeous men."

Daria blinked and fastened her gaze on her neighbor. "What?"

Stella's fan picked up speed. "You heard what I said. If you were smart, you'd invite that fella down to earth where the rest of us live."

Daria stood and began to gather her things. "There is no fella—except my Nicky. When he gets back, please send him straight up to dinner."

Stella harumphed. "Just 'cause these eyes are old doesn't mean they don't see things, Daria. As much as that boy needs a father, you need a man. You are too young and pretty to let yourself go to waste. You know what happens to body parts you don't use—atrophy."

Daria laughed. "And you have a one-note song." Daria patted Stella's shoulder. "I'll see you tomorrow."

That night when she went to tuck Nicholas into bed, she found him scribbling furiously on a notepad. Given his enthusiasm and concentration on the task, she doubted his writing could be school-related. Crossing her arms, Daria leaned against the doorjamb. "What are you doing?"

Nicholas's head snapped up and he immediately turned his pad over and rested his folded arms on top of it. "Nothing."

For a moment alarm raced through her. Every now and again Nicholas got it into his head to contact his father. Usually it took one heck of a disagreement to stir Nicholas's interest in Connor—or a punishment he thought unfair. But those times he was defiant, not secretive.

Daria willed herself to relax. Nicholas might be up to something, but she suspected setting himself up for one of Connor Johnson's patented rejections hadn't made his agenda. She decided to try another tack. "I hope you're not writing a love note to some *girl*."

A horrified expression crossed his face. "*Mo-om!*"

Daria grinned. Despite her son's protests, she knew he had a special fondness for a girl who'd been in his class since first grade. But, as usual, she refrained from teasing him about it. "Did you brush your teeth?"

He bared his teeth showing a couple of gaps where baby teeth were missing but grown-up teeth hadn't grown in yet.

She walked to her son's bedside, leaned down, and placed a soft, maternal kiss on the top of his head. "Lights out in ten minutes."

Surprisingly he nodded without protest. Daria backed away. When she reached the door she said, "I love you."

"Love you, too, Mom."

Daria smiled as warmth suffused her. Nothing mattered to her more than her son's love, his happiness, and his well-being. Maybe Stella was right; maybe they both needed a man in their lives. She knew she'd never seek one out, but if the right man happened to stumble into their lives, she wouldn't fight it either. Despite everything, she hadn't given up on love. Only time would tell if love had given up on her.

~

Two hours into his show a week later, Alonzo pressed the console button to run a series of commercials, pulled the headphones from his ears, and placed them on the desk. He stood and stretched his back before heading to the stacks of CDs that spanned the length of the broadcast room wall. Although the control room was equipped with more modern equipment that could play his cuts almost like a jukebox would, he preferred the "old-fashioned" method of finding and playing his own music.

Despite public opinion to the contrary, radio personalities were subject to the decisions of their programming director, not the other way around. He'd always enjoyed more autonomy than most of the jocks at the station, as management wanted to keep him happy. Luckily, he and the programming director shared the same vision of the show's strengths and focus, so he had little to complain about.

Alonzo found the trio of CDs he wanted. When he turned around, Diana Chambers, the station manager, was leaning on the desk facing him. Diana was a lethal combination of beauty, intelligence, and earthbound common sense that won her the allegiance of nearly everyone at the station, himself included.

Diana crossed her arms in front of her. "Got a minute?"

Alonzo's eyebrows lifted. Diana rarely deigned to make personal appearances during the talent's broadcasts. Somebody wanted something badly if Diana had come down from on high to secure it. "What can I do for you, boss?"

"I hear the Mother's Day contest was your idea."

"Most of it." He'd proposed the makeover part. The promotion department had tacked on the date part after one staffer had suggested that giving a woman a makeover without providing anywhere to show it off was like dressing a horse in racing colors just to stand in the stable. "Why?"

"As you know, the response so far has been phenomenal. It seems every kid in America thinks his mom deserves a makeover."

Alonzo set the CDs on the desk beside Diana. "Glad to hear it, but—"

"And . . . we think we've come up with a way to increase interest in the contest."

He waited as Diana took her time brushing some imaginary lint from her blazer.

"Some of the affiliates have suggested that you should be one of the eligible bachelors."

Alonzo snorted. "You're kidding, right?" He hoped so. He didn't mind putting up with the publicity engagements the station or his own publicist arranged for him. That was part of the game. Going on a date, properly chaperoned or not, was different. He liked his private life just that: private. "Absolutely not."

Diana gave him a sharp, assessing look. "Why not? You're young, single, attractive. You're not seeing anyone who'll scratch my eyes out for suggesting this, are you?"

His love life was as dried up as an old prune, but for a moment the temptation to lie assailed him. "No."

Diana stood. "Then that's settled. You can announce it tomorrow morning." She started to leave, but he called her back.

"On one condition. Let me know if you get a letter from Nicholas Johnson."

"As in Daria Johnson's son?"

"The same. If her son sends in a letter, make sure she gets picked."

Diana folded her arms in front of her. "You know I can't do that. The moms are supposed to be picked on the strength of their child's letter."

He folded his arms in imitation. "Those are my terms."

For a moment she assessed him with a sharp gaze, then grinned. "Announce it tomorrow."

As Diana turned to leave the room, Alonzo stroked his chin with his index finger and thumb wondering what had prompted the cat-who-just-chomped-on-the-canary smile that had lit up Diana's face. He didn't dwell on it for long, though. He figured he'd find out soon enough.

Two

"Would you mind explaining this to me, young man?"

Nicholas looked up from his homework to gaze at the letter written on WLIS stationery that Daria dangled from her fingertips. He swallowed audibly. "It's a letter."

"No kidding. A letter from a radio station telling me I won a contest that I never entered. Do you know anything about this?" She'd known Nicholas was responsible, even before he succumbed to a sputtering attack in which no intelligible words came out of his mouth. Who else would have done it? Despite Stella's conviction that the Johnson family required a man's presence, even she wouldn't have encouraged Nicholas to enter her name in any contest.

Daria had heard the contest announced numerous times on the radio and wondered what poor women would get pulled into that disaster waiting to happen by their children. Little did she know she'd been considering herself. Even when she'd received a phone call from someone claiming to be from the station notifying her that she'd won the contest, she'd hung up on them, swearing it was someone playing a trick on her. She never imagined her son would consider her needy enough to want to win such a contest. "Why would you do such a thing?"

Nicholas's eyes widened and he shrugged in a way only the young can get away with. "I—I thought you'd like a makeover."

"Why?"

He flexed his shoulders. "You dress worse than Ms. Stella."

Daria winced. "Ouch, kiddo. I'm not that bad." That's what she said, but she admitted in the past few years she'd dressed more for practicality than for style. She didn't think she'd become downright dowdy as her son's demeanor suggested. Then again, being fashionable had never been her strong suit.

So, maybe her closet could use an overhaul, but not at the expense of the Alonzo Clark show. Nor would she subject herself to any mystery date to appease her son. "I'll make you a deal. Let's go shopping on Saturday. I'll let you help me pick out some new things."

Nicholas's shoulders drooped and the line of his mouth became stubborn. "You mean instead of the contest?"

"Sweetie," she began in a supplicating voice, "I really appreciate you thinking of me and entering me in this contest, I really do. But I don't need some radio show to make me over and I'm certainly not interested in dating anyone, even if it were a one-shot deal. You can understand that, can't you?"

Obviously, he couldn't. Nicholas focused on the book in front of him, refusing to look at her.

Daria let out a long breath. In some ways, she couldn't blame him for his disappointment. In Nicholas's position, she'd probably feel the same way. She left his room, knowing that she would probably never convince her son of her position. However, there was an older male who wouldn't have any trouble seeing her point—she'd make sure of that. She intended to let Mr. Alonzo Clark know in no uncertain terms that she had no intention of participating in his silly contest. She'd take care of that first thing Monday morning.

~

Monday morning, Alonzo looked up from his spot at the console to find Daria pacing the corridor outside the control room door. Seeing the taut expression on her face and the rigidness of her posture, his first concern centered on Nicholas's well-being. Then it occurred to him that even if something were wrong with Nicholas, she wouldn't come to him about it. Whatever brought her to his doorstep was probably personal—and adult in nature.

He slipped the final cut of his show into the player, bade his listeners good-bye, and pulled the headphones from his ears. Vanessa hadn't bothered to show up at all that day. Ever since that morning he'd rebuffed her, she'd taken to showing up at the last second or calling in sick, in all likelihood a petty means of paying him back. Whatever her motives, her machinations were enough to earn her a reprimand from the station manager to put an end to this foolishness.

He left the control room and walked to where Daria waited. Just to be sure, he asked, "How's Nicholas?"

"He's fine. I wanted to talk to you about this."

He hadn't noticed the crumpled paper she held in her fist until she unfolded it and extended it toward him. He recognized it as her notification letter that she'd won the contest. "What's the problem?"

"The problem is, I did not give my son permission to enter me in this contest."

"That's all right. Most of the kids entered their moms in the contest without telling them. That doesn't have any bearing on you claiming your prize."

She shot him an exasperated look, one that said he should know better. "That's just it, Mr. Clark. I don't want it."

Alonzo blinked. He had not heard her say she didn't want the prize he had sold his soul to the devil to get for her. "I beg your pardon."

"I don't want your makeover or your date, so you'll just have to give it to someone else."

"Why not?"

"If I want new clothes or a trip to a spa I am perfectly capable of paying for them myself. My son and I are not charity cases."

"I never meant to imply that you were. I had no idea you'd be opposed to winning a simple contest."

"Well, thanks, but no, thanks." She pushed the crumpled letter into his palm and turned to leave.

"Before you make that decision, maybe you should read what your son wrote about you."

She snapped around to face him. He didn't know why he'd made a copy of Nicholas's e-mail or why he'd been carrying it around these last few days. He pulled out the single sheet of paper, unfolded it, and handed it to her. Her fingers trembled slightly as she took it from him, as if she were afraid to see in black and white her son's opinion of her.

Her lips pressed together as she read, and when she looked at him again, the sheen of tears clouded her eyes. He couldn't blame her for the emotion. Every staffer who'd read the letter, himself included, had been moved by it. She looked at him as if she expected him to say something, but no words sprang to his mind, so he remained silent.

"I'll think about it," she said finally. This time when she turned to leave he didn't stop her. Otherwise he might have blurted out his own personal stake in seeing Nicholas's dream for his mother fulfilled, or worse yet, how much he found himself wanting to do something for her himself.

~

That evening, after Nicholas had gone to bed, Daria joined Stella out on the porch. She'd barely taken a seat when Stella said, "What has you looking like Sad Sack tonight? Everything's okay with Nicholas, isn't it?"

A rueful smile turned up Daria's lips. Why was it that when she showed any emotion at all, everyone assumed Nicholas to be the cause of it? Daria set her own swing in motion to match Stella's momentum. "I'm not sad, I'm pensive." Daria focused on the stars overhead. "You know that Mother's Day contest they're giving on the Alonzo Clark show?"

"Who doesn't know about it? I hear the man himself will be escorting one of the single moms. It's enough to make me wish I had a child to send my name in."

Daria laughed. "That man is young enough to be your son."

Stella stopped swinging and put her hands on her hips. "That's how that other Stella got her groove back. I'm still working on mine."

Daria pushed the swing a little harder with her foot. "Well, I do have a son, and he entered me in the contest, and I won."

Stella whooped. "Then what's wrong with you, girl? Seems to me you'd be celebrating rather than moping around or bein' pensive, as you put it. Nothing wrong with a free mud bath and a new pair of shoes from where I sit."

Daria sighed. "You know that sort of nonsense doesn't interest me. Especially not some date with a stranger who'll probably bore me to death with his life story while I bore him to death with mine."

"I still don't see a problem. Just turn it down. Although you'll probably break your son's heart if you do."

"There's no need to guilt me. I read his letter." Daria pulled it from her skirt pocket. "Here's what my little urchin had to say about me." Daria unfolded the paper and began to read.

Dear Mr. Clark,

I think my mom deserves your Mother's Day makeover because she is the greatest mom in the world. She takes me lots of places, shows me how to do lots of things, like throw a curve ball. Even when she gets mad at me she tells me she loves me, just what I did was dumb. She tells me she wants me to have a happy life and she does everything she can to make me happy.

Mr. Clark, my mom hasn't had an easy life. When my dad used to live with us, he wasn't nice to her. He used to yell at her and call her names. And now that he's gone, she has to do everything herself. She works real hard to buy me stuff and pay for my karate lessons. I wish my mom would buy more stuff for herself, but she never does. She says she's saving up for things I'll need later, like college. She never complains, but sometimes at night, when she thinks I'm asleep, I hear her crying in her room. I know she doesn't want me to know, so I don't say anything, but I wish that I could go to her and give her a hug like she does for me when I am sad about something.

Mr. Clark, if my mom could win the makeover, I could show her how much I love her and appreciate everything she does for me. I want her to have a happy life, too. Please, please, please consider giving my mom the free makeover. Thank you for your time.

> Sincerely,
> Nicholas Alexander Johnson

Daria folded the letter, feeling tears sting her eyes. Both the child he was now and a glimpse of the man he would become were evident in his words. Daria looked over at Stella to find the older woman's eyes had misted.

"Oh, honey," Stella said, dabbing at her eyes with the edge of a lace handkerchief.

Daria sighed. She'd had no idea her son remembered what life with Connor had been like, or that he felt this way about her. "I'm going to have to do this, aren't I?"

Stella nodded.

"That's what I thought."

"And there's something else to think about. The contest announcement said that every woman would win a date with an eligible bachelor in her hometown. Considering your hometown is New York, who do you think your date will be with?"

"Alonzo." She didn't know why that hadn't occurred to her before or why he hadn't mentioned that fact this afternoon when they'd spoken. After reading Nicholas's letter, she could only imagine what he thought of her now, the poor downtrodden divorcée. He'd probably let her win because he felt sorry for her. If he'd honestly wanted to date her, he'd had two years in which to try. She didn't need any man's pity dates, especially not his. But she'd go along with it for Nicholas's sake. She only hoped her son appreciated the only true sacrifice she considered making on his behalf.

～

For the second time in two days, Alonzo looked up to find Daria pacing outside the control room. Obviously she'd come to a decision, but her demeanor gave no clue as to what that decision might be. Luckily, she appeared close to the hour when the traffic and news reports would give them a minute to talk. He felt Vanessa's gaze on him, but he ignored her. He left the control room and joined Daria. He took her arm and led her to a spot where they wouldn't be seen by prying eyes.

"Why didn't you tell me you would be my date?" she asked without preamble.

There was no rancor in her voice, only curiosity. "I didn't think it made a difference. How did you know?" None of the winners would be given the name of their dates until May 1.

"I didn't until you just confirmed it, but I had an inkling considering we live in the same city."

"Does it make a difference?"

"I guess. You're not a dreadful bore or an egotist. You don't behave like an octopus with an extra set of tentacles—at least not so far."

She smiled, just a hint of one at the corners of her mouth. He wondered if she was referring to that one dance they'd shared at the Christmas party the year before. It occurred to him how rare it was to see her smile, if he ever had before. He wouldn't mind if he saw that smile and the little twinkle it brought to her eyes again and again.

"I only have two hands, and I promise to keep them to myself."

"I'm only doing this for my son's sake."

And she was letting him know she didn't consider this a real date that could possibly lead somewhere. That was fine with him, as his only interest was in helping fulfill Nicholas's wish to do something nice for his mother. Or that had been his only interest when this thing had started. He wasn't so sure anymore. "Does that mean you're accepting the prize?"

"Yes."

No coyness, no beating around the bush, simply straightforwardness. That was one of the things about her that appealed to him most. He figured he'd give her a shot of his own honesty as well. "I'm glad. I understand how Nicholas feels. I was raised by a single mother myself. At his age most boys are too self-involved to consider doing anything nice for their mothers. I'm glad you didn't deprive your son of that opportunity."

She cleared her throat, obviously uncomfortable with his praise. "I'd better get back to work."

"There are some papers you need to sign, some releases. I'll send someone over to your office to take care of it."

"Thank you." She graced him with another of her minismiles and turned to leave. As she walked away from him, he noted the sexy sway of her hips. He'd never noticed that before. He shook his head to clear it. He went back inside the control room to finish his show wondering what other surprises Daria Johnson might have in store for him.

$\sim$

From the day Alonzo announced the winners to the day before her shopping spree, Daria had been subjected to all manner of teasing from her officemates. The women, all of whom knew Alonzo at least in passing, speculated on the strength and dimensions of his masculine charm. The men volunteered alternately to take Alonzo's place or defend her honor should he get out of line. One of the lawyers volunteered to draft the prenuptial agreement should one become necessary. In an act of unprecedented generosity, her boss had given her three days off to rest and enjoy her winnings from the contest.

By the time she was ready to leave her office on the day before the shopping spree, she felt pretty good about her decision to go on the date. She'd appreciated her coworkers' humor, and the few times she'd seen Alonzo he'd been his usual charming self. Knowing they were to share this date hadn't changed anything between them, for which she was grateful. All he would tell her about their date was, when the store's presonnel helped her select an outfit, to choose something suitable for evening wear. The station had provided accommodations for each of the dates. Although most of them were to take place Friday night, hers was set for Saturday. Obviously, the station planned something splashy for her and Alonzo to capitalize on the publicity. She would have preferred something quieter, less public, but unfortunately she wasn't calling the shots.

"Good night," Daria called to the receptionist as she passed her desk on the way to the door.

"Night," she called back. "And remember, we want details, lots of details."

"We'll see," Daria shot back, although she had no intention of sharing any information about her date with anyone. She'd been brought up by Selma Hyatt, who believed nice girls didn't kiss, or not kiss, and tell. But as she strode toward the elevator, she couldn't help the small smile that turned up her lips. She wouldn't admit it to anyone but herself, but she was looking forward to the next day's shopping spree.

A lone woman stood at the elevator. As Daria approached, the woman turned around. Vanessa something or other from WLIS looked back at her with an expression of disdain on her face. That surprised Daria, as she'd never spoken more than a quick hello in passing to the woman.

"Well, if it isn't the Woman of the Hour herself. How does it feel to know the only way you can get a date with Alonzo Clark is to have your son win one for you?"

The smile eased away from Daria's face to be replaced by a narrow-eyed glare. She suspected the green-eyed monster rather than genuine dislike lay at the root of the woman's attack. Rumor had it that Vanessa was after either Alonzo's body or sole ownership of his time slot and was likely to gain neither.

Daria didn't care what ambitions the woman possessed or whether she stood to achieve them, but she didn't take potshots from anyone. She smiled sweetly. "At least I got one."

The woman's lips drew into a tight line. "You're so pleased with yourself now, but don't delude yourself into thinking he really wants you."

"I don't delude myself about anything, but what I can't figure out is why you give a damn." Daria squared her shoulders. "If you'll excuse me, I'd rather take the stairs."

Walking the three flights down to the main floor, Daria admitted the woman's vitriol had dampened her enthusiasm for the date a little. In some small way, she had been anticipating going out with Alonzo, not only for her son's benefit but because she looked forward to being with him. The prospect of being his woman for one night under whatever circumstances had excited her. But being reminded that the whole world, including Alonzo, viewed that night as charity work, was just what she needed to bring her back down to earth—until she got home in time to answer a ringing phone and heard Alonzo's deep, sexy voice on the other end of the line.

Breathless from her sprint to the phone, she asked, "How did you get this number?"

"You're listed. Look, I just wanted to let you know I'll be sending a car for you tomorrow morning. My contribution to your prize package."

"Thank you, but that isn't necessary. I can get downtown on my own."

"Nonsense. And how would you bring your packages back home? Everybody with a brain cell knows how atrocious parking around Fifth Avenue can be."

Especially if your car was in the shop, which hers was. "Then I thank you again."

"It's the least I can do. I'm really looking forward to our date."

Not knowing what else to say, she murmured, "Me, too."

"Sweet dreams, sweetheart. I'll see you on Saturday."

Now she really didn't know how to respond to that, so she just hung up.

She stared at the telephone a few minutes, wondering what had gotten into Alonzo to speak to her so familiarly. And what had gotten into her? Hadn't she just warned herself about keeping her feet glued on terra firma? Yet, hearing the endearment from his lips had sent a definite thrill racing up her spine. She'd reacted like a schoolgirl, not the utterly pragmatic mother of an eleven-year-old child. Shaking her head at herself, she rose from the sofa and went to the kitchen to start dinner.

~

The next morning, the car Alonzo sent arrived at precisely 8:30. She was instantly glad he hadn't hired a limousine, as many of her neighbors found the Town Car complete with liveried driver more fascinating than she cared for.

She felt her son come up beside her at the window. "Wow. Mr. Clark must have some real cheese to hire a car like that."

She'd made the mistake of telling her son what Alonzo had done. She glanced back at him over her shoulder. "I hope you are referring to the kind of cheese one keeps in the refrigerator." Although she knew he used it, she didn't allow slang in an adult's presence.

"Aw, Mom." He rolled his eyes heavenward.

"Don't look up to the sky. Nothing is coming down from there but rain." She dusted her palm over her son's short hair. "I'd better go. You have a great day at school and I'll put on a fashion show when I get home." He still tolerated his kisses, at least when they were alone. She kissed his cheek. "You behave for Auntie Stella." She gave him the same admonishment every day.

"I will," he answered as if for the hundredth time.

With a wink at Stella, who waited for her by the door, Daria left the house and allowed the driver to help her into the car. As it pulled away from the curb, she settled back against the plush leather upholstery.

The radio station had given her a one-thousand-dollar shopping spree at Saks Fifth Avenue, one of the priciest stores in New York. After she bought a pair of panty hose, she wondered what she'd do with the fifty cents she had left over. Daria sighed. It wouldn't be that bad, but she could certainly think of a lot better ways to spend a grand than on some overpriced clothes she didn't need.

At the store, she was met by the promotions manager from the station, the store's personal shopper, and a photographer. She had expected the first two, but not the third. "I hope he's not planning to follow me into the dressing room," she said once introductions were made.

"Oh, no, of course not."

Daria shook her head as the promotions manager continued to assure her of her privacy. Obviously the woman had no sense of humor whatsoever. It was going to be a long day.

In the end, Daria bought only two things: an evening gown that cost upwards of six hundred dollars and a pair of black satin pumps that ate up the rest of the money. She'd tried the gown on as a lark, never expecting to buy it. But once she felt the cool satin against her skin, she'd changed her mind. The thousand dollars was found money, anyway, she'd rationalized. She could do with it what she wanted without denting her budget in any way. Maybe Daria Johnson could do one utterly impractical thing without the world crashing in on her. Daria smiled into the mirror. "I'll take it."

～

Alonzo pulled up in front of his mother's house in Forest Hills, Queens, a little before six o'clock the next evening. One of his cousins was leaving for a medical rotation in Kenya in the morning. By eight o'clock, the entire family would be at the house to wish her bon voyage. He'd arrived early to spend a few quiet moments with his mother before the rest of the hordes invaded.

Alighting from the car, he looked up at the two-story Tudor house with fondness. To the rest of America he might be some sort of celebrity, but here he was just another one of the knucklehead kids, despite the fact that he was almost thirty-six years old.

He found his mother, Vivian, in the kitchen, as usual. Although almost everyone would be bringing a dish to add to their potluck dinner, the backbone of the meal, the roast, was always cooked by his mother. She stood at the stove, her back to him, stirring something, probably gravy, in a large pot.

He came up beside his much shorter mother and draped an arm along her shoulders. "Hey, good looking, what you got cooking?"

She slanted a glance up at him, a smile crinkling the corners of her brown eyes. "Is that any way to greet your mother?"

"No, Ma." A foil-covered ceramic bowl sat atop the stove. He pushed aside the edge of the foil intending to sample some of his mother's famous collard greens. Before he had a chance to pluck a taste from the bowl a wooden spoon cracked across his knuckles. "Ouch," he protested.

"I've been telling you to keep your hands out of my food since you were tall enough to look over the stove. Seems some people would learn their lesson after a while."

"It seems that way." He pulled his mother closer and placed a kiss at her temple. "You still wield a mean spoon."

"I still get plenty of practice." Teasingly, she pushed at his chest. "I just put on a pot of coffee. Pour us each a cup and we can sit for a minute."

He did as she asked, then joined her at the small circular kitchen table. He waited while she added milk and cream to her cup before taking a sip from his own. "How've you been, Ma?"

"Me? I'm the same as I always am. I'd rather talk about you. I hear you have a hot date tomorrow night."

He set his cup on the table. "It's not all that hot. It's arranged by WLIS."

"But you agreed to it, which surprises me. Do you know the girl?"

"She works down the hall from the station. And she's a grown woman with an eleven-year-old son."

Vivian's eyebrows lifted. "I see."

"It's not like that."

"No? Shoot. I'd hoped you'd rigged that contest to get a date with some girl you wanted to go out with."

Alonzo nearly choked on his coffee. In a manner of speaking he'd done just that, though when he'd insisted on Daria's son winning the contest it hadn't occurred to him that they would pair her up with him. "That would be illegal. Besides, if I wanted to go out with a woman, I'd simply ask her."

"Then get to asking, would you? It hasn't escaped my attention that you have not provided me with a single grandchild. You haven't even produced a daughter-in-law for me to pin my hopes on. I want you to get serious about this, Alonzo. I'd like to see you settled and happy before I die."

Alonzo sighed. They'd been over this route so many times the asphalt had worn thin. "Considering you have never been sick a day in your life, I don't think we need to worry about the Grim Reaper sneaking up on you any time soon. Second, I like my life the way it is right now. I have plenty of time to strap on the old ball-and-chain if I ever decide to."

Vivian gave him a sharp look. "It's my own fault. I never should have taught you how to cook or keep a house neat. I made you too self-sufficient. Otherwise you'd need a woman if only to look after you."

"It's a good thing you did, because I wouldn't want the kind of woman who wouldn't expect me to pull my fair share."

She gave him a stern look, but there was a hint of a smile on her lips. "Go on and taste the gravy and tell me if it needs more salt."

Obviously she'd said all she intended to on her subject. He knew the gravy wouldn't need more salt. It never did. He got up and sampled it anyway. "It's perfect."

"Why don't you taste some of those greens while you're over there? And use a spoon."

Laughing, he did as his mother suggested. After he'd swallowed a mouthful, he said, "This is why I'll never get married. I'll never find a woman that makes greens the way you do."

"You just find the girl," Vivian shot back. "I'll give her the recipe."

$\sim$

Early Friday morning, the same car and driver pulled up in front of Daria's house. In exactly one hour she was due at the posh new Tranquillity spa that had become the rage among the monied crowd. Owned by three women, one African-American, one Latina, and one Chinese, they combined ancient healing arts from the three cultures for a relaxing retreat. Or so the brochure from the spa claimed. A retreat in the middle of midtown Manhattan. This she had to see.

Three hours into her stay at the spa, Daria was feeling no pain. She'd been bathed and perfumed, wrapped in mud and rubbed with oil, massaged, waxed, and exfoliated. Daria sighed. If she could find a way to make money at it she'd show up here every day. She sipped her mango/papaya juice and let her gaze wander about the atrium where she had been left to relax until it was time to leave for her hair and makeup appointments. She'd never been a plant person, but she enjoyed the peaceful beauty of the exotic scene around her. She was about to close her eyes when she noticed one of the young women who worked there walking toward her.

"You have a phone call, Ms. Johnson." The young woman extended a cordless phone toward her.

Considering that Stella was the only person she'd told where she was going and Stella wouldn't call without good reason, dread rushed through Daria. Adjusting the phone against her ear, she said, "Is everything all right?"

"I was about to ask you the same question."

Hearing Alonzo's voice, Daria willed herself to relax. "I thought you were my baby-sitter calling to tell me something was wrong with Nicholas."

"I'm sorry I alarmed you."

"It's all right. My heart has gone back into my chest where it belongs." She shifted in her lounge chair to cross her legs. "To what do I owe the honor of this call?"

"The promotion department thought it would be a nice touch if I called all the women personally to see how they were enjoying their day at the spa."

"I see." For a tiny moment she'd believed he'd called because he'd wanted to talk to her.

"Would you prefer I led you to believe something that wasn't true?"

Evidently he'd heard the disappointment in her voice. "No."

"So, how are you holding up?"

"Not bad. If I could manage to win a trip here, say, every month or two, I wouldn't object."

He laughed, a deep melodious sound that did something wicked to her insides. "We'll have to see about getting you a standing appointment."

She wet her lips with the tip of her tongue. "Seriously, Alonzo, I know I must seem like an ingrate after I almost refused the prize, but I truly do appreciate the station's generosity—and yours."

"I know. I'll see you tomorrow."

The line went dead before she had a chance to say another word. She clicked off the phone just as another girl came to retrieve her to get ready to leave for her other appointments.

~

The following evening, Daria stood in front of the full-length mirror in the upstairs hall surveying her handiwork. She twisted from side to side to get a better view. "Not too bad. Not too bad, at all." The hairstylist had cut and dyed her hair and fashioned it into a sleek French twist. She'd also coated it with enough hair spray to kill half the ozone layer, so her hairdo had survived the night intact. She'd splurged and bought every cosmetic the makeup artist had applied to her skin. She'd done an admirable job of recreating the other woman's handiwork. The sweetheart bodice of the retro-style gown she'd selected clung to her curves. The straight skirt ended in a little train that gave her a touch of elegance. Thanks to Stella's generosity, drop pearls hung from her ears, and a matching choker and bracelet encircled her neck and wrist. The jewelry was exquisite, but all Stella would say about them was that she'd been young once.

Daria heard the doorbell ring. She'd have thought she would be nervous knowing that Alonzo was downstairs waiting for her, but a calmness settled over her like a cool, comforting blanket. She didn't understand it, but she wouldn't complain about it either. She grabbed her evening clutch and headed toward the stairs.

She knew the exact moment Alonzo noticed her descending the stairs. He stood directly beneath her, still at the front door with Stella and Nicholas beside him. Stella looked up first. When Alonzo's gaze traveled upward to see what had claimed Stella's attention, he did a double take and the words on his lips died a quick death. Daria paused where she was, drinking in the sight of him. He wore a traditionally cut black tuxedo, which fit him perfectly. He possessed a natural elegance evident even in street clothes, but the effect of the formal wear was striking.

For a moment no one spoke, until Nicholas broke the silence by saying, "Wow, Mom, you look like a girl."

Daria grinned at her son's choice of compliment. "Thank you."

She returned her gaze to Alonzo. In one hand he held a clear plastic corsage box. The other hand was extended toward her. She placed her hand in his warm sure one and allowed him to help her down the last few stairs. In the periphery of her vision she noticed Stella leading Nicholas away toward the front room.

When she stood level with him he said, "May I concur with your son and say, Wow!"

A playful mood seized her. "Don't be so surprised, Alonzo. I was a woman before I became a mother."

"I can see that."

She pointed toward the flower box in his hand. "Is that for me?"

He glanced down at the box as if he'd forgotten he carried it. "Yes. Would you like me to put it on?"

She extended her hand toward him. "Please."

He extracted a single white orchid from the box and slid it onto her wrist. She flexed her hand and gazed down at the flower. The blossom was exquisite and the sweet smell of it tickled her nose. "Thank you." When her gaze slid to Alonzo's face, he stared back at her with a bemused expression on his face.

He shook his head. "Forgive me. I can't get over the transformation."

She cocked her head to one side. "Do I look that bad every day?"

"No, just different. I never expected to find a glamour queen hidden under the earth-mother clothes you usually wear. I feel like I'm about to step out with Dorothy Dandridge or Lena Horne on my arm."

His low, husky voice reverberated through her, thrilling her. "Let's go before my head gets too big to fit through the door."

While she got the matching wrap to her dress from the closet, Nicholas and Stella returned to bid them good night. Daria wouldn't be surprised if they'd both listened to every word she and Alonzo had said to appear on cue like that. "You two behave yourselves while I'm gone," she said as she hugged her son.

"I'd give you the same advice," Stella shot back with a wink. "But what would be the fun in that?"

Laughing, Daria grasped the arm Alonzo extended to her and headed out into the warm spring night. But the applause that started the moment she and Alonzo stepped through her front door and the smattering of flashbulbs that went off startled her, making her draw back against Alonzo.

His hands went to her waist, steadying her. "I would have warned you, but I thought you already knew."

"It's okay." She supposed she shouldn't be surprised to find that a crowd of her neighbors had gathered outside her home to watch her departure with Alonzo. Anyone who listened to his radio show had to know tonight was the night and the white stretch limousine parked at the curb must have alerted them that now was the time. She waved at her neighbors who called out well wishes as Alonzo led her toward the car.

Once they were both seated and the limousine began to pull away from the curb, she glanced up at him. "Do you cause this much of a stir everywhere you go?"

He grinned at her. "Not everywhere."

But he would tonight. She was as sure of that as she was of her own name. And she would be part of that because she was with him. Oh, joy.

~

Alonzo looked out the window as the driver turned right on Edson Avenue on his way to the New England Thruway. Daria lived in a middle-class enclave of attached and semidetached homes that appeared clean and well cared for. Though they couldn't claim much surrounding land, there were plenty of backyards and drives perfect for children to play in. A nice place for a kid to grow up. He wondered if she'd chosen this area specifically with Nicholas in mind.

He turned his attention to her. She gazed out the opposite window, giving him a moment to study her without her notice. Daria Johnson was a surprisingly beautiful and voluptuous woman. He'd suspected that her matronly outfits hid more than they showed, and that a mascara wand might be a dangerous implement in her hands. But he'd been as floored as her son by the total package. For the first time, he'd really seen her as a woman, and his libido had immediately kicked into overdrive.

That had been shocking enough, but then she'd actually teased him over his reaction. That had surprised him more, because he'd never glimpsed the humor in her, never imagined it was there. Before that he'd have sworn Daria Johnson was all business and it pleased him to know he'd been mistaken. But it reminded him how little he knew about her and conversely how sharp his desire to know more about her was becoming.

He laced his fingers with hers and gave a gentle tug. "You're awfully quiet over there."

She turned to face him, a gentle smile turning up her lips. "It occurs to me I have no idea where we're going."

"The National Arts Council is hosting a party at the Palace Hotel downtown. One of those music industry events anyone who's anyone is supposed to show up to."

"Oh."

"I have to warn you, the invitation says black tie, but you'd be surprised at what manner of black tie some of the folks will be wearing or what it will be tied to."

"Not a very conservative crowd."

"To put it mildly. We don't have to stay long if you don't want to."

"It'll be fine, really. I haven't been to the circus in a long time."

He threw back his head and laughed. She certainly had the evening pegged correctly. "As I said, we can leave whenever you want to." But as they made their way down the narrow, winding path of the FDR Drive, she wondered, which would offer up more surprises tonight, the crowd or the woman sitting beside him?

Three

Daria thought she knew what to expect from this evening once Alonzo explained where they'd be going. She'd seen similar events broadcast on television. Fans screaming, photographers snapping away, posing on the red carpet to see and be seen. What she hadn't anticipated was the energy coming from all these people packed into one small space. Or the noise. It closed in on her like a physical presence, making her claustrophobic. As she stepped out of the limousine, she had the urge to cover her ears with her hands. But then Alonzo was next to her, steadying her with an arm around her waist. He led her through the crush to the open doors of the theater, to a bank of elevators dedicated to servicing those guests going to the top-floor ballroom.

"Are you okay?"

"I feel like Clint Eastwood in *The Gauntlet*, only they were hurling flashbulbs at us instead of bullets."

Alonzo laughed, a rich baritone sound that reverberated through her. "Now there's an idea. Next time we'll come with our own armor-plated bus."

"Next time? Do you go to these things often?"

"Only the ones I can't get out of."

The elevator came. When they reached the top floor, he reached for her hand. "Ready?"

She swallowed. *"Gauntlet,* part two?"

He led her off the elevator. "Not exactly. You may not have noticed it, but you caused quite a stir downstairs."

"Me?"

"Believe me, in the scheme of things I am a very minor celebrity. I've never gotten one-tenth the reaction you witnessed downstairs. Everyone wanted to know who you were."

Looking up into hs eyes, Daria bit her lip, unsure if he spoke the truth or if he was trying to flatter her. "You're joking."

"No, I'm not. You are a stunning woman, Daria. I'm going to have to beat the rest of the men off with a stick if I intend to keep you all to myself tonight."

His huskily spoken words sent a thrill of excitement up her spine, emboldening her. "Do you intend to keep me all to yourself tonight?"

"You can count on it."

~

Alonzo smiled to himself as he led Daria down the narrow hallway toward the ballroom. He doubted she took what he said seriously, but he'd meant every word. If she thought he'd let any other man get near her, she'd find out otherwise.

He drew to a halt as they reached the threshold of the ballroom. This year's theme was Cinderella's ball. The waiters were dressed as Princes Charming, with jackets, gold epaulets, and all. The tables were covered in gold and white linen and topped by elaborate coach centerpieces. An enormous gold coach sat in one corner of the room. A white swan, the symbol of the arts council, dressed in black and white livery served as coachman. He gazed down at her to gauge her reaction.

She shook her head as if to clear it of a mirage. "I hope that swan is stuffed."

"My sentiments exactly. Shall we go in?"

Nodding, she adjusted he grip on his arm and allowed him to lead her into the room. He was pleased to discover that his friend Nathan Ward and his lovely wife, Daphne, were already seated at their table. As they approached, Nathan stood to greet them. Although Alonzo appreciated having an ally at the table, he dreaded Daria's reaction to the infamous Nathan Ward. Nathan had retired from his career as a singer a few years ago, but Alonzo didn't know a woman alive, young or old, black or white or even tone deaf, who didn't swoon over Nathan's looks and devil-may-care attitude.

"Long time no see, buddy," Nathan said, extending his hand. "They been keeping you locked in that control booth, or what?"

"Something like that." He stepped aside. With an arm around Daria's waist, he brought her forward. "Nathan, this is Daria Johnson. Daria, this is Nathan Ward."

He held his breath and waited. Daria extended her hand toward Nathan. "It's a pleasure to meet you, Mr. Ward."

Nathan grinned, grasping her hand in both of his. "Please call me Nathan. My father is Mr. Ward and he's dead."

"All right, Nathan." She extricated his hand from his and extended it toward his wife. "I guess that makes you Daphne Thorne, owner of Woman's Work."

Daphne shook her hand. "Guilty as charged."

"We've never met, but your company helped me get my job at Williams and Barnett. I'm their office manager."

"I'm pleased we could help you out."

Daria looked up at him, an expectant expression on her face—probably wondering when the heck they were going to sit down. For an odd moment, he wanted to laugh. She'd shown no reaction whatsoever to meeting Nathan. That had to be a first. Feeling unaccountably pleased, he sat her next to

Nathan, then made introductions with their other tablemates, most of whom he knew.

Two chairs on the other side of Daphne remained unclaimed. Daria leaned closer to him and whispered, "Do you know who we're waiting for?"

"Probably no one." He leaned across Daria to ask Nathan, "Are those Michael's seats?"

Daphne answered for Daria's benefit. "My brother buys tickets to this thing every year." She shrugged. "It's for charity. But he never shows up. He hates these things."

"Lucky dog." If the station hadn't footed the bill this time, he'd have stayed home, too. Hell, he probably would have blown it off if his date was with anyone but Daria. For some unknown reason he felt the need to impress her. He turned to Daria. "Would you like a drink?"

"Please. White wine."

"Coming right up." He motioned to Nathan to join him, and the two men walked to the bar in the corner of the room.

After the men had gone, Daphne scootched over a seat to sit next to Daria. "You know they make fun of us for traveling to the ladies' room in packs, but when was the last time you saw a lone man get up and go to the bar?"

Daria laughed. "I hadn't thought about it that way." She stole a glance at the two men talking amiably while waiting their turn in line. "Do you suppose they do the same thing we do when we go to the ladies' room?"

"You mean talk about us? Sure. For about two seconds. Then they start looking around for the woman with the biggest hooters in the room."

"And here I thought my ex-husband was the only one who did that."

"It's all of them. It's programmed into their blasted DNA. As long as they just look, who cares?"

Daria shrugged, not knowing how seriously to take Daphne's comments. She had to admit she found the other woman's security in her husband's regard for her refreshing. Daria had never felt secure of Connor's feelings toward her, not even when they were dating.

"Alonzo's a good guy. How did you meet him?"

She recognized the shrewdness in Daphne's gaze. Alonzo was her friend and she sought to protect him in case his date for the evening had less than his best interests at heart. Since she liked Daphne, she wanted to put her fears to rest.

"I've know Alonzo for two years. His radio station is on the same floor as the law firm I work for. But this isn't a real date. I'm the New York winner of the Mother's Day contest." She shrugged. "This is purely a duty date."

Daphne swirled the remains in her wineglass. "Oh, really? Then why do you suppose Alonzo looked like he wanted to deck my husband just for holding your hand?"

"I wouldn't know." She glanced in the direction of the bar to see the two men returning. When her gaze met Alonzo's he winked at her. That was a very heady notion, that Alonzo could actually feel possessive of her. She refused to buy into it, though. She intended to keep her head out of the clouds and her feet solidly planted on earth. She refused to invest anything more into this date than was written in black and white on the release form they'd asked her to sign. He'd take her out, he'd bring her home. End of story. Monday morning they'd go back to being two people who passed each other in the hall from time to time.

Alonzo slid into his seat beside her and deposited her drink in front of her. "Did you miss me?"

Daria lifted the glass to her mouth and swallowed. How was she supposed to retain any sense of equilibrium when he smiled at her that way? When his sexy voice sounded so close to her ear that it sent a shiver up her spine? "Maybe a little."

He flashed her one of his killer grins. "I'll have to work on that, then. Make sure you miss me next time."

She'd been teasing him, but he didn't appear to be teasing back. His dark brown eyes held a curious intensity and he sat much too close to her. Did he think that she required the full date treatment—attentive companion and all? She didn't. She simply wanted to get through this night and get back to her nice normal life tomorrow.

He took her wineglass from her and set it on the table. "Come dance with me?"

"Now?"

"No, in twenty minutes when they'll play another one of those god-awful Motown medleys everyone loves. Of course now."

"I haven't finished my drink."

"It'll still be here when you get back."

The band was playing a slow, sultry rendition of a Luthor Vandross song, she couldn't remember the name of it. She opened her mouth to refuse, but he didn't wait for her answer. He stood and held out his hand to her.

She sighed. Now she couldn't refuse without making a fool of herself and him. She took his hand and allowed him to lead her to the dance floor.

~

Out on the dance floor, Alonzo took Daria into his arms. She tried to maintain a discreet distance between them, like at the Christmas party, but he wasn't having that. She might not consider this a real date, but he aimed to change her mind. He wanted this chance with her, to see where things would lead. Gently, he pulled her closer until their bodies touched.

She glanced up at him, a questioning look in her eyes. Even in four-inch heels, the top of her head barely came to his shoulder. "Alonzo, I—"

He cut her off with a finger against her lips. "Please, baby, just let me hold you." He pulled her closer still, until her face nestled against his neck. Her scent, a combination of floral perfume and the woman herself, reached his nostrils. Her breath heated his skin, heated him. His fingers found their way under the crisscross straps of her gown to touch her soft, warm flesh.

With a sigh, she melted against him. Her fingers strummed his nape in an erotic manner. He wondered if she was aware of what she was doing or how swiftly his body had hardened in response to her. He lifted his head to look down at her. The dreamy expression on her face spoke volumes to him. She wasn't as immune to him as she wanted him to believe, not by a long shot. With a self-satisfied smile, he brushed his lips over her temple.

Her head snapped up and she stared at him with eyes that had darkened to a deep brown. "Alonzo—"

He cut her off the same way he had the first time. She pressed her lips together, fueling him with the urge to lower his head and claim her mouth. He didn't though, because he suspected he'd embarrass her. Instead he led her back to the table. He'd proved his point to himself and maybe to her. That was enough. For now.

~

Back at the table, Daria sipped deeply from her wine, wondering if Alonzo knew how deeply that one simple dance had affected her. His nearness hadn't undone her; the knowledge that he wanted her had. There was no mistaking the imprint of his arousal against her belly or the tender way he'd held her.

For a moment at the end, she'd have sworn he was about to kiss her. Disappointment had flooded through her when he'd led her back to the table instead. She wanted that kiss. She'd wanted to feel his lips on hers, as soft and gentle as they had touched her temple. So much for not pinning any hopes on the outcome this evening.

Maybe she'd been mistaken in believing that Alonzo thought of this as anything more than a pity date. She didn't know if that thought pleased her or terrified her.

"Ready for that trip to the ladies' room?" Daphne asked, drawing Daria out of her own thoughts.

Daria nodded. The men stood as the women made their exit. The ladies' room was a large oblong area, most of which was dedicated to comfortable leather chairs and a long lighted makeup bar along the far wall. The women there seemed to be using it more as gossip central than an actual place to go to the bathroom. As she and Daphne claimed two seats at the makeup table, she would have sworn she saw a number of hostile looks directed at her from women she'd never seen before in her life.

She leaned closer to Daphne and whispered, "Is it me, or are some of the women here giving me dirty looks?"

Daphne waved her hand dismissively. "Pay these fools no attention, Daria. They're simply jealous. Alonzo's a catch and they're just mad that someone else caught him."

Daria didn't agree she'd done any such thing, but she understood Daphne's point. "So I should just ignore it?"

"Either that or get a voodoo doll with lots of pins. When I first married Nathan there were plenty of people, mostly women, who felt obligated to tell me that our marriage would never last. After all, he was this megastar and I was a nobody. What could I possibly offer him? Never mind that Nathan and I had known each other since we were kids, that we were and still are madly in love with each other. Even now, some bimbette will make a play for him right under my nose.

"Most of the time I just laugh. Nathan and I waited years to be together. He isn't going anywhere. We only come to these things to support charities we care about and because I realize my husband needs the occasional dose of public adoration to satisfy his ego. Most of the time we lead a very quiet life raising our two daughters."

Daria lifted her shoulders in a small shrug and concentrated on freshening her lipstick. She didn't know how any woman could live like that, under the constant threat of other women trying to steal her husband. Connor was a nobody, but women had called their house at all hours looking for him. He'd claim they were all clients or prospective clients. She hadn't been naive enough to believe that, but she'd never really investigated to find out if that was so. She hadn't wanted to know. When she finally got fed up with him and challenged him, he disappeared. Not a week later, she discovered he was living with one of his supposed clients. Her only thought had been to wish that other woman well dealing with him. Any love she'd felt for Connor had fled a long time before that.

But how differently that must play when your husband was someone in the public eye. With Connor she'd only had to contend with women he met personally. She didn't have to worry that half the women in America were after her husband. Maybe Daphne Thorne could laugh about such a scenario, but she knew she never would.

Daria slid a glance at Daphne. Although she knew no future existed for her and Alonzo, she couldn't help being curious about him. "I never asked you how you know Alonzo."

"We all grew up in the same neighborhood in Queens. Alonzo's mom, my dad, and Nathan's grandmother still live there. Alonzo's father used to be the high school music teacher, a great guy. The kind of teacher they make movies about, you know, *Stand and Deliver, Mr. Holland's Opus*, that sort of thing."

"*To Sir, with Love.*"

"An oldie but a goodie. Anyway, he also led the band, and they were awesome. Instead of trying to force the kids to play your standard marches and other hits from the Old Fogeys' Hall of Fame, they played contemporary songs, so the kids loved it. They were good enough that they were invited around the country to various band competitions."

Daphne fell silent and laid her brush on the table. "One night after one of the competitions some of his students got attacked by members of another band who thought they should have won the competition instead. One of the guys pulled a knife and when Mr. Clark tried to intervene the kid stabbed him."

"Oh, no." Daria bit her lip as the sting of tears burned her eyes.

"The whole neighborhood went into mourning after that. And Alonzo was devastated."

"How old was Alonzo when this happened?"

"Probably nine or ten. Young. Because we liked Mr. Clark so much, Alonzo was like our kid brother. He still is."

"Why are you telling me this?"

"Because Alonzo is a sweetheart, definitely his father's son. And if you hurt him, I'm going to have to come after you. You can ask my husband. That isn't a pleasant prospect." Daphne checked her teeth for the presence of lipstick and finding none she flashed Daria a dazzling smile. "Ready to go back?"

Daria had to laugh. One minute the woman was threatening her; the next she treated her like a best girlfriend. Under other circumstances, she wouldn't mind getting to know Daphne Thorne better and finding out from her husband why tangling with her was such a big deal. She rose and followed Daphne back to the table.

∿

Dinner was a choice of filet mignon, chicken marsala, or broiled salmon. Alonzo chose the steak while Daria chose the fish. As they ate, Daria finally seemed to relax around him, especially after Daphne confided that she and Nathan were trying to have another child, a boy this time since they already had two girls. Daria regaled them all with stories of raising her own son, funny touching stories that made him admire her all the more.

But he noticed that never once did she mention her ex-husband in any of the stories. She'd been divorced from him for several years, so it didn't make sense to him that the pain of the separation lingered so close to the surface that she would keep her from talking about him. Had she left her husband out of the stories out of deference to him? Alonzo doubted that, too. In all likelihood, the man had simply been uninvolved with his family, as so many men were. It made him wonder what sort of man Daria had been married to.

"So there you are."

Alonzo looked up to find Vanessa standing over him, one hand perched on her hip, the other wrapped around a half-full wineglass. From her slurred speech he doubted the one she held was the first of the evening. The belligerent expression on her face told him she hadn't stopped by the table for a social call. She was spoiling for a fight. He stood blocking Daria from the other woman's sight. "What do you want, Vanessa?"

She took an unsteady sip from her glass. "I thought you wouldn't be joining us tonight."

"I changed my mind."

"I see. I'm not good enough for you to go out with, but here you are, with Little Miss Nobody?" She gestured in Daria's direction.

Anger flashed through him. Vanessa might be angry with him, but he refused to allow her to take it out on Daria. In a deadly voice, he said, "Go back to your table, Vanessa."

"Why? Why should I?" She swayed on her feet. Alonzo reached for her to prevent her from falling, but she smacked his hand away. "Afraid I'll embarrass your little girlfriend?"

"You're embarrassing yourself." Already diners at other tables had turned to look at them. In the scheme of things, this little exchange amounted to peanuts considering some of the outrageous behavior of the others. But word of Vanessa's drunkenness would undoubtedly make it back to WLIS and to Diana Chambers. Diana's dislike of the on-air talent making asses of themselves in public was no secret. Given Vanessa's poor performance at work, she'd be lucky to keep her job. But he didn't feel sorry for her. Any misfortune she faced she'd created for herself. Unfortunately, he'd run out of polite ways of asking her to leave.

He was about to start on the impolite ones when he noticed Nathan in the periphery of his vision, rising to his feet. Nathan stepped forward, a conciliatory expression on his face. "Come on, sweetheart. Let me take you back to your seat."

For some reason, the steam seemed to go out of her. She looked from Nathan to Daphne to Daria, then finally to him. "Oh, to hell with all of you." She whirled and took off toward the other side of the room.

Alonzo sank into his seat and grasped Daria's hand. "I'm sorry about that."

Daria shook her head. "Don't be. Even before tonight that woman had it in for me."

Nathan, who'd been monitoring Vanessa's departure, plopped into his seat and sighed. "Where else but the NAC can you get dinner and a show for five hundred dollars a pop?"

Daphne smacked her husband's shoulder, then laid her cheek against it. "What do you say we get out of here? You guys can come to our place for a nightcap."

Alonzo took Daria's hand in his. She offered him a faint smile, but the sparkle in her eyes had dimmed. Maybe it would be better if he took her home instead. He turned to Nathan. "Some other time."

After the couples said their good-byes, Alonzo led her from the hall to the bank of elevators. He used his cell phone to call the driver, so by the time they got downstairs the limousine was waiting for them.

The normally long ride back to Daria's seemed interminable. She seemed to have slipped into some sort of funk, and nothing he said worked to snap her out of it. Remembering how animated she'd been during their meal, he could gladly have throttled Vanessa for the sour note the evening ended on. When the car pulled up to the curb in front of Daria's he followed her inside, hoping to make some last-ditch effort to salvage the night.

$\sim$

Once Alonzo unlocked her door for her, she stepped over the threshold and turned to him. She didn't bother to turn on the hall light, as that would encourage him to stay. She'd spent the long minutes of the ride coming to a conclusion about them, one that didn't include extended good nights. "It's late."

He didn't take the hint, though. He stepped forward, forcing her to step back and allow him into her home. He closed the door behind him, plunging them into near total darkness. Only the small night-light plugged into a wall socket illuminated the hallway. Daria braced her back against the wall just to have some bearing. "It's late," she repeated.

"I know. I'm going."

Although she couldn't see his face clearly she felt the heat of his body. He was too close and she had nowhere to go since she'd backed herself against the wall.

His fingertips touched her cheek. "I'm sorry you didn't have a better time tonight."

Although she wanted him to leave, she didn't want him to think she hadn't enjoyed herself. "The evening was fine, though the last act could have used a little work."

"To say the least. I really am sorry that happened."

"I know."

"Good night, Daria."

She expected him to withdraw, but he didn't. The hand at her cheek moved to tilt her chin upward and a second later, his mouth touched down on hers. He pulled away from her almost immediately, but the brief contact left her breathless. Slowly she opened her eyes to gaze up at him as best she could. Though a faint smile curved his lips, his eyes had darkened to black in the dim light.

He stroked the knuckles of one hand across her cheek. "I've wanted to do that since the moment I saw you walk down the stairs."

She swallowed, not knowing how to respond to that admission. Or how to handle a man's desire. Connor had been her one and only lover, and passion hadn't been his forte. She'd never felt he truly wanted her more than say any other female body on the planet. He made love like he lived the rest of his life: haphazardly and without much effort.

Instinctively she knew Alonzo would be a different kind of lover: thoughtful, tender, giving instead of greedily snatching whatever he could get. She wasn't ready for sex with him or anyone. She doubted she could even handle a decent kiss. But she wanted him. Fearing he'd read her emotions in her eyes she lowered her head and buried her face against his chest.

His arms closed around her, his hands making soothing motions on her back. "I'm sorry, baby," he crooned against her ear.

She shook her head, silently denying that he had anything to be sorry for. If anything, she regretted leading him to believe she wanted less from him, not more. She lifted her head and gazed up at him. She knew she could never tolerate life in his world, nor would she subject her son to it either. But pragmatism and practicality be damned, she could have a little piece of him if she dared to take it.

She slid her arms around his neck and molded herself against him. Going on tiptoe, she pressed her open mouth to his.

His reaction was immediate and all-consuming. His tongue swept into her mouth, scalding her with his heat and his passion. She squeezed her eyes tight and gave herself over to the kiss. Surrender, though there had never been any struggle. She moaned her pleasure, and the kiss turned wild, out of control. Her hands roved over his back and her spine arched as she strove to get closer to him.

Daria was trembling by the time he broke the kiss. He buried his face against her neck. His whiskers scratched the delicate skin of her throat but she didn't care. She clung to him, dragging air and the heady masculine scent of him into her nostrils. Beneath her fingertips his heart beat a wild tattoo in his chest.

Finally, he lifted his head and touched his knuckles to her cheek. "I should go."

"Yes." But suddenly his mouth was on hers again. One of his arms circled her hips. The other hand rose to mold her breast with his palm. She whimpered from the sheer pleasure of having his hands on her.

"Mom, is that you?"

Light flooded the entryway. Her son stood at the top step by the upstairs light switch. All she could see were his feet, so she knew he couldn't see them. But what had he heard? Guiltily she sprang away from Alonzo. In the most normal voice she could muster, she said, "Yes, it's me, sweetheart. Go back to bed."

"Your voice sounds funny."

"I'll be up in a minute." She leaned back against the wall and closed her eyes as her son retreated. A moment later she heard his room door close with a faint click. She dragged in a slow breath as she contemplated what had just happened with Alonzo. How far would she have let him go if her son hadn't made an appearance? She honestly didn't know. How far would he have gone? Would he eventually have called a halt or would he have continued to take as long as she didn't try to stop him? She didn't know the answer to that either.

"Look at me, Daria," Alonzo commanded.

She opened her eyes, but kept her kiss-swollen lips pressed tightly together.

He rubbed his hands up her arms to settle on her shoulders. "We are two consenting adults. We didn't do anything wrong."

She shook her head. He'd read her emotion correctly but not the cause of it. Maybe he hadn't done anything wrong, but she questioned her own behavior. She'd known he intended to kiss her, and despite the fact that she considered a relationship between them untenable, she let him. Hell, she encouraged him in every way she knew how. She'd taken what he'd offered, knowing she offered little in return. Those were the actions of a user. Maybe she was more like Connor than she wanted to admit.

"I think you'd better go," she said finally.

He nodded, a grave expression on his face. She opened the door for him. Once he stood on the opposite side of the threshold he turned to face her. His fingertips caressed her cheek in a gentle motion. "I'll call you, tomorrow."

The tender look in his eyes almost undid her. She nodded, not trusting herself to say anything. She watched him walk out to the limousine, then closed the door. She kicked off her heels and went upstairs to check on her son. He lay facing the wall, trying to hide from her, but she knew he wasn't asleep. She sat on the bed beside him and stroked her palm over his hair. "Checking up on me, were you?"

Nicholas turned toward her. Moonlight and the Yugi-Oh night-light that burned at the head of his bed illuminated his face. "I just wanted to know if your date with Mr. Clark went okay."

"It went fine." But by the excited expression on her son's face, she doubted if all that concerned him was whether she'd had a good time. "Why?"

"You like Mr. Clark, don't you?"

"He's a very nice man."

"You were kissing him, weren't you?"

Heat rose in Daria's cheeks. To put it mildly. If she were back in high school, she would have called it making out. She tickled her son's sides. "That's none of your business, sport."

"I know." He sat up and braced his elbows on his knees. "But you like him, right?"

"Yes." Daria inhaled deeply and asked the question she dreaded getting an answer to. "Why?"

"I like him, too. Not like that but you know what I mean."

Daria nodded. "And . . ."

Nicholas pressed his lips together, averting his gaze to the pattern on his comforter. "Every boy needs a father, Mom. Dad's a real jerk, but Mr. Clark is cool. He talks to me like a person, not like some kid he doesn't have time for."

Like his own father treated him. Daria sighed and bit her lip. How could she make her son understand that the man he idolized was not the father for him? "Listen, Nick, I like Mr. Clark a lot, and it's okay that you do, too. But because of his career, he lives a different sort of lifestyle than I want for you or myself. When grown-ups get together, there has to be more to it than just liking each other. They have to have compatible goals, they have to want the same things. They—"

She stopped speaking, realizing her son had already tuned her out. Already he'd become a master of the male-only trick of not hearing whatever he didn't want someone to say. "It's complicated. We'll talk about it more tomorrow, okay?"

He nodded sullenly. "All right."

She bent and kissed his forehead. "Get some sleep."

Daria rose from the bed and went to her room. Like an automoton she undressed and pulled the pins from her hair. Once she'd donned a pale peach nightgown and brushed out her shoulder-length locks, she surveyed her image in her dressing table mirror. She touched her fingertips to her kiss-swollen lips and then to a spot on the side of her throat where Alonzo's whiskers had burned her skin.

She couldn't deny she'd enjoyed every moment of being in his arms, or every moment being with him, period. But she was no longer some starry-eyed girl who could cast aside any concerns other than if a man turned her on or not. She had to consider her son and what kind of life she could make for him, by herself or with a man.

Daria put down her brush and settled herself under her covers. Why couldn't anything in her life be easy? Plenty of women went on dates without their sons immediately pressing them for a new father. She'd been mistaken in thinking she alone could be enough to satisfy Nicholas's parental needs. But did her son have to pin his hopes on the one man Daria could never give him?

And worse yet, why was she cursed with the desire to be with him, to find out where things with them might lead if left to follow their own course? She'd known from the beginning this date would lead to disaster. Why hadn't she stuck to her guns and turned Alonzo Clark and his mystery date down?

Tears formed at the corners of her eyes. She tried to blink them away, but it didn't help. She wished she could blame her melancholy on PMS or the aftereffects of the wine. In truth, she was merely tired and frustrated and half in love with a man she could never have. She buried her face in her pillow and let the tears fall. A good cry could sometimes clear the mind and cleanse the psyche.

Oh hell. There wasn't any point to trying to rationalize her emotions. She hurt, ached somewhere way down deep, somewhere primal and unchecked by logic. Somewhere where she feared she would never be less alone than she was at this moment, and it terrified her right down to her bones.

Four

Daria woke to the aroma of brewing coffee and bacon sizzling in the pan. Her stomach rumbled and her mouth watered. Stella must be responsible since Daria didn't allow Nicholas near the stove. Time to start her day, even though she felt like burying herself under her covers.

Downstairs she found Nicholas already seated at the kitchen table, while Stella was busy scooping the bacon from the pan.

When Stella saw her, her face split in an impish grin. "Well, if it isn't Cinderella the day after the ball. Sit down, child. Breakfast is almost ready."

"Happy Mother's Day, Mom." Nicholas beamed at her as she slid into the seat across from him.

"Good morning, sweetheart." What devilment was her little angel up to now? And she was sure it was something.

"Do you want your present now?"

"My present?" She'd assumed her Mother's Day makeover would be it this year.

"I'll be right back." Nicholas returned with a small garment box wrapped in flowered paper and ribbons. "Open it."

"This had better not be another snake," she teased. The Mother's Day he was four, Nicholas had found a garter snake in the backyard and boxed it up for her. She'd nearly died of surprise, but the snake had gone on to live a happy life in the earth behind their house.

"It's not a snake."

Gingerly, she removed the ribbons, then tore off the paper. She opened the box to find a sleeveless black dress. She stood and held it up against her body. The hem fell to midthigh. She glanced at Stella. No way had her son picked this out himself. Stella shrugged and popped another set of toast out of the toaster.

She turned to her son. "It's lovely, Nicholas."

"You can wear it on your next date with Mr. Clark."

Daria pressed her lips together. She didn't bother to remind her son that there would be no more dates with Mr. Clark. Better to let him have his moment for now. She leaned down and kissed his forehead. "Thank you so much. I love it."

"Then you'd better get it away from the table. Hot food coming through."

Daria stepped aside, went to the living room, and laid the dress across the sofa. Later, she'd have to ask Stella the story behind the dress.

After their meal, Daria dabbed her mouth with her napkin and placed it on the table. She nodded in her son's direction. "Clear your place and then start getting ready for church."

"Aw, Mom, do we have to go?"

Daria almost smiled. Her son's interest in the divine was less than enthusiastic. "Yes, we do. It's Mother's Day. I want to show off my son."

Nicholas made a face, but did as his mother asked. Once he was out of the room, Daria turned to Stella, who sat beside her. "How on earth did my son afford that dress?"

"He took out a loan from *his* fairy godmother. He has to rake my leaves this fall and shovel my snow this winter. Then we're even."

"He does that anyway, Stella." Despite the older woman's dislike of physical displays of emotion, Daria threw her arms around her neck. "Thank you."

"Quit hugging on me," Stella protested. "You'll smush my brooch."

Stella fingered the item that she had pinned to the lapel of her robe. "And while we're on the subject, how do you think your son managed to afford that?"

Daria shrugged and feigned innocence. Stella had confided to her recently that as a young woman she'd had two pieces of jewelry that she treasured. Both were lost in a fire that had consumed her home. "How do you suppose it will look with this?" Daria pulled a jewelry box from her robe and handed it to Stella.

"Now what did you go on and do?" Stella's fingers trembled as she tore the paper from the tiny box. She removed the lid and pulled out a tiny gold locket on a gold chain. "Oh, my."

Daria grinned. She'd actually rendered Stella speechless. "There's an inscription on the back."

"With all our love, Nicholas and Daria." Stella glanced up at her with tear-filled eyes. "Oh, child, you don't know what this means to me. My mother gave me those things."

To Daria's surprise, Stella threw her arms around her and hugged her. She pulled back almost immediately, embarrassment coloring her cheeks. "I'd better get you your present, shouldn't I?"

Stella went to the pantry and pulled out a square box wrapped in silver paper. "Happy Mother's Day."

Inside the box lay a lavender silk lounging outfit. "Oh, Stella. It's beautiful."

"And perfect for entertaining a man."

Daria brought the garment down to her lap. "Just because I went out with Alonzo last night does not mean—"

Stella patted her hand. "I know, child. Don't think I didn't hear you crying in your bed last night, 'cuz I did. And the good Lord knows, there are only two times when a woman cries over a man: when she's got one and when she doesn't. Either way, a little silk never hurt no one."

Daria shook her head. "You shouldn't have. With the dress and all, it's too expensive."

"Well, you shouldn't have done what you did, neither. Just think, we'll all go to the poorhouse together."

Daria laughed. "We'll have worse places to consider if we don't hurry up and get dressed for church."

"You got that right. But don't think I want to see you going back to your old frumpy ways. When I saw you come downstairs last night, it was like I was seeing a vision and Alonzo Clark's eyes nearly bugged clean out of his head."

After she and Stella cleaned the kitchen, Daria went back to her room to change. With Stella's words ringing in her ears she stood at her closet surveying the garments that hung there. Frump city, as Stella would say. She had to admit that in the last few years she had really let herself go, dressing more like someone's maiden aunt than a young woman in her thirties. If her makeover had taught her anything it was that she liked looking pretty and feminine. Her dowdy days were over.

Reaching into the back of her closet she pulled out a multicolor linen sundress, a remnant of earlier times. The form-fitting bodice ended in a flared skirt that fell to just above the knee if she remembered correctly. It was still wrapped in cellophane from the cleaners, so it hadn't wrinkled. But would it still fit? Daria shrugged out of her robe and pulled the dress over her head. Aside from being just a tad tight across her breasts, it fit perfectly.

Daria beamed at her reflection in the mirror. "Not too shabby, old girl," she told her reflected self. "Not too shabby at all."

Ten minutes later, with her hair floating around her shoulders and her makeup in place, Daria descended the stairs. She'd thrown on a navy blazer on top and her most daring pair of navy pumps on her feet to complete her outfit. "Is this unfrumpy enough for you?" she asked Stella when she reached the bottom step.

"Honey chile, when Pastor sees you, he's going to forget all about Mother's Day and start preaching about the wages of sin."

Daria's gaze rested on her son, dressed in a navy blue suit, white shirt, and colorful tie. He was nearly as tall as she and starting to get the look of a man, not a boy. "Are you ready to escort two lovely ladies to church?"

Nicholas grinned. "I don't know, but since you and Miss Stella are already here . . ."

Daria ran her hand over his hair. "My son the comedian. Are we ready to go?"

Stella waved her hands in the air. "Oh, gracious, I can't believe I almost forgot. I'll be right back." She hurried back toward the kitchen.

Daria glanced at Nicholas, who shrugged. A moment later, Stella rushed back holding a square florist's box. "Couldn't let these go to waste."

"What are they?"

Stella opened the box to show three perfect carnations, two white and one red. "Mother's Day flowers."

"Stella, they're beautiful. When did you have time to get them?"

"I didn't. Alonzo Clark brought them last night and asked me to put them in the refrigerator for you." She handed Daria a tiny envelope. "Here's the card."

Daria took the envelope, then cast a disgruntled look at Stella. The card had obviously been opened and probably read. "Why don't you tell me what it says?"

Without missing a beat, Stella said, "Happy Mother's Day, Daria. Hope it's all you want it to be, Alonzo."

Daria slid the card from the envelope to read those exact words.

"An old-fashioned custom for an old-fashioned man?" Stella ventured.

Daria didn't answer. In truth Alonzo's thoughtfulness touched her on a very feminine level. She slipped it back in the envelope, placed the envelope inside the box, and concentrated on pinning the flowers on everyone.

"How come I get the red one?" Nicholas asked, admiring the flower.

"According to tradition, you wear a red carnation if your mother is alive and a white one if she isn't."

"Oh, I thought it was because I'm a guy and you guys aren't."

Daria shook her head at the illogic of that sentence. "Let's go."

When service was over, Daria drove the three of them to the Cross County shopping center in Yonkers.

"Why are we stopping here?" Nicholas asked as she pulled into a space in the parking lot. He put shopping on the same level of torture as eating broccoli and taking out the trash.

"I thought I'd buy a few things while the sales are on." She turned to Stella. "Defrumpify myself a little."

Stella grinned. "You know you got my vote, but I thought you were headed for the poorhouse."

Daria shrugged. "I'm expecting a hefty refund check this year. I was going to put it all in Nicholas's college fund, but I guess I can spend a little of it on myself."

"Atta girl," Stella said, getting out of the car. "Let's hit that new Victoria's Secret store they got here."

"Mo-om," Nicholas protested. "I have to look at underwear?"

"Hush up, child," Stella admonished, laughing. She leaned closer to Daria and whispered, "One of these days he's gonna be begging to see some poor girl's underwear."

Daria laughed, but she hoped that time was a long way off.

～

Two hours later, Daria thought she had Victoria's real secret figured out—she charged too much. Even so, Stella had talked her into buying a set of skimpy black underwear to wear with her new black dress. She'd also bought some separates that she could pair with some of the items already in her closet. She didn't want to replace her entire wardrobe, but she had a sewing machine and enough ingenuity to modify much of what she owned.

Once she got home, she went to her room to change and to put away her purchases. Immediately she noticed the button flashing on the answering machine. She supposed the call must be from Alonzo, as most people who knew her knew she reserved Sundays for spending quality time with her son and left her alone. She pressed the play button, and immediately Alonzo's deep voice filled the room.

"Daria, this is Alonzo. I guess you must still be at church. I hope you liked the flowers. Call me when you get a chance."

Alonzo rattled off the numbers for his home and his cell phone before hanging up. Daria sank down on her bed and stared at the machine. Given the easy, familiar tone of his words, she had definitely left him with the wrong impression last night. How could she not, after the way she'd thrown herself at him? She bit her lip. That left her with the unpleasant task of correcting that impression. But not over the phone. She'd have to see him Monday and explain herself face-to-face.

"Aren't you going to call him back?"

Daria glanced over her shoulder to find Nicholas eyeing her with a suspicious scowl. She rose from the bed. "No, I'm not."

"Why not? Didn't you have a good time last night?"

"Yes, I did. It's complicated."

"Everything adults do is complicated."

A dull ache began to throb at her temple. Even if she wanted to, she doubted she could explain her feelings to her son. "Nicholas, please. Change you clothes and I'll take you to the park, the one by Two Thirty-third Street. We'll work on your pitching."

Nicholas had been begging her to take him to Van Cortlandt Park where there was enough space to really let loose. For the past three weeks, she hadn't found the time. Both of them recognized it as a bribe, and Nicholas didn't appear to be too pleased to have gotten what he wanted in this way. She watched him clomp back to his room. She'd have to make it up to him, though how she had no idea. For now, she turned off the answering machine. That way Alonzo couldn't leave another message for her son to question her about. She changed into jeans and an old sweatshirt. Within fifteen minutes, she and Nicholas were out the door.

~

". . . and then Michael Jordan called to ask if I wanted to go bowling on Mars with Shaquille O'Neil and Magic Johnson."

Alonzo blinked and focused his gaze across the table to his mother. "What did you say?"

"I could have been reciting the Pledge of Allegiance for all the attention you've been paying me. What woman's got you mooning over her so bad that I can't enjoy a Mother's Day dinner with my son?"

"I am not mooning. I was thinking."

"Right, about some woman. How did your date go last night?"

Alonzo shifted in his seat. His mind had been on Daria, and the fact that she hadn't called him back yet. Had he misread her passion in the way she'd kissed him the night before? He didn't think so. He'd told her he intended to call her and she hadn't protested. So if both she and Nicholas were all right, why hadn't she returned his call?

"It isn't polite for a man to kiss and tell."

"So you got that far. I was beginning to wonder if my boy had lost his touch. Tell me about her, then. Should I start writing out my recipe?"

He knew he'd live to regret that comment about her greens. "Daria is . . . different than what I expected."

"What do you mean?"

"In the office she's no-nonsense, very off-putting. Last night she was funny and warm and . . ." He cleared his throat and sat up straighter, realizing he'd stopped short of telling his mother that he'd wanted her from the moment he saw her on the stairs. "I, um, we had a good time."

An astute woman, Vivian studied her son with a speculative glare. "And she hasn't returned your call."

"No."

Vivian wiped some imaginary bolognese sauce from the corner of her mouth and dropped her napkin to the table. "What a refreshing change—a man waiting on a woman to call."

He didn't find a thing refreshing about it. "I'm concerned that they are all right."

"How old is this woman?"

"Thirty-two."

"Imagine that! She managed to live thirty-plus years without you fussing over her." Vivian patted his hand. "Relax, sweetie, they're fine. What do you say we have some dessert?"

His mother might be right, but his gut told him otherwise. He remembered the anxious look in Daria's eyes when he'd left. He wondered if she regretted letting things between them go as far as they did. He hadn't intended for them to get that serious himself. But once she'd put her sweet mouth on him, he'd gone a little crazy. He couldn't remember wanting a woman the way he'd wanted her. It had taken the appearance of her son to draw him back to sanity.

He didn't intend to spend much more time speculating about it. After he got home that night, he dialed Daria's number. Nicholas answered the phone.

"Hey, little man. Where's your mother?"

"In the shower."

For a moment Alonzo's mind flooded with images of Daria's nude body sluiced with water. He cleared his throat, suddenly aware of the curtness of the boy's answer. "Is she okay?"

"I don't know. She was weird today, and last night I heard her crying. Did you treat my mom bad, Mr. Clark?"

Alonzo closed his eyes, not knowing what to respond to first—the knowledge that something he'd done might have made Daria cry, or the accusation in the boy's voice and the accompanying trust inherent in his question. "I haven't done anything that I'm aware of to hurt your mother."

"Okay. I gotta go."

The boy hung up, obviously satisfied with the answer he'd received. However, Alonzo's concerns had only intensified. After pacing around his living room for a half hour, he got in his car and drove to Daria's.

∼

Daria had just kissed Nicholas good night when the doorbell rang. She figured it was Stella coming to have another go at her about her feelings for Alonzo. When she opened the door to find Alonzo himself on the other side, she froze with her mouth hanging open.

"Hi, Alonzo, won't you come in?" he said, as if speaking for her.

Despite the humor of his words she sensed an undercurrent of intensity in him, saw it reflected in his dark eyes. Why was he here? If she'd suspected this would be the result of not returning his phone call, she'd have rung him up right away. She still hadn't come up with the words she wanted to say to him, but she couldn't leave him standing on her doorstep either.

She pushed open the screen door. "Please come in."

He stepped inside, crowding her in the small foyer. The citrus smell of his cologne reached her nose, and the warmth of his body seared her. She turned and preceded him to the living room. "Please have a seat."

He crossed her small living room, made smaller by his presence in it. She glanced around the room, wondering what he thought of her modest furnishings. Comfort, not style, had been her guide in decorating. Although he'd grown up in a small neighborhood in Queens, his circumstances had risen far above that.

He stopped at one corner of her beige tweed sofa, but didn't sit. "You have a lovely home, Daria. Very inviting."

"Thank you." She realized she'd gripped her hands together and dropped them to her sides. "Can I get you anything? Tea or coffee? A drink? I don't have much."

"Nothing, thank you."

"Then why are you here?"

"I want you to answer a question for me."

"If I can."

He hadn't really been looking at her before, but now he fastened a steady, intense gaze on her. "Did I make you cry?"

"Why would you th—" Nicholas. Earlier that day when she'd been in the shower, she'd heard the phone ring. Nicholas told her it was a wrong number, but obviously her son had lied to her about Alonzo being on the phone. What else had her little angel told him?

"I was crying last night, but not because of you, not the way that you think." She fiddled with the sash on her robe, trying to come up with the words to explain what she'd been feeling. "Did you ever feel that you were living this perfectly nice life until something came along and made you question your choices or what you thought you wanted?"

"Going out with me made you regret your life?"

"No, not exactly. For the first time in a long time I wished I had someone to share it with. Everyone tells me I'm supposed to be looking for a man, a life partner. If not for myself, then for Nicholas's sake. Even he tells me he needs a father. Last night was the first time I felt the lack myself. I don't know."

Realizing all she'd confessed to him, she turned away from him, wrapping her arms around her waist. Now she'd really managed to make a fool of herself, but good. She thought to ask him to leave, but her mouth couldn't seem to form the words. A moment later, his arms closed around her from behind. The heat of him was so intoxicating she leaned against him without thinking.

His lips brushed her temple. "Would it surprise you to know I felt the same way?"

He had to be joking. Here was one of the most famous radio personalities in the country, who had women falling all over him, and he wanted to metamorphose his life after one evening spent in her company? That she could not believe.

She pulled away from him to a safe distance and turned to face him. "Let's get real here, Alonzo. The only reason you went out with me last night is that I won that contest. Pity the poor single mom and her wretched little life. The only way she can get a date is if her son wins one for her. Don't think I don't appreciate all that you've done for me and for my son. But I'm not foolish enough to believe that the evening was anything more to you than a career obligation."

His eyes, which had held such warmth only moments ago, turned hard and cold as glass. "Tell me, how was I advancing my career when I kissed you last night? And what about you? I didn't hear any words of protest coming from your lips. In fact, you encouraged me. Tell me, what kind of woman shares that kind of passion with a man she believes is using her?"

She squeezed her eyes shut and lowered her head, not knowing what to say to him. "I never said I thought you were using me."

"What else would you call it? If I have no real interest in you as you claim, then I must have been out for what I could get from a vulnerable woman. If you think that's true, then you don't have a very high opinion of me."

Her head snapped up. Not for a minute did she mean to imply that she faulted him for anything that happened last night. "That's not true."

He lifted his shoulders in a fatalistic shrug. "I'll tell you something, Daria. Even before I saw your son's letter I had asked the station manager to make sure you won. It was my price for getting involved with this ridiculous contest in the first place. Somewhere in the back of my mind I must have known that would mean we would be paired together, but I wasn't really thinking about that. I saw you as a devoted mother who could use something nice to happen to her. Not out of pity, but as a kind of cosmic thank-you for being there for your son.

"After I read Nicholas's letter, I have to admit I was looking forward to our date, looking forward to knowing more about a woman who would inspire such love and devotion. And when you walked down those stairs in that gown . . . you took my breath away. I didn't try to hide the fact that I wanted you. I still do.

"Pity was never part of the equation, Daria, not until now." He stepped back from her, turned to leave, then pivoted back. "I'm going home. You don't have to worry about me bothering you again."

She stood rooted in place, her eyes riveted to him until he disappeared around the curve in the hallway. A few moments later she heard the door open and close and the screen bang. She hadn't tried to stop him because she hadn't known what to say if she did.

Maybe it was best that she let him leave without comment. It, whatever it had been between them, was over. She supposed she should be happy to conclude something that never should have existed in the first place, but she wasn't. Not one little bit.

~

"So how did it go last night? Give Mama all the gory details."

Diana waylaid him on his way out to the candy machine. "Not you too, Diana." Not one person he'd run into at the station had failed to ask him about the date. He hadn't told any of them a single thing.

"I have a vested interest in knowing. I heard about the stunt Vanessa pulled. Is it as bad as everyone says?"

"Without knowing what everyone is saying, I'd guess probably."

Diana made a disgusted face. "Damn. I was afraid of that." Diana sighed. "I don't know what to do with that girl. But that isn't your problem. Tell me how the rest of the evening went."

"Don't tell me you have a vested interest in that, too."

Diana offered him a sheepish look. "Actually I do. True Confessions time. I already had Nicholas Johnson's letter in-house when I asked you to become part of the contest. His letter knocked my socks off, and I knew if nothing better came in his mother would win the makeover."

"And . . ." Alonzo prompted, not quite sure where this story was heading.

"And the consensus around here was that one man in particular would make the perfect match for her: you."

He didn't know if he should be angry or amused. "You folks took a vote on it?"

"Not exactly, but we all remember seeing you two at the Christmas party. You were off in your own little world on the dance floor. We were surprised either of you noticed when the music ended."

"The affiliates had nothing to do with you trying to get me into the contest?"

She shook her head. "I was prepared to let you off the hook if you protested too much, but when you asked me to make sure Nicholas's mom won, I knew I'd made the right decision."

Alonzo shook his head. He'd cooked his own goose, but he didn't regret it. He only wished he hadn't come down so hard on Daria the night before. She hadn't deserved it, and he'd regretted walking away from her the moment he'd gotten outside her door. He couldn't blame her if she never spoke to him again after some of the things he'd said.

The night was supposed to be a treat for her, but Diana had turned it into a publicity opportunity for the station. Page Six of the *Post* boasted a picture of them on the red carpet above a caption that read: WHO'S ALONZO CLARK'S MYSTERY WOMAN? Beneath that the blurb talked about how Daria had won the contest and speculated on a future between the two of them. Undoubtedly the head of the publicity department had made sure that item got into the paper.

He never should have gone along with that idea in the first place. He wouldn't have if he hadn't felt the need to impress her. But what had made him think she'd be enamored of a group of shallow, self-absorbed individuals he could barely stand himself? If he had it to do over, he'd have taken her to someplace quiet where they could have focused on each other. Now, all he could hope was that she would give him another chance.

"So—" Diana prompted.

He appreciated Diana's matchmaking attempts, but in truth she'd done just as much harm as good. At any rate, he had no desire to tell her anything. "I'll have to let you know." He winked at her and walked away.

~

At exactly 11:50, Alonzo claimed a spot outside the office building that housed the radio station and settled in to wait. Daria left her office every day at noon for lunch. He hoped to waylay her as she departed.

A wave of people exited the building, Daria included. Alonzo almost didn't recognize her. She had on the same sweater set he'd seen her wear before, but the matching skirt was tighter and shorter than it had been before and she was wearing heels. Her hair was down and her face was made up. The total effect was quiet alluring.

But she hadn't noticed him. When he called her name she turned to face him, but she didn't look happy to see him. He walked to where she waited. "We need to talk."

"I can't see why. I would think you'd said all you had to say last night."

"About last night—" He was cut off when a fellow pedestrian bumped into him, muttering as he passed. He couldn't blame the guy. Every New Yorker knew the sidewalk at lunchtime was no place to hold a conversation.

"Let me take you to lunch. My treat."

He saw the hesitation on her face before she answered him. "I have to be back in an hour."

He took her to a little café around the corner, too pricey to do much business with the working crowd. They were seated at a windowside booth.

Daria folded her hands on the table and eyed him with a penetrating gaze. "What did you want to say?"

She was back to being all business, which didn't surprise him. "I wanted to apologize to you for what I said last night."

"There's no need. You were right. I had no business kissing you when I had already made up my mind that it wasn't wise for us to see each other again. I didn't mean to accuse you of using me, when actually it was the other way around."

"Why did you? Kiss me, I mean."

"It's been a long time since a man has shown the slightest interest in me. I missed that. After dealing with my ex-husband, I didn't want any male attention and I made sure I didn't get any. But in doing so, I gave up a part of myself, a part I'm glad to have back. For that, I thank you."

But she didn't want anything else from him. He doubted Vanessa's histrionics had anything to do with that decision, but what did? Had her ex-husband hurt her so badly that she didn't want to try again? He pondered that while the waitress took their orders. When she left, he leaned back in his chair. "What was he like?"

"Who? My ex-husband?"

He nodded.

"A vain, spoiled, self-involved child, who never had any real regard for anyone other than himself."

Somehow he couldn't imagine Daria with such a man. "Why did you marry him?"

She gave a rueful little laugh. "Looking back on it, I have no idea. Connor was a good-time guy. I'd been raised very strictly and the thought of being with such a freewheeling man appealed to me. I think he married me because he wanted to sleep with me and that was what I required. But I became pregnant with Nicholas almost right away. Maybe if we'd had a few years to cement our relationship first, things might have turned out differently, but I doubt it. The only responsibility Connor ever honored was his job."

She blinked and looked at him as if she were seeing him for the first time. "I don't know why I am telling you all this."

Because on some level she trusted him. He saw that even if she didn't. "I don't know what your husband did to you, Daria." He didn't want to know. Already he wanted to hunt the guy down and throttle him. "But I'm not him."

"Believe me, I know that."

"Then what made you decide not to see me again?"

She sighed as if relieving herself of a heavy burden. "You travel in some pretty lofty circles, Alonzo. You may belong there, but I don't. I want a nice, stable life for myself and my son. I don't want to have to wonder where my man is or what he's doing or who he's doing. Been there, done that, watched the videotape."

And that's the kind of grief she thought he would bring her? "Daria, most nights I'm in bed by nine o'clock. I get up at four in the morning to make it to work on time. I am not a party animal by any stretch of the term."

"I saw you last year at the Video Music Awards with that singer, what's her name, Jameilah?"

"Her name is Janet Watson and her family lives across the street from my mother. She asked me to go with her because, unlike her boyfriend at the time, she knew I wouldn't embarrass her in public. But what has that got to do with anything? I am a public person because of my job, but I am not some Casanova on the prowl. It might surprise you to know that the only woman besides my mother I've been out with in the past six months was you, Saturday night."

He leaned across the table and took her hand in both of his. "Listen, Daria. I know it was a mistake to bring you to that dinner, but are you saying that all a person gets with you is one shot? Blow that and it's over forever? Whatever happened to giving a guy a second chance?"

He looked at her with an expression of entreaty on his face. At the same time, his thumb rubbed against her palm. Her fingers flexed and she tried to pull her hand away, but he held it gently but firmly.

She let out an exasperated breath. "You don't play fair, Mr. Clark."

"Nope."

His dual attack on her conscience and on her senses must have worked, because she lowered her head and sighed. "When?"

"Can you get a baby-sitter for Saturday night?"

She slanted a glance up at him. "I think so."

"I'll pick you up at seven."

The waitress came with their food, a cheeseburger for him and a salad for Daria. As the waitress set down the plates he could sense Daria's eyes on him, measuring him. He met her gaze, one that said, *Please don't let this be another mistake.* He smiled. He'd make sure it wasn't.

Five

Daria hadn't seen Alonzo for the rest of the week at work, and when he called Saturday morning to ask her if she wouldn't mind if he sent a car for her instead, she was immediately filled with trepidation. She couldn't handle a change in plans, not when her stomach was already a knot festival at the prospect of going out with him again. She'd told him that would be fine, but by the time seven o'clock rolled around, she jumped when the doorbell rang.

"Simmer down, girl," Stella admonished. "Or you're going to give yourself a thrombosis."

Daria rose from the sofa and smoothed the skirt of her black dress over her hips. "How do I look?"

"Like ten million dollars, child, 'cuz one million's not enough."

Daria snorted over Stella's exaggeration. "Seriously."

"You are a damn handsome woman, Daria Johnson, and you know it, so stop fretting about how you look. Now go on and get out of here before your ride up and leaves without you."

"I'm going, I'm going." Daria walked to the hall banister where she'd draped her black and white pashmina. She arranged it around her shoulders, then picked up her black purse. "I'm going."

Stella chuckled, a deep melodious sound in her throat. "Have a good time."

"I will."

Nicholas appeared out of nowhere to give her a good night kiss. He seemed almost as excited as she. She smoothed her hand over his hair. "You two behave yourselves."

"We ain't makin' no promises, isn't that right?" She elbowed Nicholas. "And if I was you, I wouldn't be makin' no promises neither."

Color rose in Daria's cheeks, but she had no intention of being seduced by Alonzo Clark. She'd agreed to have dinner with him, not be his dessert. With a wave she opened the front door and headed out into the warm spring night.

Surprisingly there wasn't much traffic for their journey into Manhattan. At least she assumed that a restaurant in Manhattan was their destination—until the driver bypassed the last exit on the FDR Drive and headed for the Brooklyn Bridge. She leaned forward and asked the driver where they were heading. The address he gave her held no meaning, but as there were many fine restaurants in the outer boroughs she didn't question their destination.

Finally, the driver came to a stop on a block full of historic brownstones. This had to be a mistake, she thought as the driver opened the door to help her out. But directly in front of her was the address the driver had mentioned.

This was no restaurant, it was someone's home. Alonzo's home. "Would you wait until I get inside?" she asked the driver, though she had no intention of staying. This was not what she'd agreed to.

"Certainly, ma'am."

She walked up the stairs and used the brass knocker to summon Alonzo. She didn't have to wait long before the door opened and he stood in front of her. He wore a pair of cream linen pants topped off by a black silk shirt. Simple and elegant, and to her he'd never looked more handsome.

He leaned forward and kissed her cheek. "Welcome to my home, Daria."

She shook her head. "I thought we were meeting at a restaurant."

"We are. *Chez* Alonzo." He bowed. "May I show you to your table?"

"Not funny."

"Look, Daria, I didn't bring you here with any wild seduction schemes in mind. I wanted to prove to you that I am not the man you think I am. What better place to show you that than in my own home? If you like, Paul can wait outside to take you home whenever you want to go."

She huffed out a breath. She saw the earnest look in his eyes and it swayed her. "That won't be necessary."

"I'm glad." He stepped back to allow her to enter. "You look lovely tonight."

"Thank you."

He closed the door behind them. "Would you like a tour?"

"All right."

With a hand on her back, he led her down the hallway, across hardwood floors covered by oriental runners, to a large living area. Though the furnishings were more expensive, his living room reminded her of hers in the simplicity of the decor. One corner of the room was dominated by what appeared to be a stuffed carpet.

"What's that?"

"Believe it or not, it's a rocking chair."

She eyed him skeptically. "Really?"

"Want to try it out? It's the most comfortable spot in the house."

"Maybe later."

"I'm going to hold you to that."

Daria slanted another glance at him. How did you hold someone to a maybe?

He led her to other rooms: his study, the dining room where silverware and glasses for two had already been laid out on a white tablecloth, and finally to the kitchen. Stark white and enormous compared to hers, it boasted every amenity Daria had ever dreamed of owning. Delicious smells issued from the stove, but she couldn't see anything cooking.

"What are we having?"

"Steak. Which reminds me, it's time to turn them." He went to the counter to get a pot holder and a meat fork. "If you'd like some wine I'll get it for you in a minute."

She notice the open bottle on the counter. She wouldn't mind a glass to help take the edge off her nerves. "I can do it myself."

"Absolutely not." He straightened from the task of turning the steaks and shut the broiler. "In my family we have a rule: the first time you visit, you're a guest, so as host, it is up to me to see to all your needs." He filled a glass halfway and handed it to her.

"Thank you." She took a small sip, watching him over the rim of her glass. "What happens the second time you visit?"

"You're still company, so we let you get a little more comfortable. You can get your own drink, maybe." He grinned at her like a schoolboy. "By the third time, we have you doing the dishes."

She laughed, then hiccuped, as she'd been drinking her wine. "I'll have to make sure to stop at the second time."

His eyes narrowed and his smile became one of challenge. He reached for his own glass and took a sip. "We'll see."

She took another sip, watching him. Something about him was different tonight. She couldn't put her finger on it or define it, but she had the feeling she was seeing him for the first time, the quintessential man without the trappings of success or fame getting in the way. A smile tilted up her lips. "So, I take it I would be going against the rules if I asked you if I can help with anything."

"Yup." He set his wineglass on the counter. "Everything is ready anyway. If you'll have a seat in the dining room, I'll be in to serve you right away."

He'd spoken the last words as if he were the maître d' of a snooty restaurant. "All right," she agreed. "I shall await you directly."

~

After she'd gone, Alonzo set about arranging their meal on two plates. He'd planned a simple meal since he'd lacked the concentration to prepare anything more involved. Steaks, wild rice, and a medley of fresh, steamed vegetables. It would have to do. He set the two plates, the wine bottle, and his glass on a tray and carried it to the dining room.

He stopped in the open doorway, thoughts of food completely forgotten. Daria stood by one of the paintings in his living room, admiring Tom Feelings's handiwork. She glanced over at him, one of her treasured minismiles on her lips. She'd taken off her shawl and draped it over the back of her chair. For the first time he got a good look at what she was wearing: a little black dress that bared her arms and most of her back. Her legs were bare, her feet encased in high-heeled black pumps. Although her attire pleased him, the little smile did him in.

He was falling, sinking like a stone in a pool of water. He'd always liked her, always admired her, but in the past few days, she'd burrowed a little place under his skin and didn't appear to want to get out. He didn't want her to. And he knew the reason he'd reacted so harshly when she'd made that comment about him using her was that she'd been right about him wanting what he could get. In truth, he wanted all of her, but at that moment he'd been willing to settle for less.

What he didn't know, and what plagued him, was whether she felt anything real for him in return.

She took a step toward him. "Is something wrong?"

"Not at all." He walked to the table to set down the tray. "Dinner is served."

As he arranged the plates, she took her seat. He unfolded his napkin on his lap. With her strict upbringing, he figured her to be a religious woman. "Would you like to say grace, or should I?" he offered.

He thought he detected a hint of a smile on her face as she said, "Please, go ahead."

Now he'd sunk himself. He folded his hands and tried to remember the words his father had spoken at every mealtime. "Bless us, O Lord, and these thy gifts which we are about to receive." If he were still a practicing Catholic he would have crossed himself in thanks for whatever divine intervention that helped him remember that prayer.

She patted his hand. "Very good. I didn't think you could do it."

He leaned back in his chair, his gaze riveted to her smiling face. "I believe in God. It's religion I can't stand. That doesn't bother you, does it?"

She lifted her shoulders in a delicate motion. "You and my son should get together. He thinks church was invented to give sinners insight into the tortures of hell." She shrugged again. "Everyone has to believe in their own way."

"And I believe I'll have some more wine. How about you?"

She held up her glass. "You're incorrigible."

"So they tell me." He sipped from his glass. "How was your week?"

She swallowed before answering. "Hectic. We've got a big trial coming up at the end of the month. How about yours?"

"About the same as it always is. Although next week I'll be flying solo, unless they find someone to replace Vanessa before that."

"She was fired? Not because of what happened at the dinner."

"No. She had it coming before then. I didn't know it until now, but she was the station manager's niece, which is why she got so many chances to mess up, but Diana finally got fed up."

"I'm sorry to hear that. But I got the impression from Vanessa that she was used to having her own way. That's why I don't spoil my son. I don't want him to grow up thinking the world owes him something like his father does."

Although he admired Daria's skill in raising Nicholas, he wanted this evening to be about them. He carefully steered the conversation to art, given her interest in his painting. From there they discussed music, books, the current lineup of television shows, which neither of them knew much about. It didn't surprise him that they agreed on many things. Though he wouldn't describe his upbringing as strict, it was old-fashioned as he supposed hers was.

As they finished off coffee and slices of caramel cake, he found her silently observing him with a curious expression on her face.

"Why are you looking at me like that?"

She shrugged and looked down at her coffee cup. "Like what?"

"Like there's a big bump on my head and you're trying to figure out what's in it." His heart skipped a beat, when she started to laugh. He'd finally gotten a real smile out of her and the effect was breathtaking.

When she composed herself she said, "I was thinking that I really didn't know much about you before tonight."

His eyes narrowed and his voice lowered an octave. "And what have you discovered?"

She tilted her head to one side and bit her lip.

His goal hadn't been to make her uncomfortable, but that question obviously did. He stood and held out his hand to her. Kenny G's saxophone was moaning a plaintive lover's call over the dining room speakers. "Come dance with me," he said.

She placed her hand in his and rose from the table. He led her closer to the door where there was room enough for them to move. He pulled her into his arms and she melted against him. For a moment he simply held her, reveling in the feel of her soft body next to his. Despite the difference in their heights, the fit was oh, so sweet. Slowly he began to move, more of a sway than an actual dance. His fingers drifted over her back, then upward to curve around her delicate nape. He was rewarded with a soft purr as she snuggled closer against him, her cheek resting against his shoulder. He could stay like that forever, but he knew the final chords of the song were only moments away.

~

As the song ended, Daria lifted her head to look at Alonzo. He might not have brought her here to seduce her, but he was doing a fine job of it anyway. Being in his arms moved her in a way no man's touch had before. But just being with him, talking about their lives and what mattered to them, had moved her more. When he'd asked her what she'd discovered about him she hadn't answered, afraid she'd blurt out that she'd learned that she was in love with him. Although she knew it was true, she wasn't ready to share that with him yet.

He regarded her with hooded eyes that had gone almost black. She swallowed. If he kept looking at her like that she'd forget all her mother had taught her about cows and free milk and do what she wanted. And she wanted him so much, it was like a taste in her mouth that needed satisfying. She stepped away from him and fixed her gaze on a nice safe spot, his chest. "Maybe I'll try that rocking chair now." Surely she could maintain some decorum on that innocuous-looking piece of furniture.

For some reason, he grinned. "If you say so." He motioned for her to precede him.

When they got to the living room she took one more look at the contraption while Alonzo busied himself at the bar in the corner. "How do you get on this thing?"

"Sit down and swing your feet over, but take your shoes off first."

She slipped off her heels and held her skirt to cover her derriere as she sat. She leaned back and pulled her feet over, setting the chair into a gentle rocking motion. She shrieked and giggled at the unfamiliar sensation, making Alonzo look back at her with an engaging grin on his face.

"Are you all right back there?"

"I'm fine." Once she settled into the chair, she realized how soft it was, like sitting on a giant carpeted pillow. She spread her arms and sighed. "I could stay here forever."

Laughing, he turned and walked toward her, holding a brandy snifter in each hand. "I suppose that could be arranged. I'll call your job on Monday and tell them you won't be coming in." He toed off his shoes and lay down beside her, extending one of the glasses toward her.

She accepted it and took a small sip. The strong liquid burned its way down to her stomach. A comfortable warmth suffused her body. She turned her head so that she could look at Alonzo. He lay with his body tilting toward her and his head propped up on his hand. "I do believe you are trying to get me drunk, Mr. Clark."

"I just want to see to all your needs. I am the host, remember." He trailed a finger across her cheek. "Have I seen to all your needs, Daria?"

She swallowed and shut her eyes, because there was one need that no one had seen to in a very long time. Her body throbbed with it, and her breasts ached with it. She pressed her legs together in a vain attempt to quell it. But she wanted him too badly for any half measures to suffice.

"Look at me, Daria."

She opened her eyes to find Alonzo's concerned face hovering over hers. "What is it, sweetheart?"

She looked away from him, not knowing what to say. She wanted him, but she was raised to look for love before falling into bed with a man. It was something she believed in, too. But Alonzo had never said anything about caring for her, only wanting her. At this late stage in her life, she refused to play the fool. "I think you'd better take me home now."

"Why?" With his thumb and forefinger he turned her face toward him. He looked at her with a sharp expression she didn't understand. Then his features relaxed, softened. He pulled her into his arms so that she lay on top of him.

For a moment, she was too stunned by his gesture to do anything but lie there with her cheek against his shoulder.

His hands moved over her back in a soothing, nonsexual manner. "I'm sorry, Daria," he whispered against her hair.

She didn't understand his apology, either. "It's okay," she said, more to have something to say than because her words meant anything.

"Can I ask you something?" he said in a subdued voice.

She nodded.

"Your husband was your first lover, right?"

She nodded again.

"And your last lover?"

"Connor was my only lover, if that's what you're getting at."

He turned them so that they lay side by side on the chair. He brushed her hair away from her face with the backs of his fingers. That tender look was back in his eyes, and a rueful smile curved his lips. "I'm not even going to pretend that I don't want to be with you, Daria. That would be a lie and we both know it. But I would never try to force you into anything you aren't ready for. Do you believe that?"

"Yes."

"Do you want me to take you home?"

She didn't want to leave yet, not on this sour note. She didn't want to leave, period. "No."

"Tell me what you want."

She gazed up into his dark eyes. Only one answer sprang to mind: you. She'd been kidding herself to think that she could walk away from him so easily. Not when every fiber of her cried out for his touch. If there were hell to pay, she'd pay it tomorrow, but she would not give up her chance for one night in his arms.

Cradling his face in her palms, she brought his mouth to hers. The contact was electric, like lightning dancing along her nerve endings. She gasped, and his tongue invaded her mouth, sending another electric thrill racing through her body. She once thought she wanted gentleness from him, but his passion, like an internal inferno, consumed her, fired an ache in her so profound she moaned into his mouth.

Alonzo leaned back on one elbow and looked down at her. Her eyes had darkened in passion and her lips were already swollen from his kisses. Like his, her chest heaved with the exertion of breathing. She looked up at him expectantly, as if waiting for him to act, but he didn't know what to do.

When she'd suggested they adjourn to the rocking chair, he'd assumed she'd done so as a prelude to becoming more intimate—probably because that's what he wanted. He wanted her to want him. And when she'd asked him to take her home, he'd assumed she was playing some game of turning him on only to shut him out, as punishment for the words he'd said to her the other night. He'd known enough game players and phonies to make that a reasonable assumption. But he should have known better when it came to Daria.

He suspected that despite having been married, she was as innocent as they came. Otherwise she never would have gotten on this chair with him if she expected her virtue to remain unchallenged. He'd never used it as a seduction tool before, but it put her too near to him, too accessible, and—considering the way she looked reclined on it—too sexy for him to ignore.

But he hadn't lied to her when he'd said he wouldn't take advantage of her in any way. Yet, she'd been the one to kiss him. Again. He didn't want any misunderstandings this time.

He stroked his fingertips along her cheek. "Baby, tell me what you want. I need to hear it from your own lips."

She rolled toward him and leaned up so that her lips were flush with his ear. "Make love to me, Alonzo."

A wave of heat rolled through his body at her whispered entreaty. His groin tightened as he pulled her to him. Their mouths met and their tongues mated. His fingers found the zipper to her dress and rasped it down. Pushing aside her dress revealed the unexpected: a daring black demibra with satin straps. He traced the lace edging of one of the cups, before dipping below to stroke her nipple with the back of his finger. She squeezed her eyes shut, and a soft sound issued from her throat.

"Do you like that, baby?" he asked her, while giving the same treatment to the other breast.

She nodded.

He found the front clasp of her bra, but before he could unfasten it, she placed her hands on his.

"I want to see you, Daria."

"Not yet." She rose to her knees and stared down at him. "I want to see you, too." Her fingers tore at his clothes and they didn't stop until he was as nude as God made him. She sat back on her heels and surveyed him. He lay back unself-consciously awaiting the verdict. He was no hard-body, but he wouldn't frighten little children either.

"You're beautiful," she said finally.

"Isn't that supposed to be my line?" Laughing, he pulled her down to him and kissed her. She writhed against him, driving him crazy. He put his hand on her hip to still her movements, but his hand encountered the smooth bare flesh of her buttocks. With a groan, he slipped her panties the rest of the way down her body and tossed them aside. He did the same with her bra, then laid her beside him.

He ran his hand over her stomach, which was lined with the faint remnants of stretch marks, her body's testament to her motherhood. Lord, she was exquisite, a black Madonna come to life, just for him. He ran his hand upward to caress one breast and then the other. Her eyes drifted shut and her neck arched, as if offering them to him. He lowered his head and took one of her turgid nipples into his mouth and suckled her.

She made a sharp sound in her throat and her body arched toward him. One knee lifted and rested against his hip. Gently, he pushed it back down and spread her legs. His fingers traveled upward between her thighs until he reached the sensitive juncture at their apex. Her flesh was already damp and engorged, but after so much time without a man he'd probably hurt her. He took her other nipple into his mouth to tease it with his tongue, as he circled her sweet flesh with his fingertips.

She moaned and called his name, the sweetest sound he'd ever heard. From the tautness in her body, he knew she was close to the edge, close to ecstasy. He sheathed himself with the condom he'd left in his pants pockets for just such an emergency, feeling her gaze on him. He turned back to her and slid his hands under her bottom to pull her on top of him. He'd wanted to give her control, but she looked down at him, a confused expression on her face.

She had to be an innocent if this minor variation on the sex act threw her. "Take me inside you, baby." He lifted her hips and set her down so that the tip of his penis pressed against her vagina. She sank against him so slowly that the pleasure of it was almost more than he could stand. His fingers dug into her hips, and his back arched. Through narrowed eyes, he looked up at her. "Are you okay?"

She nodded, setting her hair dancing. "Very okay."

He would have laughed if simply breathing didn't take up all his energy. He lifted her again, but this time she began to set the pace herself. With her hands braced against his chest, she moved over him. She might be an innocent, but she was a fast learner. His hands explored her soft body while his mouth sought hers. Between the rocking of the chair and the motion of her hips, she took him on an incredible ride, one he didn't want to end. He pulled her down to him and buried his face against her throat.

He knew the instant her orgasm overtook her, because she froze and then her hips bucked wildly against him. He growled her name as his own release claimed him, arching his back, plunging him into the sweetest sense of bliss he'd ever known.

For a while they lay together, damp, limp, sated. Daria lifted her head to look down at Alonzo. She was rewarded with a lopsided, exhausted grin. She leaned down and kissed his mouth. She'd never known making love could be this stirring, this mind-blowing. She felt cheated and blessed at the same time. "Thank you," she whispered against his lips.

He stroked her hair back from her face. The ringing of his telephone interrupted whatever he was about to say. He pulled her back down to him. "The machine will get it."

She snuggled against him, until an urgent female voice pleaded for Alonzo to pick up the phone. She felt him tense beneath her, and suddenly he was disentangling himself from her.

"I'd better take this," he said. With a kiss to her nose, he got up and padded the few feet to the phone. He had his back to her, and though she couldn't hear his words, she sensed the cadence of his voice, low, steady. The antithesis of the voice on the phone. She wondered about the nature of the call if he could respond to it so calmly.

After a moment, he hung up the phone and turned to face her, a benign expression on his face. But what he said shocked her: "I'm sorry, Daria, but I'm going to have to send you home."

She blinked and pressed her lips together. He was asking her to leave when the scent of their lovemaking was still fresh in the air? And why the sudden decision after some woman called him on the phone? All she could manage to say was, "I see."

He began to dress, not with haste, but with a certain deliberateness. She found her clothing and pulled it on, keeping her back to him so that he wouldn't read the confusion and disappointment on her face. She had just given herself to the only man she'd been with since her husband, and all he could think about was getting her to leave.

Once she had her shoes on and her bag in her hand, she turned to face him. She offered him a brittle smile. "All ready."

He walked to where she stood and wrapped his arms around her. "I'm so sorry, Daria."

She stood rigid, refusing to be pulled closer into his embrace. If the call was no big deal, what exactly was he sorry for?

He didn't seem to notice her uncooperativeness. He pulled away and took her arm, leading her toward the front of the house. Once they got outside, she noticed the car was still there. She looked up at Alonzo questioningly.

He shrugged. "I had Paul wait just in case."

She said nothing to that, but allowed him to seat her in the car once the driver opened the door. "I'll call you," Alonzo said, stepping back to close the door.

She turned her head to face the opposite window as the car door slammed. Right, he'd call her. That was man talk for "See you around, sister." On the long drive home, Daria promised herself she wouldn't cry, but she didn't quite succeed.

When she got out of the car, the driver gave her a sympathetic look. "Is there anything you want me to tell Mr. Clark?"

"Yes. Have a nice life." She ascended the steps in front of her house, let herself in, and quietly got ready for bed. She lay down, but every time she closed her eyes she saw Alonzo, the look of relief on his face a moment before he closed the car door and stepped away. He was happy to get rid of her, eager to rush off to whatever woman had called on the phone. Well, whatever misery she felt now, she'd brought on herself. She'd practically begged him to make love to her when she knew full well what the consequences might be. She hadn't expected said consequences to be shoved in her face in such an offhand manner. Daria sniffled and wiped a tear from the corner of her eye. If what didn't kill you made you stronger, she'd be Superwoman come morning.

~

Alonzo paced the narrow strip of unoccupied waiting room floor at Lennox Hill Hospital in Manhattan. The last time his family had gathered, there had been lots of laughter and good times. Now they huddled together with grim-set faces, each in their own purgatory wondering if one of its members would survive. One of his young cousins, Cassius, had "borrowed" his mother's car so he and a friend could pick up some girls that needed a ride. The boys were blindsided by a van driver who blew a red light. The fact that the kids hadn't been at fault was little consolation to either family.

While the friend who'd been driving escaped with only a broken leg, the doctors suspected Cassius suffered from a concussion as well as internal injuries. So now the family kept vigil hoping that they wouldn't hear the worst from some doctor they didn't even know.

But what kept Alonzo pacing were thoughts of Daria. He'd rushed her out of his apartment. He had no idea if she got home safely or not. It was too late to call her for fear of waking her son. He supposed he could call Paul to find out, but one of his cousins had borrowed his cell phone to check on her family and hadn't returned from outside and none of the pay phones worked.

"Would you please sit down?" his mother complained. "You're wearing a hole in the linoleum."

He turned to his mother, the family rock, to see her patting the seat beside her. Ever since he was a boy, she alone had been there for him, to count on, to listen to his dreams, to provide for him. And for the life of him, he couldn't remember giving her anything but grief, as Cassius gave his mother now.

He sat next to her and put his arm around her delicate shoulders. "How are you holding up?"

She rested her head on his shoulder. "I'm fine. It's you I'm worried about."

"Why?"

Vivian lifted her head. "Take a walk with me down to the vending machines. You can buy your old mother a cup of coffee."

Which meant she wanted to speak to him out of the earshot of the others.

When they reached the small coffee room at the end of the hall, the circular table was unoccupied. Vivian sat, while he got a cup of black coffee for her and a bag of peanut M 'n' M's for himself.

He slid into the seat opposite his mother. "What's up?"

Vivian looked heavenward. "I spend tens of thousands of dollars on a college education and he still says, 'What's up?' "

Alonzo laughed, the first time in hours. "You didn't ask me here to discuss my choice of vocabulary."

"No. I was worrying about that long face of yours."

"Mama," he said in a droll tone, "we are here waiting to find out how serious Cassius's injuries are."

"Yes, but as many scrapes as that boy has been in, I never saw your face hang so close to the ground before. Something tells me it wasn't that boy you were thinking about. Something tells me that whatever is on your mind wears Shalimar perfume and a delightful shade of red lipstick." Vivian lifted her hand to dab away a spot of it on her son's cheek.

He touched his hand to the same spot. "Had he been wearing that the whole time? Despite his mother's correct assumption about the direction of his thoughts, he wasn't ready to tell her about the depth of his feelings for Daria yet. "Actually, I was thinking about us, wondering if you have any regrets about my growing up."

"Alonzo, every mother has regrets. Lord knows I tried to be the best mother I could, but we all make mistakes, we're not perfect."

He patted his mother's hand. "No, I meant did you have any regrets about what kind of son I was to you?"

She sat back, casting him an incredulous look. "What kind of question is that?"

"A legitimate one. Were there times when you'd wished I'd been a better son to you?"

Vivian shrugged and let her shoulders fall on a heavy sigh. "I wish you'd done your chores more often without me having to ask you all the time."

"That's not what I meant."

"What do you want me to say? Were you the perfect son? No, there is no such thing. Did you drive me out of my mind worrying about you sometimes? Yes, but that's what sons are for." Vivian sighed. "But would I go back and change it? Not one thing. You always have been the light of my life and you always will be."

Despite the fervency of his mother's words, he knew she spoke a lie. Although he'd been young, he remembered his father and what he and his mother had been like together. They'd shared one of those rare and magical marriages that got better with the passage of time rather than being diminished by it. Until he died, Arthur Clark had been the sun in Vivian Clark's world.

Another memory flashed across Alonzo's mind of another man, his father's best friend. He'd been around for a while after his father had died. He remembered walking in on them once and pitching a fit because he was holding his mother.

"Whatever happened to Uncle Jack?"

"Now, why do you want to bring him up after all these years?"

Alonzo shrugged. "I haven't thought about him in years."

"Well then, he doesn't need to get thought about at all." His mother stood and smoothed out her skirt. "We'd better get back to the others." His mother walked away without waiting for him.

Alonzo shook hs head. That was strange. He cleared the table and followed her. He got back to the waiting room in time to hear the doctor's report that Cassius had no internal injuries but because of the concussion they'd be keeping him at least overnight.

After hugging one another in relief, most of the family prepared to go home. His cousin, Angela, found him to return his cell phone.

"By the way," she said, "your phone rang, but when I answered it, whoever was on the other end hung up."

"Probably a wrong number," he answered. He stared at the phone for a moment, considered calling Daria, then thought better of it. There would be plenty of time to tell her what happened the next day.

Six

After a fitful night of tossing and turning, Daria rose earlier than usual to collect herself and read the Sunday paper. Stella was the next to rise. She came into the kitchen, took one look at Daria, and said, "Well, at least I didn't hear you crying last night."

Daria set aside the funnies. "I've cried all the tears I intend to cry over Alonzo Clark. Do you want some eggs?"

Stella's eyebrows lifted as she slid into the seat across from Daria. "It's like that, is it? And to think he struck me as a smarter man than to leave a woman riled up two times after two dates. What'd he do this time?"

"Nothing." If she was angry with anyone, she was angry with herself. He was only being a man. What was it that comedian said? A man was only as faithful as his options? Alonzo must certainly have plenty of those. She should have behaved like a wiser woman.

Stella folded her arms in front of her. "Do you mean nothin' nothin' or didn't make a pass at you nothin'?"

Daria sighed. "Oh, he made a pass all right. And I went after it like a wide receiver."

For a moment, Stella simply stared at her as if she'd grown another head. "Are you telling me what I think you're telling me? 'Cuz if so, I gotta lie down."

"Don't look so shocked. I am a woman. I have needs, too."

"Honey, I know every woman has needs. I just wasn't aware you was aware you had 'em."

She covered her face with her hands. "Oh God, Stella, I've been so stupid."

"How so, child? There ain't nothin' stupid about making love to a man you care for and who cares for you."

"I know. But what if he doesn't care for you? What if you deluded yourself into thinking he cared because that's what you wanted?" Without going into detail, she told Stella about the phone call and how Alonzo had rushed her out of his apartment.

"Did you ask him who was on the phone or why he was so hell-bent on leaving?"

"No." In truth, it hadn't occurred to her to do so. She'd been too stunned from the fact that he wanted her to leave at all.

"Then you can't know why he asked you to leave. For all you know, it could have been a family emergency."

Daria shook her head. She remembered Alonzo's calm demeanor during the call. And she had tried to give him the benefit of the doubt. "When I got home, I called his cell phone, just to make sure he was all right. A woman answered the phone." Daria drew in a long breath and let it out slowly. "The truth is some woman called him and he went running. End of story. Since he got what he wanted from me, I doubt we'll be hearing from Alonzo Clark again."

She got up from the table, went to the refrigerator, and began gathering ingredients for their usual Sunday breakfast of bacon and eggs.

"I'm sorry, honey. I thought for sure the man cared about you."

"That makes two of us." Daria cracked the eggs into a bowl, then stopped, her shoulders drooping. "What on earth am I going to tell Nicholas?" She twisted around to face Stella. "He thinks the sun rises when Alonzo gets out of bed in the morning."

"You'll think of something." Stella walked to her and took the whisk out of her hand. "Let me do this. You'll have us eating rubber instead of eggs."

Daria didn't protest. She slumped into her chair, knowing that no matter what she said or how she said it, she'd have to disappoint her son. She wasn't looking forward to it.

~

Have a nice life. What the hell was that supposed to mean? It was what you said to someone to kiss him off, not someone you'd just spent a phenomenal night making love with. But that was the message Paul said Daria had sent for him.

He'd assumed when she hadn't questioned him that she understood he only asked her to leave because he had to. Obviously, he'd been mistaken. Exactly what she did think, he didn't know, but he doubted it was pleasant. When he'd called her, her machine had answered. If she was home, she wasn't answering, which wasn't a good sign.

It was his turn to sit watch by Cassius's bed. Because of the concussion, Cassius had to be woken every few hours. For the first time the young man roused on his own. He stretched and looked at him sleepily.

"Hey, man, what's happening?" Cassius said in a sleep-roughened voice. "When do I get out of here?"

"I don't know. How do you feel?"

"Like someone took a sledgehammer to my head." He touched his fingertips to the bandage on the side of his head. "This is so whack. We've got class pictures coming up next week."

That's what he was concerned about? How he'd look in a school photo?

Despite his foolish actions, Alonzo hadn't really been angry with him before. He understood youthful exuberance, as he'd had his own share of it. But Cassius's cavalier attitude, after worrying his whole family half to death the night before, changed things.

"Maybe you should have thought about that before you went joyriding in your mother's car last night."

"We weren't joyriding."

"Then what would you call it? You take a car that neither of you owns the pink slip for. Let's not get into the fact that neither of you has a license."

"Jay has a permit," he said defensively. He struggled to sit up straighter in bed, a belligerent expression coming over his face. "Back up off me, Uncle Alonzo. It's not like you're my dad or anything."

Maybe that was the problem. Cassius's parents had divorced the year before, which seemed to be when Cassius suddenly started getting into trouble. "No, I'm not your father, but that doesn't mean I don't care about you and want what's best for you."

The boy's features softened. "I know."

"Then I can't figure out for the life of me why a smart kid like you would risk so much over some girls?"

Cassius ducked his head. "It wasn't some girls, it was one girl. This girl in my class. She has problems at home."

Alonzo's eyebrows lifted. He wondered what Cassius meant, but didn't question him on it, fearing he'd clam up. "Your girlfriend?"

"Sort of. I like her, but she's a friend, too. She called me and told me she had a fight with her parents. I'm not sure but I think they, you know, hit her. I just wanted to go get her. I talked Jay into driving."

Cassius looked up at him, a plea for understanding in his eyes. Alonzo did understand that urge to help someone else in need, sometimes at your own peril. He patted the boy's leg, which was close enough for him to touch. "Why didn't you tell anyone else what happened?"

"Nobody asked. They just assumed I was being wild."

A knock sounded on the door and a second later a male head popped in. "Is this where they're keeping the knuckleheaded boys?"

"Dad!" Cassius's face lit up.

With a nod to him Cassius's father went to the head of the bed and embraced his son. "How's that hard head of yours?"

"Still attached."

Alonzo smiled watching the two of them together. He let himself out of the room, went outside, and called Daria on his cell phone. When the machine picked up this time, he didn't bother to leave a message. He got in his car, headed for the FDR and Daria's house in the Bronx. If she wanted to send him another message, she'd have to do it face-to-face.

～

Daria sat on the sofa after church, trying to concentrate on the *Times* crossword puzzle. Nicholas was doing his best to distract her, finally laying his head on her arm preventing her from writing. She put down her pencil and draped her arm around his shoulders. "What is it you want, little boy? You're driving me nuts."

"Tell me how your date went with Mr. Clark last night." He folded his hands in supplication. "Please."

Daria sighed. She'd put off the inevitable as long as she dared. She dropped the newspaper to the coffee table and shifted so that she faced her son. "I know that you've been hoping that things will work out between Mr. Clark and me, but that is not going to happen."

The expectant smile on his face faded to a belligerent scowl. "Why not?"

Daria huffed out a breath. What could she tell him that he'd understand. "Sweetheart, a woman expects a certain amount of deference and respect from a man. When she doesn't get it, she has no choice but to move on."

His eyes widened. "You dumped Mr. Clark."

"Not exactly, but I decided I don't want to see him anymore."

"Oh, Mom. What could Mr. Clark have done that's so terrible, huh?"

Daria sighed. Her son had plenty of time to learn about late-night booty calls and fast women. She'd discussed Alonzo all that she cared to. "Go finish your homework. Tomorrow is a school day."

A mixture of emotions played across Nicholas's face, confusion, distrust, anger, and finally resignation. "All right." He stalked off in the direction of the stairs, clomped to the second floor, and slammed his room door.

He'd been disrespectful, but she couldn't really blame him. He deserved an answer, but she couldn't give him one that would make sense to an eleven-year-old psyche. Besides, Daria suspected her son wouldn't tolerate well any derision of his hero Mr. Clark. Clearly, Nicholas's allegiance was with Alonzo, not her. While that stung, she also recognized that her son needed to believe that there was some man he could look up to. Until the night before, she wouldn't have faulted him for seeking that man in Alonzo Clark.

Daria got up from the sofa intending to start dinner. Halfway down the hall, the doorbell rang. Since she wasn't expecting anyone, she went to the front window to check who was at the door. At the same time, Nicholas bounded down the stairs and yanked the front door open.

"Mr. Clark!"

She heard her son's excited voice and momentarily shut her eyes praying for strength. It was bad enough to try to explain to Nicholas that she wouldn't be seeing Alonzo again, without him showing up on her doorstep, apparently giving the lie to everything she'd said. What could he possibly want now? She'd already given him everything she had to offer.

Sensing Alonzo's presence in the room, she turned to find him standing behind her. "We need to talk," he said.

That's what he'd said last time, and she'd foolishly given in to him. She cast her gaze on her son. "Please go to your room so Mr. Clark and I can talk."

"Sure, Mom." This time he exited with a grin, no stomping up the stairs or slammed doors. Obviously, Nicholas thought Alonzo would straighten everything out. But Daria knew her son was headed for disappointment for the second time in a day.

Daria fastened a narrow-eyed look of displeasure on Alonzo. "What are you doing here?"

He stared back at her for a long moment with an expression in his eyes she didn't understand. He shoved his hands in his trouser pockets. "Apparently we have some sort of misunderstanding between us."

"Apparent to whom? I don't know what you're talking about."

"What exactly do you think happened last night?"

"I wouldn't know. Some woman called you on the phone and you rushed me out of your apartment like the latest plague victim."

"That was my cousin on the phone," he said in a patient voice. Her s—"

"Don't." She cut him off. "Spare me the convenient excuses after the fact. I've heard them all before."

Anger bloomed in his eyes, and he took a step toward her. "I am not your damn husband, Daria. I was trying to explain to you that I had a good reason for leaving you like that. If you ever want to hear it, you know where I'll be."

He walked out leaving the front door open and letting the screen bang. She rushed after him in time to see him get into a black sports car and drive away. Tears welled in her eyes, but she blinked them back. He might be telling her the truth, but she couldn't afford to believe him. She couldn't risk the heartache for herself or her son that lay at the end of the road of trusting an unworthy man.

She closed the door and rested her back against it. In the periphery of her vision she saw her son on the stairs. She focused on his face and his expression of utter betrayal. He said nothing, but then he didn't need to utter a word. He turned and walked up the stairs as silent as a stone.

∼

Two weeks later, Alonzo lay on the rocking chair in his living room trying to get through the third novel of an author slated to be on the show the following week. The writing lacked any depth whatsoever, yet the man had made it to the top of the Blackboard best-seller list. Alonzo closed the book and dropped it on the cushion beside him. He would never understand the American public's buying habits if he studied them for a million years.

His doorbell rang. Automatically, he checked his watch. Twelve-thirty on a Saturday night. Who could be calling on him now? Checking the peephole he frowned seeing his mother standing on the other side of the door. He pulled it open. Dressed in a black silk pantsuit, she looked as if she was coming in from a night on the town. "What are you doing here?"

Vivian breezed past him to enter the brownstone. "Can't a mother visit a son, a son that hasn't returned her phone calls in a week?"

"Not at twelve o'clock at night."

"I wanted to make sure you were home."

He opened his mouth to ask her why she assumed he'd be home on a Saturday night, but closed it. They both knew his mother had a more active social life than he did. "What can I do for you?"

She walked past him into the living room. He shut the door and followed her. He found her standing in the middle of the floor, eyeing the rocking chair. "You didn't tell me you had company."

"I don't," he said, momentarily confused by her comment. Then he noticed Daria's shawl lying on the rocking chair where he left it. He gathered it up and tossed it onto a chair. "A remnant from another night."

Vivian eyed the rocking chair again, but eschewed it for a more conventional seat. "The young lady from the contest? How is she?"

"I wouldn't know." Every day of the past two weeks he spent half his time with his eye on the area outside the control room, hoping he'd see Daria there, hoping she'd give him a chance to explain himself. She hadn't shown up and he doubted she ever would. "She's not speaking to me. Seems she has me confused with her ex-husband."

Vivian raised a brow. "How did that happen?"

Alonzo sighed, shoving his hands into his pants pockets. "She was with me when I got Joannie's call. She thinks I brushed her off to be with another woman."

"Didn't you tell her where you were going?"

He shook his head. If she'd have asked him, he would have told her, but she hadn't.

"Why didn't you bring her with you? No one would have minded."

"She has an eleven-year-old son. I thought she might find sitting vigil for another woman's son distressing." That's why he'd tried so hard to keep an even tone to his voice on the phone. He hadn't wanted to alarm her.

"I'm so sorry, son. It seems to me you really care about this girl."

"Glutton for punishment that I am, I'm in love with her."

"Then don't give up on her, Alonzo. Give her time to come around. When a woman's been hurt by a man, really hurt, it takes a lot to make her trust again."

He narrowed his eyes on his mother and the way she worried the hem of her blouse. Something told him she spoke from personal experience, but to his knowledge his father had never done anything to hurt her. He sat in the chair opposite her. "Does this have to do with Uncle Jack?"

She bit her lip and considered him. "I don't know if I should tell you this."

"Go ahead."

She lifted her shoulders and let them drop. "When your father died, Jack and I were both devastated. In our own ways we had both loved him. When he was gone, we turned to each other for comfort." She sighed. "There had always been this attraction between us that neither of us had wanted to explore. We were loyal to your father. But once he was gone . . ."

"You explored it?"

"Not the way you think. We'd barely kissed when you—"

She trailed off and he finished for her. "I burst in and gave you hell for betraying Daddy. Are you saying I'm the one who hurt you?"

"Not at all. It was Jack who did that. You have to understand, if I'd made up my mind to be with that man, nothing on heaven or earth could have stopped me, not even you. But we were both so guilty for what we were feeling, all it took was someone's censure, anyone's, to put an end to what was blossoming between us. I told Jack we needed to be apart, but I only meant for a while until you could adjust to your father being gone and we could decide what we really wanted."

She stood facing away from him, her arms wrapped around herself. "But he left. He never even told me he was going. He sent me a note saying that he couldn't come between a mother and her son. I never heard from him again. I lost both men I loved in a matter of months."

He had always wondered why his mother, as socially active as she was, had never remarried, never shown much interest in men. He'd assumed she remained loyal to his father's memory, never suspecting a darker reason. He stood and went to her, wrapping his arms around hers and resting his chin on her shoulder. "I'm sorry for whatever part I played in that happening."

She patted his cheek. "It wasn't your fault. It was his. I always thought he took the easy way out, running away instead of fighting for what he wanted." She sighed and pulled out of his embrace to face him. "So don't give up on her, make her see that you love her. Don't walk away if there's any chance for you to stay."

After his mother left, Alonzo paced around his living room, too wired to sit down. He had no intention of giving up on Daria. He just didn't know what to do. Show her that he loved her. Great advice, but how?

~

The next Friday night, Daria flounced into the swing next to Stella and covered her face with her hands. "I can't take this anymore, I really can't." Daria sighed and ran her hands through her hair.

Stella patted her knee. "The boy giving you a hard time?"

"Not exactly. He does what I tell him, and only what I tell him. But he's angry with me, and there's no way I can make him understand my position."

"Run that position by me again, because I kinda got lost with it myself."

Daria's shoulders drooped and she cast Stella a hard look. "Not you, too."

Stella shrugged. "I could see you being mad at him if he actually did what you think he did, though I'm not sure he did."

Daria's brow furrowed. "Now you've lost me."

"Listen, child, I don't know what happened, and let's face it, neither do you. You told me he said he had an explanation, but you wouldn't listen to it. As I said, I can understand your being angry with him. But I know he's called you in the last week and you wouldn't talk to him, because I answered the phone. Heck, he even dedicated a song to you on the radio the other morning."

She already knew that. "You Don't Know Me" by Ray Charles. The receptionist at work had brought her portable radio over to Daria's desk so she could listen to it. And he'd shown up at her office, on the pretext of returning her pashmina. She'd taken one look at him and her breath had stalled and her heartbeat had trebled. He hadn't touched her at any time, but still she'd started to tremble. Even now, she missed him more than words could describe. She crossed her arms under her breasts as if that could cover the hollowness she felt inside but it didn't. She turned to Stella. "What's your point?"

"Child, even if he did do wrong by you, he's obviously trying to make it up to you. Why won't you give him another chance?"

"I can't afford to, Stella."

"Why not? What are you afraid the man will do to you?"

"It's not him I'm afraid of, it's me. Do you know what it's like to get sucked up into a man's life? That's what happened to me with Connor. I gave up everything I had, everything I wanted for myself or out of life to be with him. The only thing that Connor cared about was what he wanted. I got, I don't know, lost. Connor never asked me to do that, to give up myself for him, not in words anyway. I did it because I wanted to please him, and maybe I wasn't strong enough to hold my own ground when it came to what I wanted."

Stella laughed, a harsh sound. "You not strong? You're the strongest woman I know. You don't sit around whining and complaining, you just do what needs to be done. If that's not strength, I don't know what is."

"If I'm so strong, why did I allow myself to behave like the kind of woman I detest, one who rolls into a man's bed at the slightest provocation?"

Stella shook her head. "Because you love him. Let me tell you, I'm a God-fearing woman, but if a man as fine as Alonzo Clark wanted to be with me, I'd say, 'Forget the money, show me the bed.'"

Daria laughed, as undoubtedly Stella expected her to. But suddenly, the older woman seemed to grow introspective, quiet.

"There was a man who loved me once," Stella said in a somber voice. "I loved him, but I was foolish. I thought I'd play hard to get. I wanted to make him prove how much he loved me. He never got me, but life did. While I was busy playin' he got serious with another woman. Now he's still married and a grandfather three times over, and what do I got?"

Feeling the older woman's regret, Daria put her arm around Stella's shoulders. "You've got us."

Stella shrugged off the embrace. "No offense, but I'd rather have my man, too, and some of my own grandbabies to give that son of yours some playmates."

Daria looked up at the darkening sky, contemplating Stella's words. Stella had loved and lost and never quite recovered from it. Daria saw the same anguish, the same regret waiting for her at the twilight of her life. Up until now, her chief concern had been providing a safe, secure life for her and her son. But at what cost? True happiness for both of them? And what if she was wrong? What if she risked everything only to be hurt? Caught between her options, she didn't know which way to go. She turned plaintive eyes to Stella. "What do I do, Stella? What do I do?"

"Go to him. Tell him how you feel. If he understands, then you know you've got a good man. If not? You can deal with that, too."

Daria nodded, feeling more at peace than she had in weeks. "For now, I'd better check on my son. Lord knows what he's up to in there. I'll be back in a minute."

When she got upstairs, Nicholas wasn't in his room. She checked her own room and the bathroom. He wasn't there either. A frisson of alarm skittered up her spine, but she ignored it. Nicholas was probably in the kitchen and she hadn't noticed. But he wasn't anywhere on the first floor. While she and

Stella had talked, night had fallen. Daria stood at the back door, scanning for signs of her son in the backyard. Finding none, she went to the basement door and called down. "Nicholas." Only silence answered her.

"Nicholas," she screamed, panic starting to set in. She ran down the stairs, checked all the nooks and crannies that hid the washer and dryer, the boiler and a small meat freezer. She raced back up the two flights to his room. Still no sign of him, and his backpack and some of his clothes were missing. She pulled open the drawer by his bed. The binder where he kept his Pokemon and Yugi-Oh cards, his most prized possessions, was missing too.

Tears clouded her eyes as she raced downstairs to where Stella still sat in the swing. "Oh, God, I think Nicholas ran away."

Stella was on her feet before Daria finished her sentence. Together they phoned all of Nicholas's friends' houses, hoping that he'd shown up at one of them. No one had seen him.

She called Connor, on the off chance Nicholas had called him at his home in New Jersey. On the fourth ring, the line was picked up. "What?"

"Connor, this is Daria. Has Nicholas called you?"

"Why would he do that?"

Why, indeed! Connor sounded as disinterested as if they were talking about the weather. "I think he's run away. We were having some problems. I thought he might have called you."

"Sorry. If he turns up here, I'll call you so you can pick him up." The line went dead.

Daria bit back the curse that sprang to her lips at Connor's total lack of concern for their son. She stared at the phone as she held her lip between her teeth. Only one more number to call. It made sense that she would find him there. By now, Nicholas must have been gone long enough to make it to Alonzo's.

She dialed his number, and almost immediately he answered the phone.

"Alonzo, this is Daria." She stopped, her throat too clogged with emotion to continue, because if he wasn't at Alonzo's she didn't know what to do next.

"I was just about to call you. It seems I have something here that belongs to you."

A moment later, she heard her son's contrite voice. "Hi, Mom. I'm sorry if I worried you."

The tears that had threatened in her eyes tumbled over as relief rushed over her. *If* he had worried her.

"I'm bringing him home now." This time Alonzo's voice reached her.

All she could manage was to nod and mumble a strangled "Thank you." She hung up and sank into a chair. "He's at Alonzo's," she told Stella, who still looked at her with an anxious expression. "He's bringing Nicholas home."

Stella let out a relieved breath. "Thank you, sweet Jesus." After a moment Stella fastened a steely gaze on her. "After you straighten out things with your son, maybe you should set things right with your man."

Daria inhaled, gathering strength. "I think you're right."

Her newfound conviction didn't keep her from pacing until she heard a car door slam out front a moment before her doorbell rang. She'd barely gotten the door open when Nicholas rushed in and threw his arms around her. She gave him back a fierce hug, raining kisses on the top of his head, his cheeks, his forehead. "Don't you ever scare me like that again, young man."

Nicholas looked up at her, an earnest expression on his face. "I won't. Mr. Clark said he would take a strap to me himself if I ever did anything that stupid again."

She glanced up at Alonzo, who stood framed by the screen door behind him. Whatever happened between them, she had to express her gratitude for keeping her son safe. "Thank you," she mouthed. He inclined his head in a single nod.

She turned her gaze to her son. "What else did Mr. Clark say?"

Nicholas inhaled deeply. "Lots of things."

She almost laughed, imagining the lecture Alonzo must have given on the long ride home.

"Mostly, he said if I were going to grow up to be the right kind of man, I had to start practicing now. He said I had to think about other people's feelings and what they want, not just what I want." He looked over his shoulder at Alonzo. "Did I get it right?"

"You got it perfect, son."

Something went soft in Daria hearing the word *son* on Alonzo's lips pertaining to her son. She was grateful when Stella ambled forward and demanded to know where her hug was. Before Daria knew it, Stella had whisked Nicholas, backpack and all, through the front door, claiming she'd return him tomorrow. Obviously Stella meant for her to settle things with Alonzo. Since her son was in good hands she didn't mind.

For a moment, both she and Alonzo stared after the departing pair. When he turned back to her, she focused her gaze on him. "How did he get to your house in the first place? How did he know where you live?"

"He looked it up on the Internet. According to boy genius, you can find out where almost anyone lives if you know where to look."

"That computer is coming out of his room tomorrow."

"Don't be too hard on him. He took the subway to my house. By the time he got there, he was terrified and on the verge of tears."

"What did you do?"

"I let him cry."

Oh, Lord, how this man pleased her. She could imagine Alonzo comforting her frightened son. How many men would do that for some other man's child? Nicholas's own father couldn't be bothered with so much as a phone call. "I guess that means I shouldn't threaten him with a strap, too?"

Alonzo shrugged. "I was pretty upset myself to find your son on my doorstep. Anything could have happened to him out there, alone and unprotected."

A momentary chill of alarm rushed up her spine contemplating the possibilities. "I know, but I'm grateful that if he found the need to run away he ran to you. I can't thank you enough for taking care of him and bringing him home."

He shrugged again, obviously uncomfortable with her gratitude. "I'd better be going, I guess."

That's what he said, but he didn't move. He'd laid his words down like a challenge, waiting for her to tell him what she wanted. She didn't hesitate. "Or you could stay and tell me what happened the other night."

She took his hand and led him into her living room. Alonzo sat at one corner of her sofa. She settled next to him, tucking her feet underneath her. As she listened to his story of rushing to the hospital to check on his injured cousin, she felt smaller and smaller, incredibly petty for what she'd thought. "Oh, Alonzo. I'm so sorry."

He touched his fingertips to her cheek. "Don't look so worried, sweetheart. It turned out not to be too serious. He cracked his head on the dashboard because the airbag didn't deploy. He's fine now. And some good came of it, too. His parents are divorced. He got the chance to see his father and tell him how much he missed him. He's agreed to come around more."

"I guess all's well that ends well."

He took both of her hands in his and gazed at her with a piercing intensity in his eyes. "How's it going to end with us, Daria?"

"That depends on whether you can forgive me. I admit to being scared to death of getting involved with you and as blind as my son in considering what other people wanted."

"What do you mean? Did you think I was out to hurt you?"

She shook her head. "No, but I figured you would. I told you that no man had paid me the least attention in years. I couldn't believe you were actually interested, or that the interest would last."

"I always have been, but what interested me wasn't primarily what was on the outside. It was what's in here." He laid his palm against her heart.

She shut her eyes at the onslaught of emotion that welled in her. A second later she felt his lips on hers, gentle, loving, and so sweet it took her breath away.

When he pulled back he cradled her face in his hands. "I love you, Daria. I want to marry you and help you raise your son and be a family. Tell me you love me."

At last she could give him what he wanted. "I love you, Alonzo. I love you." She pressed her lips to his for a lingering kiss full of tenderness and promise.

When they separated, he reached into his pocket. "I have something for you. It's from my mother." He extended a folded piece of paper toward her.

"Your mother wrote me a note?" By the grin on his face, she knew he was up to something. She unfolded the paper and read: "Wash greens thoroughly before cooking. Brown one-quarter pound bacon in the bottom of a five-quart saucepan. . . ." She gazed up at him, confused. "What is this?"

"My mother's recipe for collard greens. I thought you might like to have it."

"You want me to cook for you?"

"Tomorrow." He took the paper from her and set it on her coffee table. He pulled her closer and pressed his lips against her throat just under her ear. "There'll be plenty of time for food, tomorrow."

Epilogue

Vivian Clark checked her watch for the fourth time in fifteen minutes. Alonzo had asked her to meet him here, but there had to be some mistake. First off, the ambience of the restaurant was all wrong. Several small, intimate tables filled the dimly lit room. Scented candles on each table provided most of the light, and most of the atmosphere. Soft music wafted into the room via invisible speakers. If she weren't mistaken, this was a place for lovers.

Second, she'd bred into her son the value of punctuality. He would never keep her waiting, not if he could help it. She didn't know if the knot of anxiety that settled in her stomach was due to worry that something had happened to Alonzo to make him late, or the fear that she might be waiting for him in the wrong place.

She scanned the room again for signs of him. Her gaze snagged on a lone man sitting at the bar. A handsome brown-skinned man with a wicked smile and a full head of salt-and-pepper hair, he wore a stark black suit and white shirt. Somehow his features seemed familiar. Maybe she needed to put on her glasses. As she watched, he lifted his glass in a silent salute to her.

Vivian glanced away. If she weren't waiting for her son, she might have found the man's interest in her intriguing. Oh, who was she kidding? She hadn't let a man near her in thirty years, not that none had ever tried. But she'd had two chances with love and both times it had slipped away. No need in tempting fate a third time.

She checked her watch again, but looked up sensing another's presence near her. Her gaze traveled upward, until it settled on a man's face, the man from the bar. He was standing behind the other chair at her table, Alonzo's chair.

"Hello, Vivian," he said.

She blinked, startled by the basso profundo of his voice and the fact that he knew her name.

Before she could recover, he motioned toward the empty seat. "Mind if I sit down?" Without waiting for a response from her, he slid into the seat. He folded his hands in front of him and rested his elbows on the table. "You don't remember me, do you?"

Vivian scanned his face in the dim light. Most of his features could have belonged to anyone, but his eyes, brown with flecks of gray and green. Her hand went to her chest and the air rushed from her lungs. "Oh, my Lord! Jack? Is that you?"

He smiled. "It's been a long time."

She shook her head as if to clear it. "What are you doing here? How did you kn—" And then she realized Alonzo had never intended to dine with her. He'd arranged this meeting without telling her. "What were you doing at the bar?"

"Getting up my nerve to come over here and talk to you. You look fabulous, Viv. The years have been kind to you."

"And to you, too." The only sign of his true age was the gray in his hair. He still possessed the same proud carriage and good looks he'd had as a younger man.

"Thank you."

For a moment they lapsed into silence. Then they both rushed to ask and answer what they had been up to the past thirty years. She had continued with her career as a secretary for one of the most powerful men in the publishing industry, or an executive assistant as they called it these days. He had moved to Arizona to be near his sister, had married and divorced and fathered two beautiful girls.

When they fell silent again, Jack speared her with an intense look. When he took her hand in his she didn't protest. "You know, Viv, there hasn't been a day that's gone by that I haven't thought of you. Walking out of your life was the hardest thing I've ever had to do and the biggest mistake of my life. Do you think we could go back to the beginning, start again?"

She gazed down at their hands, entwined on the table, his larger, darker, hers more delicate and fairer. Did she dare risk it? Could she give up her comfortable, boring life for the chance of love with a man she had always desired? The answer was a no-brainer.

She lifted her hand enough to shake his. "Hi, I'm Vivian Clark, and you are?"

He shot her a dazzling smile. "I'm Jack Hunter. It's a pleasure to meet you."

And from the speakers, Louis Armstrong sang, ". . . what a wonderful world."

Dear Readers,

I hope you have enjoyed reading Daria and Alonzo's story. Although I am not a single mother, I know many women who are, who struggle with the same issues that Daria faces. As mothers, we want to do what is best for ourselves and our children, but sometimes the road isn't so clear. All we can do is make our choices and hope for the best.

My next book, COULD IT BE MAGIC?, will be out next month. This book, too, deals with the issue of motherhood, as in what makes someone a mother. My heroine, Jacqueline (Jake) McKenna, takes in her brother's child after her brother dies and the child's mother abandons her. This newfound motherhood as well as other changes in her life (including a sexy new boss) throw Jake for a loop, but she comes out fighting. I hope you will enjoy that story, too.

I would love to hear from you. You can contact me at DeeSavoy@aol.com or at P.O. Box 233, Bronx, NY 10469. Or stop by my Web site at www.deirdresavoy.com.

In closing, I wish for all the mothers out there the same thing Alonzo wished for Daria—that your Mother's Day is all you hope it to be.

All the best,
Dee Savoy

ABOUT THE AUTHOR

Native New Yorker Deirdre Savoy spent her summers on the shores of Martha's Vineyard, soaking up the sun and scribbling in one of her many notebooks. It was there that she first started writing romance as a teenager. The island proved to be the perfect setting for her first novel, SPELL-BOUND, published by BET/Arabesque Books in 1999.

SPELLBOUND received rave reviews and earned her the distinction of the first Rising Star author of Romance in Color and was voted their Best New Author of 1999. Deirdre also won the flrst annual Emma award for Favorite New Author, presented at the 2001 Romance Slam Jam in Orlando, Florida. This year, Savoy has been nominated for three Emmas, including Author of the Year.

Deirdre's second book, ALWAYS, was published by BET/Arabesque in October 2000. ALWAYS was a February 2001 Selection for the Black Expressions Book Club. ONCE AND AGAIN, the sequel to ALWAYS, was published in May 2001, and was also selected by the Black Expressions Book Club. MIDNIGHT MAGIC, the third book in the Thorne family saga, was a 2001 holiday release.

Deirdre's fifth book, HOLDING OUT FOR A HERO, will be published September 2002. HOLDING OUT FOR A HERO features fictional hero NYPD detective Adam Wexler and real-life hero fireflghter Paul Haney, the winner of the 2001 Arabesque Man Contest, on the cover. HOLDING OUT FOR A HERO was also picked up by Black Expressions.

In her other life, Deirdre is a kindergarten teacher for the New York City Board of Education. She started her career as a secretary in the school art department of Macmillan Publishing Company in New York, rising to Advertising/Promotion Supervisor of the International Division in three years. She has also worked as a freelance copywriter, legal proofreader, and news editor for CLASS magazine.

Deirdre was graduated from Bernard M. Baruch College of the City University of New York with a Bachelor's of Business Administration in Marketing/Advertising.

Deirdre is a member of Authors Supporting Authors Positively (ASAP) and the founder of the Writer's Co-op writers' group. She lectures on such topics as Marketing Your Masterpiece, Getting Your Writing Career Started, and other subjects related to the craft of writing. She is listed in the American and International Authors and Writers Who's Who, as well as the Dictionary of International Biography.

Deirdre lives in Bronx, New York, with her husband of ten-plus years and their two children. In her spare time she enjoys reading, dancing, calligraphy, and "wicked" crossword puzzles.

The Price of
a Mother's Love

Jacquelin Thomas

One

When Kree Mansfield's relatives traveled down to North Carolina, they usually commented on the green and fertile landscaping. Today, however, no one said a word about the trees or the colorful blooms bursting up throughout the city as they rode in a caravan of cars led by two long sleek limousines, parading down Lynn Road.

The twenty-third day of March brought with it an air of sadness as the funeral procession climbed the paved driveway leading to Kree's home. The driver from the first limo assisted her out of the car. Kree made her way somberly to the front door, her sister, Candace, following on her heels.

She stepped off to the side to allow her sister entry. Kree remained in the doorway watching in silence as her ex-husband helped their son outside of the car and into his wheelchair. She felt the familiar stirrings of guilt whenever she looked at Korey.

Emotionally drained, she pushed herself into the living room and dropped down onto the sofa. People were still piling out of the cars and Kree was grateful to have a few seconds alone. With everything she'd gone through over the past few weeks, her sanity demanded it. Kree ran her fingers through her short auburn hair, weariness draining her.

She felt as if she could give up on life. She didn't care about the dark shadows beneath her eyes, the paleness to her otherwise bronze complexion, or her lack of makeup.

Well-wishers and family gathered in the house, murmuring words that were supposed to be comforting to her. Their words were like the brisk spring weather outside, bringing a chill to her body.

Her brother, Charles, had been missing for almost a month until four days ago when a homeless person found his body hidden behind some bushes on the south side of Raleigh. He'd been shot to death—a product of the type of life he led.

"Kree, honey, can I get something for you?"

She shook her head. "I'll be fine. Thanks, Aunt Martha." Kree's head began to ache from her overwhelming grief. She looked pensively around the room, suddenly wishing everyone would leave. She couldn't seem to summon the strength to be sociable.

Her son navigated his wheelchair toward her. Her heart tugged at the look of sadness in his eyes. Kree met his gaze and smiled.

Korey positioned himself beside her and set the brake.

"How are you holding up, sweetie?" she asked.

He gave a slight shrug. "It's still hard for me to believe. I keep expecting Uncle Charles to walk in any moment now."

"Me too," Kree admitted. She glanced around the room searching for her sister. "Where did Candace go?"

"I think she's in her room."

"She was complaining of a headache earlier. Maybe she went to lie down."

Korey nodded. "Have you talked to Dad?"

"No. Is he still here?" Kree hadn't seen Stone since watching him with Korey earlier. She hoped he hadn't gone home. Just having him around made her feel better somehow. The truth of the matter was that Kree had never stopped loving Stone.

"He said he was going to hang around for a while. He wants to make sure you're okay."

Kree eyed her son in disbelief. When she didn't think Korey was paying attention, her eyes searched the room again and the hallway beyond it. There was no sign of Stone.

"He's still here," he reassured her.

She pretended not to know whom he was talking about. "Who?"

This caused her son to explode into laughter. *"You know who.* You're not slick."

Kree couldn't help but smile. "I don't know what I'm going to do with you." She reached out and stroked his cheek.

Gently removing her hand, Korey said, "Mom, don't do that. I'm not a baby. I'm fourteen years old."

"I was there the day you were born, remember?"

Korey stood his ground. "But you still try to treat me like a little kid—always hugging and kissing on me all the time."

"I just want you to know how much I love you." Kree's eyes misted over. "I want to cherish every single moment I have with you. You never know what can happen . . ." Her voice trailed. Kree would never forget that day, ten years ago, when they almost lost Korey.

"I love you, Mom. You're my best friend."

Wiping away a tear, Kree smiled weakly. "I'll try not to baby you so much. I promise."

Korey weaved his fingers through hers. "Mom, you have my permission to baby me all you want when we're alone—just not in public, okay?"

"I can handle that." Kree blinked, trying to hold on to the tears.

Releasing her hand, Korey announced, "I'm going to go check on Aunt Candace. I'll be in her room if Dad comes looking for me."

"I'll tell him." Kree wiped away another tear as she watched her son maneuver his wheelchair through the room. Korey had learned to handle with strength and courage the blow fate had dealt him. She was extremely proud of him.

Although confined to his wheelchair, Korey was a very active teen. He counseled other teens with disabilities at a local youth center, played keyboards for church, and was a member of several organizations at school. Korey didn't lack the attentions of the opposite sex either. Girls were constantly calling Kree's home as well as Stone's.

Guilt surged through her pores. Kree had never forgiven herself over what happened to Korey. He was in that wheelchair because of her. Now Charles was dead because of her too, she acknowledged sadly. She had failed at motherhood. Kree groaned at the truth.

Kree heard Stone's voice and she felt her heartbeat return to normal. He was still there. She had a feeling Stone was in the kitchen. Kree could smell the floating aroma of fried chicken, spicy seasoned collards, and freshly baked corn bread. People were still bringing food into the house. She smiled at her neighbor carrying a chocolate layer cake toward the kitchen.

Stone probably has his head buried in a plate, she thought with amusement. He went running most mornings to keep his athletic physique in shape. Stone was proud of his six-three height and muscular build. He kept his head shaved and his face free of facial hair. Stone was deep brown to the bone with beautiful eyes the color of Hershey's dark chocolate.

For a thirty-eight-year-old man, Stone was in excellent shape. Outside of special events like this—he was very careful about what he ate.

Some mornings, Kree would run with Stone but she hadn't done it within the last month. She'd been worried about Charles and hadn't wanted to leave the house.

Kree concentrated hard—wanting to remember her last conversation with her brother. Charles had been talking to her about church. He was sup-posed to attend church with her but that day he disappeared. Initially, Kree wasn't worried, just figured he'd changed his mind, but when two days passed and there was no sigh of Charles, worry became a cloak, heavy and dark. She knew something terrible had happened.

Two

"I don't know about this, Korey. This could turn out badly."

"It'll work, Aunt Candace," he reassured her. "I know it will. We send this letter to the *Alonzo Clark Morning Show,* and Mom will win a makeover and the shopping spree. After all she's been through lately, I really want her to win."

Candace smiled at her nephew. "Hundreds of kids will be writing letters to the radio station." She tilted her head in curiosity. "What makes you so sure Kree will be chosen?"

"Because of this letter. It's touching and all that."

Candace stuck her hands in the pockets of her jacket, shrugging in doubt. "Your mother is going to kill us, Korey. You know Kree doesn't like stuff like this." She looked around tentatively, not wanting to be overheard by anyone.

"She'll like this," Korey promised. "You'll see. Besides, this is just the first part of my plan."

Inclining her head, Candace inquired, "What's the second part?"

"I'll tell you later," he replied cryptically.

"I really hope you know what you're doing."

"It's going to work."

Glancing toward the doorway, she questioned, "How was Kree holding up when you last saw her? She was a wreck at the funeral." Candace wanted to wipe away the memory of her brother lying in that coffin. Instead she wanted to remember him as he was the last time she had seen him—a handsome and vibrant young man.

"I think she's much better. She wasn't saying a whole lot when I was in the living room."

Candace rose to her feet. "I guess I'd better go out there. I'm surprised Aunt Martha hasn't burst in here already to get me. I can't believe she came all this way here to take control of everything. I have to tell you, Kree's a better woman than me. I would have gone to blows with Aunt Martha."

"Mom didn't care. She was so upset over Uncle Charles's death. Miss Washburn down the street could've planned the funeral for all she cared."

Shaking her head in sadness, Candace stated, "Kree still blames herself. I love my sister and I've tried to tell her that she did the best she could for Charles. He was my brother too, and I miss him . . . but this is not her fault."

"Mom blames herself for what happened to me. I know that's why she and my dad got divorced. I think he kind of blames her too."

"It wasn't just what happened to you, honey. I think Kree and Stone's marriage started to fall apart when they took in Charles and me after our parents died. Your parents were young and hadn't been married quite three months. I appreciate all they've done but what I really wanted was for them to stay together. I hated when Stone left."

"Sounds like we all blame ourselves for the divorce. That's why we should be the ones to fix it. That's what Uncle Charles wanted too. He wanted us back as a family. He felt that would only happen if he were gone."

Candace looked surprised. "Is that what he told you?"

Korey nodded. "We talked the day before Uncle Charles disappeared. He had planned to move in with this girl. You saw her today at the funeral. The one with the orange hair—"

Candace's brown eyes crinkled in laughter. Playing with her diamond engagement ring, she said, "You mean Racine? I think she'd prefer honey blond."

"Looks orange to me," Korey responded nonchalantly. "But anyway, they were planning to get a place together. Uncle Charles was even going to church with her. She and Uncle Charles have been together for almost a year. Racine wanted to get married, but Uncle Charles kept stalling."

Candace shook her head in dismay. "My brother . . ." Disappointed, she sank down onto a chair.

"He didn't want to get married until he had himself together," Korey explained.

Her mouth parted in surprise. *"Charles told you all this?"*

"He sure did."

"You believed him?" Charles had a talent for knowing exactly what people wanted to hear. It enabled him to easily manipulate others.

"Aunt Candace, I believed him. I could see that he was changing his life."

"He did seem different," Candace admitted. A new wave of grief swept through her. "I wish Charles and I had not grown apart. We used to be so close. I wanted so much to help him."

"It's too late for us to help Uncle Charles, but not for my mom," Korey pointed out. "We can still help her."

~

Candace went in search of food. She was going to prepare two plates—one for her and one for Korey. They were planning to eat in her bedroom, away from everybody else. She paused in the hallway to talk to a couple of her cousins from Greenville before continuing on to the kitchen.

From where she was standing, she could see into the living room and spotted Kree standing by the window. She was looking out the way she used to when she was watching for Charles.

Their brother had put Kree through so much unnecessary anguish. Candace found a small measure of peace knowing that in the end Charles was trying to make positive changes in his life.

She decided against disturbing Kree. Candace saw Stone in the den as she entered the kitchen. He was talking to Aunt Martha. Strolling around the huge kitchen she stole peeks at the only man her sister had ever loved.

He caught sight of her, smiled, and waved.

Candace waved back.

Stone had been a good father to her even though he and Kree were divorced. Throughout school he was there at all of the important events, including the Father-Daughter Dance. Candace hadn't asked him because it was during a time when he and Kree weren't speaking to each other. She'd decided not to attend, but on the night of the dance, Stone showed up with the most beautiful dress she'd ever seen. He was the most popular father at the dance. The memory bought a smile to her lips.

Korey was right. His parents deserved a second chance.

When she'd prepared their plates, Candace returned to her bedroom. Her nephew was still there working on the laptop computer.

Placing a plate of food on the desk, she asked, "What are you working on this time?"

"I wanted to add something else to the letter. I'm done now."

"I wasn't sure about this before but now I am. I think you're doing the right thing. Kree and Stone should be together and maybe this will give them a chance."

"It's important that we send this letter to Alonzo Clark, Aunt Candace. Once he reads it, he has to choose Mom as one of the winners. My mother's happiness depends on it."

Taking the letter from her nephew's hand, she murmured, "I'll make sure it goes out tomorrow via Federal Express."

～

"I heard you and Charles were planning to get a place together," Kree announced to Racine. She'd noticed the young woman standing in a corner crying softly and joined her.

Racine wiped away tears with both hands. "We'd talked about it but changed our minds. He was saved. Did you know that?"

Kree shook her head no. "He'd been asking me questions about God and salvation, but no, I had no idea."

"He got saved a couple of weeks before he died. He left to go to church with you the Sunday he disappeared." Racine's eyes filled with tears again. "Charles desperately wanted to get his life back together. He didn't want to hurt you anymore, Kree."

She recovered quickly from the surprise of Racine's statement. "Were you and Charles going to get married?"

"Y-yes," came Racine's broken reply.

Kree embraced her. "I'm so sorry for your loss."

"I loved your brother with my entire soul. He didn't have to die like this. Charles just wanted to make amends . . . then he ends up in the wrong place at the wrong time and now he's dead. People are saying that he was an informant for the police and that's why he was killed."

"He was an informant?"

Racine shrugged. "I really don't know, Kree. Charles never said anything to me."

She didn't know what to think or how to feel. Could Charles have been helping the police? If Kree had known about it, she would have tried to stop him from making such a dangerous decision.

"I miss him so much," Racine was saying.

"Me, too." Kree's eyes filled with unshed tears. "I can still remember when my mother brought him home. He was the sweetest baby." She heaved a soft sigh and added, "I hope Charles knew how much I loved him."

"He did," Racine affirmed. "He used to say that you always had his back. Charles wanted to make you proud of him, Kree. He really wanted to please you because he loved you so much."

"I just wanted him to be happy."

"He was. Right before he died, Charles said he'd never been happier. This was the happiest time of his life."

"I think that's why this seems all the more tragic."

Racine shook her head. "No, this was the best time—while Charles was saved, happy, and at peace. As much as I miss him, I'm glad God chose this time to take him from us. It would have been so much more painful if he'd left this earth never knowing what it felt like to be happy."

Kree nodded in understanding. "But there is this selfish part of me that wishes he were still with us."

Three

Stone stared down at the program in his hand. *Homecoming services for Charles Jacob Jackson.* Twenty-six years old was too young to die, he thought. Stone and Charles hadn't gotten along well but it didn't make his grieving for the young man any less. He'd loved Charles like his own, but not even time could erase the stain of bitterness Stone felt toward him whenever he looked at Korey.

When Charles was sixteen, he broke the number-one Mansfield law by bringing a gun into the house. Then on top of that, he was showing it off to one of his friends when he should have been baby-sitting Korey, who was only four at the time.

The teenage boys had been playing around when the gun went off. The bullet ricocheted off a table and struck Korey in the back. The spinal cord injury rendered him paralyzed from the waist down.

Stone had been so angry with Charles that he ordered the boy out of his home immediately. Kree, on the other hand, refused to throw her brother out on the streets. She couldn't stand the thought of sending him to any of the other relatives, including Aunt Martha.

The Mansfield house had become extremely tense as they struggled to make the adjustments needed for Korey. Kree and Stone tried to make their relationship work; however, the incident was the deathblow to their already fragile marriage.

In the beginning, Stone put all the blame on Kree. Even now, he still felt she was mostly responsible for things going wrong, although now he was able to share some of the blame.

Instead of speaking up, he held his tongue and did not reveal his true feelings about Charles and Candace living with them. He loved his in-laws but believed that he and Kree had been too young to take on such a tremendous responsibility. They had been married only a few months and had not planned on having their own child for a couple of years.

Stone strolled into the living room where Kree sat surrounded by her relatives. Her aunt Martha had lapsed into a tale about Charles and Candace when they were younger. Kree would smile and nod every now and then, but she didn't offer any comment.

He could see the pain and grief etched all over her face. Stone knew without a doubt that Kree loved her siblings as much as she loved her own son. She'd sacrificed her own marriage for them.

"How are you, Stone?" a woman standing nearby asked.

Stone recognized the sound of Clara Jean's singsong voice. "I'm fine. And you?"

She inched closer. "I'm doing okay. I was sorry to hear about Charles's passing. It came as such a shock." Clara Jean tossed a look over her shoulder. "Kree isn't taking his death too well."

"It's been hard on her," Stone confirmed. He wasn't fooled by her false concern for Kree. The two women merely tolerated each other.

Placing a hand on his arm, she asked, "Are you sure you're okay?"

She'd been throwing herself at him for years so her gesture didn't surprise Stone.

He nodded. Stone glanced over at Kree. She looked as if she was listening to her aunt Martha, but he knew her well enough to know she had zoned out. Kree always played with her hair when her mind was on something else.

Stone had forgotten that Clara Jean still had her hand on him until Kree glanced his way. Her expression was unreadable. Suddenly she stood and left the room abruptly.

Removing her hand, Clara Jean stated, "Times like this usually bring people closer together."

Stone tossed a quick look at her. "You said that to say what?"

"It's obvious you and Kree still care for each other. Maybe you two should work on getting back together."

Stone glanced at the woman in surprise. *"You want me and Kree back together?"*

"No," Clara Jean admitted. "But since I can't seem to take your mind off your ex-wife, she might as well have you."

He laughed. "You're crazy."

"Nothing crazy about it. I just know when I've been beaten."

There was never any competition, Stone wanted to shout, but he wisely held his tongue. He had never held an attraction for Clara Jean but he didn't want to offend her.

Nodding toward the group of women gathered around Kree, Clara Jean said, "She looks like she needs rescuing. Why don't you go over there?"

Stone agreed. "I think I'll just do that."

"Remember now . . . If Kree don't have the good sense to take you back, just give me a call. You still have my phone number, don't you? You've never used it."

Giving her a smile, Stone walked away in quick strides.

~

Stone would never fall for a woman like Clara Jean.

Kree knew this deep in her heart but she'd still found herself consumed with jealousy when she saw them together. Clara Jean had her claws on Stone as if the two were lovers.

The image was too much for Kree and she had to leave the room. In addition to that, her cousins and Aunt Martha were driving her crazy with their funeral stories. She stopped in the foyer just long enough to catch her breath. She didn't want to linger for fear of someone else wanting to express his or her sympathy. It was simply too much for her to bear at the moment.

Kree found herself in Charles's bedroom. She picked up a discarded shirt that once belonged to her brother and held it close to her heart.

"I miss you so much, Charles."

She felt a hand on her shoulder. Kree turned and looked up into the face of her ex-husband. The way he was looking at her filled Kree with drops of joy in her sea of grief. Her eyes halted at the tiny scar that trailed through his right eyebrow, breaking through their otherwise breathtaking symmetry.

Tearing herself from his gaze, she said, "Thank you for coming."

"I wouldn't be anywhere else. Charles was a part of my family."

His words stabbed at her. Charles had been mostly a source of trouble for Stone and Kree from the moment she brought him home. Now that he was dead, she refused to focus on those times and pushed them back into the recesses of her mind.

Stone knelt down beside her, his smile soft and gentle. "I noticed you haven't eaten anything. Would you like me to fix you a plate?"

"I'll be fine, Stone. Thank you though."

"You haven't eaten much since Thursday."

Her full lips smiled in delight. "You're keeping tabs on me?"

Stone nodded. "Yes, I am. I know how you are." He took her hand in his, the touch warming away some of her pain. "What happened to Charles—you shouldn't blame yourself. He was running around with the wrong people."

"I keep trying to figure out if I could have done something different. Maybe I should have let Aunt Martha take Charles when she wanted to. I just didn't want him and Candace split up." Kree's eyes shined with a film of water. "Maybe I was wrong." She wiped away her tears with the back of her hand.

"You did the best you could, Kree. We did what we could. Charles changed after your parents died. Perhaps we should have considered some form of counseling. I don't know."

"I failed, Stone," Kree whispered as her lips trembled and more tears welled up in her eyes. I failed as a wife and a parent." Her forlorn heart felt as if it might break.

"We all make mistakes."

"I've paid a high price for mine," she responded softly.

After a moment of uncomfortable silence, Stone asked, "Would you like Korey to stay over here tonight?"

"You don't mind?"

"It's fine. I think it might do you some good to spend time with your son. He's taken Charles's death pretty hard."

"Do you . . . are you planning on leaving soon?"

"Not for a while. Why?"

"I just can't deal with all these people right now. A part of me wants to run to my room and hide." Kree glanced around the room, and lowered her voice. "I know Aunt Martha means well but she's getting on my nerves."

Stone smiled. "She needs to be in control."

"That's fine. I just want her to leave me alone. She's been hinting that she's willing to stay longer. I feel bad because I want her to leave." Kree folded her arms across her chest.

"How long will she be here?"

"She's supposed to go home day after tomorrow. She *needs* to take Benny and Saul with her."

"What are they doing?"

"What have they been doing in all the years you've know them—they're drinking nonstop." Kree allowed her irritation to show. "Benny went to the funeral drunk."

"I assumed as much. I thought for a minute he was going to fall into the coffin."

Kree put her hands on her face brushing away the wetness. "This brings back so many painful memories for me. I've buried my parents and now my brother."

Stone embraced her. "I'm sorry, baby."

"You two look so good together," Aunt Martha said from across the room. "I don't know why y'all don't make it legal. Korey needs both his parents."

"Korey has both of his parents, Aunt Martha," Kree replied. She knew her aunt meant well but she didn't want her putting Stone on the spot like that.

"You know what I mean."

Kree decided to let the matter drop. She didn't want to risk getting into an argument with Aunt Martha. Changing the subject, she asked, "Could you do me a favor and make sure Benny eats something? He needs to put something else in his stomach other than alcohol."

"I told that boy not to come here with that mess. I don't care where they go, him and Saul can always find a liquor store."

Stone took Kree by the hand, surprising her. "We should join the others," he said.

Aunt Martha's lips curved into a smile. "Thank you, Jesus," she hollered. "Oh, His mercy is sooo good. . . ."

Kree stole a peek at Stone. He was openly amused.

She allowed him to lead her into the kitchen. He wanted her to eat some-thing and wasn't going to let up until she did. "You win, Stone. I'll fix a plate."

Right behind her, Aunt Martha said, "Honey, you go on and sit down. I'll bring you a plate. Stone, take Kree out of this kitchen."

"You heard your aunt—you're banished from the kitchen today."

She threw up her hands in resignation. "Fine. I'm going." Kree walked a few feet into the den and took a seat on the sectional sofa. Stone left the room to take a call.

Aunt Martha strolled through the den carrying a plate laden with food. "You sure have a pretty place here, Kree. This house is beautiful. Huge too. I told all the folks back home in Philly that you're crapping in high cotton now."

Korey and Candace chose that moment to enter the room. Her son looked perplexed by the statement, but Candace and Kree fell back in laughter.

Kree rolled her eyes heavenward when her aunt sat down beside her. "You and Stone considered getting back together yet?"

Kree smiled. "You don't give up, do you?"

"I know the two of you still got the hots for each other. I can see it every time I look at you both."

"Get her, Aunt Martha," Korey encouraged. "I keep telling Mom that."

Kree shot her son a warning look. She then sent Candace a look.

"I didn't say a word."

"But you were thinking it," Kree stated. "It takes *two* people to make a re-lationship work."

"Now if you need me to help you get your man, I can stay for a little longer."

"What are you going to do, Aunt Martha?" Candace asked.

"I've learned a trick or two in my day. Girls, y'all should've seen me back then. Course now, I was a bit slimmer in those days and things were sitting up and not dropping down—y'all know what I'm talking about. . . ."

Korey shook with laughter.

Kree reached over and gave him a playful pinch.

"When I met your uncle Elliot . . . girl, I had him eating out of my hands and at my kitchen table in no time. We got married after a five-month courtship."

"Stone and I have been through our courting period. We made it down the aisle and everything. Things just went crazy after that."

"Honey, you can get him back. Or maybe you don't want Stone. Is that it?"

"Aunt Martha, I love Stone. That will never change."

"Then what on earth are you sitting around for? If you're not careful, some woman is going to snatch him up." She gave a slight nod toward the kitchen. "That one over there sure has been running Stone down with those eyes of hers."

Candace gave her aunt a knowing smile. "That's Clara Jean. She's been after him for years."

"She's not his type," Kree stated flatly. "Clara Jean is much too flashy for him."

"She look like she fast," Aunt Martha muttered. "Look at that dress she's wearing. Looks like she painted it on."

"I like it," Korey threw in.

"You would," Candace shot back. "Just don't forget she's old enough to be your mama."

Kree eyed Clara Jean with disdain. The woman couldn't seem to take her eyes off Stone. Kree couldn't believe Clara Jean was just standing there staring at him so hungrily in the open like that. Didn't the woman have any decency about her? she wondered.

Turning around, Clara Jean met Kree's gaze. She gave her an innocent smile before moving on to engage one of their neighbors in conversation.

Kree felt the hair on the back of her neck stand up. She found Stone watching her and wondered if he'd caught her looking at Clara Jean. He knew she didn't care much for her. From the moment Clara Jean found out that Stone and Kree had separated, she determined to be the next woman in his life.

But Stone hadn't wanted Clara Jean. He dated a couple of women before landing into a committed relationship with Angela.

Kree didn't like Angela, but it was mostly because she feared losing Stone forever. She thought he would end up marrying the woman, but Stone ended it five years later. She was pressing for marriage and he decided he just wasn't ready.

When Stone and Angela's relationship ended, Kree and Candace went out to dinner to celebrate. They made a conscious effort to keep the real reason for their special dinner a secret from Stone.

Kree didn't like the fact that he seemed to be hurting from the breakup, but on the other hand, she had another chance. If only she weren't such a chicken.

Four

"Korey, I love having you here with us," Kree announced while washing dishes. "The house always feels so much more alive whenever you're here." Their guests were gone and she was relieved. Kree was grateful for the show of support tragedy offered but she needed some time alone with her grief. Her mourning had been public since the day Charles's body was found.

Propping his hands on the armrests of the wheelchair, Korey complained, "I wish Dad and I didn't live two blocks away. We should be in the same house—as a family. Why can't he see that?"

"Your father is stubborn," Candace stated. "You know how he is."

"Have you told him how you feel, Mom? Why don't you just tell him that you want to be with him?"

Korey's question caught Kree off guard. She tried to think of an answer and failed. "Honey, I don't think we should really be discussing this. This is not something a child should really be worrying about. Your father and I will handle our relationship, whatever that may be."

"Mom—"

Kree interrupted him. "This will work out the way it's meant to be, son."

He backed off. "If you say so."

Kree put away a stack of dishes. She wanted the same thing—Stone and Korey back home with her. Candace was engaged and would be getting married soon. She and her husband would be leaving for Los Angeles shortly after that.

A round of laughter brought her attention to the couple in the den. Candace and her fiancé, Trey, were going through the collection of photo albums. Kree wanted her sister to select some of the pictures of Charles and their parents for her own family album.

Korey dried the last of the pots and put them away. He and Kree joined the couple.

"Is Dad giving you away at the wedding?" he asked Candace.

She nodded. "He's been the only father I've known since I was eight." She wiped down the marble countertop. "I'm going to miss you all so much when I leave." Smiling at her fiancé, she said, "I've already told Trey that I'm coming home at least once a year."

"Candace is right. We're going to plan to come home once a year. She'll be here even if I can't make it."

"I'm going to try to come out there once a year too. Maybe Stone will agree to let me bring Korey with me."

"He will. Dad knows how close I am to my aunt."

Kree smiled at her son. "You think you have your father wrapped around your finger, don't you? One day he's going to surprise you."

Korey burst into laughter.

Aunt Martha ambled into the den, checking everything out. "Looks like y'all having a good time in here. Mine if I join the party?" She surveyed the sparkling room and said; "Now I told you I would clean up in here for you, Kree. You don't need to be worrying about cleaning during a time like this. My old body just needed a nap, that's all."

"Come on in, Aunt Martha," Kree stated. "I didn't want you to come all the way to North Carolina just to pick up behind us. We're going to watch a movie if you'd like to join us."

"Where did Benny and Saul go?"

Kree tried to remember the last time she had seen her cousins. "I think they went with Uncle Mack."

"If they're with Uncle Mack, then they're headed for the Dollhouse," Candace stated.

"The Dollhouse. What's that?" Korey questioned. "One of those houses of ill repute?"

Candace and Trey burst into laughter.

"It's something like that, I guess." Kree eyed her son. "I know I'll never have to worry about Korey going there."

"You're right, Mom. I don't need to go see strippers."

"Lord, have mercy," Aunt Martha moaned. "My brother is still as nasty as he always was. What is he thinking—taking those boys to a place like that?"

"It was probably Saul's and Benny's idea," Candace responded. "This is right up their alley."

"Mack likes looking at naked women too. Don't let your uncle fool you."

Kree put away the last of her dish towels. "Why did Sue Anne leave?" Kree asked.

"She wanted to get back to Greenville. She said she had to work tomorrow." Candace finished off her water and tossed the empty bottle in the trash. "Pearl Lynne rode back with her."

Kree regretted not spending more time with her cousins, especially since she didn't have much family left.

"I need to get up and do some laundry," Candace announced.

"Might as well throw me in with it. Girl, look at this body. I got wrinkles, creases, and folds," Aunt Martha said.

Korey threw back his head and burst into laughter.

"Don't worry about it tonight, Candace. We'll get up early tomorrow and take care of everything," Kree said.

"Y'all a-do no such thing. Just leave it outside your room and I'll take care of it in the morning." Aunt Martha wagged her finger at Kree. "And I mean it too. I'm here to take care of my babies."

"Yes, ma'am," they replied in unison.

"Aunt Martha, you've been in Philly more than twenty years but you never lost your southern twang."

"Honey, I'm what you call a southern Yankee."

They spent the evening watching a movie and talking about Candace's upcoming wedding. The only thing that would have made the night perfect was having Charles there with them.

Shortly after midnight, Kree made her way upstairs to her room. She lay across her bed, every muscle aching. She didn't move for almost an hour, too tired even to get undressed. Memories of the past came at her and Kree felt the sting of tears. This was not the way she'd wanted her life to be.

~

Stone stared at the ranch-style home for a moment before getting out of his car. Kree had bought the house shortly after their divorce with her portion of the insurance money she'd received after her parents died in the plane crash. She hadn't wanted to live too far from Korey. She'd deposited the balance into accounts for Charles and Candace.

After Korey had been shot and paralyzed, Stone filed for divorce and sued for custody of Korey because he could think of no other way to protect his son. Kree didn't fight him on his motion for physical custody. After she recovered from the shock of everything, she became angry. Over time they managed to move past the bitterness and eventually become friends.

Stone stepped out of the car and headed to the front door and pressed the doorbell. His mind was busy, trying to think of what he would say.

Kree opened the door a few minutes later. She looked surprised to see him standing there and said, "I didn't expect you this early, Stone. Did Korey have something to do today?"

"No, it's nothing like that. I knew Aunt Martha would be up with the sun cooking breakfast so I came hoping that you all would take pity on me."

Kree laughed as she moved aside to let Stone enter. "She must have known you were coming. Aunt Martha's made all of your favorites."

"You don't mind, do you? I've never been much of a breakfast cook—"

"Much of any kind of cook," Kree interjected with a smile. "You know you're always welcome here."

In the back of Stone's mind, he could remember a time when that wasn't the case. They had come a long way and he was grateful.

Kree looked as if she was in much better spirits today and that made him feel good. Stone hated to see her in pain. Her short hair had already been combed and styled and she was dressed in a pair of sweatpants and a T-shirt, looking younger than her thirty-six years.

"Is Korey still sleeping?" he inquired.

"I heard him moving around not too long ago. He should be out shortly. He loves Aunt Martha's cooking just like you do."

Stone wanted to say more, but before he could utter another word, Aunt Martha joined them.

"Well, well, well . . . look what the cat done drug in. . . ." She wiped her hands on her apron as she walked toward Stone. "I thought my homemade cinnamon raisin biscuits would bring you running down here."

"Aunt Martha must have had the window open and fanned the fumes down your way," Candace joked as she strolled into the room wearing sweatpants and a T-shirt like her sister.

They burst into a round of laughter.

"That's okay," Stone muttered. "I'll endure any and all jokes for Aunt Martha's biscuits."

"I made scrambled eggs with bits of cheese and ham just for you, Stone."

"How did you know he'd be here this morning, Aunt Martha?" Kree asked.

She dismissed her question with a wave of her hand. "You don't have to worry about none of that. Y'all just get in there to that fancy table of yours. I'll take care of the rest."

"You don't have to tell me twice, Aunt Martha." Candace headed to the dining room.

Stone followed Kree, asking, "Should I check on Korey?"

"I'm coming," they heard him say.

He and Kree shared a look of amusement. No one wanted to miss out on one of Aunt Martha's meals.

They sat around the table.

"Is Trey gonna make it for breakfast?" Aunt Martha inquired.

"He should be here any time now," Candace replied. "He was in the car when I called him a few minutes ago."

Stone glanced over at Kree. Their gazes met and held.

He was still very much attracted to her. There were times Stone felt the attraction was mutual but then Kree would retreat into a shell and he was unsure. They had never sat down to discuss their feelings. Maybe they should, Stone decided. The timing had to be perfect though.

～

Kree could have jumped for joy when Stone showed up at her door that morning. They saw each other a lot because of Korey but this time seemed different. She couldn't extinguish the tiny spark of hope igniting through her body. Maybe something good would come out of Charles's death after all.

"Smile," Candace whispered. "Don't look so uptight."

Kree gave her sister a playful pinch, and then stole a peek at Stone. He was engaged in a light banter with Aunt Martha. She couldn't get over how handsome he looked. She glanced down at the worn-looking sweatpants and wished she'd at least changed into something more presentable. Stone didn't seem to notice—in fact, he paid very little attention to her.

Her eyes traveled to Trey. His obvious devotion to Candace thoroughly pleased Kree. She was happy that Candace had been able to find a good man with whom to spend the rest of her life. Kree sent up a silent prayer that Trey and her sister would always be one.

Despite the way things ended with her and Stone, Kree still believed in happily ever after. She refused to believe that the man on the white horse did not exist. She grew up reading romance novels. Her love for reading romance gave her the foundation to recognize the qualities she wanted in a man. When she met Stone, Kree knew she'd found her very own hero. When their marriage ended, it took her for a loop. She was a much stronger woman now because of it.

"Where did you drift off to?" Stone's deep voice whispered.

Kree lifted her eyes to meet Stone's gaze. "Huh?" She'd been caught completely off guard by his question.

"You look like you were miles away from here. What were you thinking about? Charles?"

Playing with her scrambled eggs, she answered, "A lot of things, I guess."

He pointed to her plate. "Are you going to eat your food?"

Smiling, Kree inquired, "Why? Are you still hungry?" Stone had finished most of the food on his plate.

"There's plenty of food in the kitchen," Aunt Martha announced.

"That's good to hear," Korey responded. "I'm ready for seconds."

"Me too," Stone chimed in. Picking up his and Korey's plates, he added, "I'll get it."

As soon as Stone disappeared into the kitchen, Aunt Martha said, "It's so good seeing my family all together like this. It's sad when you think of the reason behind it though. Family needs to come together in times of joy, too."

"We will," Kree confirmed. "We'll all be back together when Candace and Trey get married."

"That's right." Aunt Martha turned to Candace. "Honey, I'm so happy for you."

Stone chose that moment to return, carrying two plates laden with food. He placed one of them in front of Korey. "Aunt Martha, don't you want to stay at my house for a few days?"

"You just want my aunt over there cooking for you," Kree accused playfully. "Stone, you should be ashamed of yourself."

"Don't you worry none, Stone. I've got you covered. I have a homemade chicken potpie in the freezer just for you and I brought you some beef stroganoff. I'll make you some more cinnamon raisin biscuits—you can store them in the freezer until you're ready to eat them."

"Aunt Martha, I thought you brought all that food for us," Candace stated.

"There's going to be enough left for y'all. I brought three potpies, two stroganoffs, and four dozen biscuits. That's two dozen apiece."

"You spoil us, Aunt Martha." Kree picked up her glass of cranberry juice. "I'm not complaining though."

"See, if you'd let me work with you a few days, I'd have you cooking good as me."

Kree gave a short laugh. "Like you'd really give me your recipe for the biscuits. You are the only one in the family who can make cinnamon raisin biscuits like Big Mama did. Everybody else has to come to you and you know you love it."

"Big Mama gave me her recipe right before she died. She made me promise not to tell a soul. One day I'm going to share it with you though—when the time is right."

"Why don't you tell her while you're here?" Korey questioned. "Then we can have them all the time."

Looking serious, Aunt Martha said, "It's a big responsibility. Your mama's not quite ready yet."

Stone bent his head and seemed to be concentrating on his food. Kree knew he was trying not to laugh. "Aunt Martha, what do I have to do? Go through some sort of initiation?"

"Something like that," she uttered.

The rest of the morning was spent discussing Candace and Trey's upcoming nuptials.

After everyone had eaten their fill, Aunt Martha shooed them out of the room. "I want to get the kitchen clean, so y'all go spend some quality time together in the den."

Kree and Candace exchanged a smile.

Korey navigated toward the hallway. "I'm going to watch television in my room," he announced.

Stone watched his son leave the room. He hated the fact that Korey couldn't run or play sports like the other kids his age. He was alive and well, he reasoned silently. Stone would have to be grateful for that.

"You must not be going to work today." Kree cut into his thoughts. "Kasner Computer College can actually do without you today?"

"KCC can manage on its own for a day."

"Do you ever miss IBM?" she asked. Stone had landed a job with IBM right before graduating from college. He stayed with them until four years ago when he decided to teach computer programming at KCC. Within the last year he'd been promoted to assistant dean at the college.

"Not really. I do miss the classroom though."

"Don't like all that administrative work, huh?"

"You know I was never into all that paperwork. What about you? Are you planning on working today?" Stone hoped Kree would take the rest of the week off. She was still grieving over Charles.

"It's hard to work with Aunt Martha here. She's leaving in a couple of days. With the weekend coming, I probably won't do anything until Monday."

"I'm glad to hear that. You don't need to hide your pain in your job. How is the real estate business?"

"Right now it's great. But you know it's up and down."

"You seem to manage well no matter what. I've seen all those awards you've gotten."

She couldn't stop her smile. Kree wanted Stone to be proud of her.

They heard Aunt Martha singing in the kitchen as she worked.

"There she goes," Kree murmured. "She loves gospel music."

They listened quietly for a moment.

Stone glanced over at Trey and Candace. They seemed to be in a world of their own. Gesturing toward them, he said, "Makes you feel invisible, don't you think? I doubt if they know we're even in the room."

Candace glanced his way, grinning. "We heard you. We know you're here."

Kree settled back into the chair, eyes closed and listening to Stone and Candace bantering back and forth. For the moment they were a real family once again and she was filled with happiness.

Five

"Finally!" Kree whispered when she hung up the telephone. She'd just sold the property on Creedmoor. The buyers had gone back and forth before deciding to make an offer. Then the seller almost backed out of the deal. . . . It had been frustrating but she was thrilled with the result. Kree immediately went to work on the paperwork.

She heard her private line ring but decided to let Candace answer it. A few minutes later she heard her sister say, "Kree, you have a telephone call."

"Who is it?"

Standing in the doorway, Candace replied, "Someone from the *Alonzo Clark Morning Show*."

"Yeah, right," Kree shot back. "I know it's April Fools' Day. Ha ha ha." She returned her attention to the project before her.

"I'm serious," Candace insisted. "Check it out yourself."

Frowning, Kree stated, "I don't have time for games. I have too much work to do."

"Just pick up the phone. This is no joke."

Rolling her eyes at Candace, Kree did as she was told. "Hello."

When she ended the call, her sister prompted, "Well?"

Kree was dumbfounded. "That . . . that was the *Alonzo Clark Morning Show*. I've won a Mother's Day makeover and a shopping spree. Korey sent them a wonderful letter." Her eyes teared up. "He is such a loving son. I'm so blessed to have him."

Candace moved around the desk and hugged her sister. "Congratulations. You really deserve it, Kree. You've been through so much over the years."

"I can't believe Korey did this for me."

"It really shouldn't come as a surprise," Candace stated. "You and Stone have done a great job with him." She walked over to the sofa in the office and sat down. "He put so much thought into that letter."

Giving her sister a knowing smile, Kree asked, "So you *did* know about it?"

Candace nodded. "Guilty." She traced the cabbage rose pattern on the sofa with her finger.

"I thought so. Thank you. I couldn't ask for a better Mother's Day." Kree paused for a second. "Wait. . . ."

"What's wrong?"

"I can't do this. I just remembered that they mentioned something about a blind date. I'm not interested in meeting a total stranger and then going out to dinner with him."

"Kree, you really need to get out more. This is just one date. What could it really hurt? You don't even have to see the guy anymore if you don't want to; besides the guy will be local so it might be somebody you already know."

"That would be so much better for me. Blind dates have always made me feel as if I'm desperate."

"That's not the case and you know it."

"I know but it doesn't stop me from feeling this way. But then again, this is a onetime deal."

"So you're going to do it?"

"I guess. Like you said, what could it hurt? Who wouldn't enjoy a day at Soigné followed by a shopping spree at Triangle Town Center? I haven't had a chance to visit the new mall yet." Kree wondered what Stone would say if he knew. He probably wouldn't care, she decided.

When Candace left the office, Kree picked up the telephone, and then she remembered that Korey wouldn't be home until after four. He tutored a couple of students on Thursdays. She would have to call him later.

Kree's thoughts traveled back to Stone. When their marriage ended, she stopped caring about a lot of things, including her hair, makeup, and clothes. After a while, Kree decided to cut her shoulder-length hair off and loved it. She'd been wearing her hair short ever since. Unless she went into the office or met with clients, Kree didn't bother wearing anything other than T-shirts and jeans.

A part of her wanted to have the makeover because she hoped to rekindle Stone's interest in her. The other part just wanted to feel beautiful.

∼

Candace and Korey made plans to have dinner and take in a movie afterward. She went to Stone's house to pick him up before meeting Trey at the restaurant.

She greeted Stone with a kiss on the cheek. "Hey, I didn't know you were home. I'm so used to seeing the car in the driveway."

His face broke freely into a smile. "I actually parked it in the garage this time."

Candace shrieked with surprise. "Really? I don't believe it." In all the years she'd known Stone, she never once saw him park his car any other place than the driveway or on the street. Kree used to get on him all the time about it.

"I'm going to clean the driveway," Stone confessed. "That's the only reason it's in the garage."

Candace sighed in mock resignation and said, "I don't know what you have against garages."

"I use them for extra storage. I've got a lot of stuff."

"Ever heard of a yard sale? Stone, you've got junk stored away. My rule of thumb is if you haven't seen it in a year, then you really don't need to keep holding on to it."

"Kree thinks that way too."

"Makes sense though, don't you think?"

Stone laughed and changed the subject. "What restaurant are you all going to?" Giving him a sidelong look, Candace answered, "We're going to eat at the Mayflower. You know how much Korey loves seafood." Gesturing toward the hallway, she asked, "Is he in his room?"

"Yeah. He's dressed and ready though." Stone navigated toward the kitchen. "I have a dinner meeting but I should be back here before the movie lets out. Korey misplaced his key."

"I still have my copy. I'll give it to him."

Stone nodded in approval.

"I'm going to drag your son out of here." Candace made her way to Korey's room. She knocked before sticking her head inside.

He was on his computer. "Hey, cutie. You ready to go?"

"Hey, Aunt Candace. I'm ready—just needed to finish up this letter. This is the second part of my plan."

Candace stepped all the way inside. "Another letter? Who are you writing now?"

Korey nodded. "This one is from Dad. I need you to sign it though."

"Excuse me?"

"I need you to sign Dad's name to this letter. We need this one to go FedEx too. I want Alonzo Clark to get it tomorrow."

"Korey, what are you talking about? And why are you writing a letter for your father?" She didn't listen to the radio very often, so Candace wasn't exactly sure what was going on. "I thought the contest was over."

"The first part of it is. Now that the winners have been announced, men can write in to request a date. That's where Dad comes in. He's going to win a date with Mom. He'll be her blind date."

Candace shook her head. "Why don't you just tell your Dad what's going on and have him send in the letter himself?"

"Just read the letter. You'll see why this letter needs to be sent."

"It's nice," she murmured as she read. "Very well thought out . . ."

"Candace, I really believe that our plan—"

"*Our* plan?" she interrupted.

"Okay, my plan. The point is that I feel like this is going to work. All we need now is Dad's signature. I don't want to tell him about it because he may not understand."

"You mean he may not go along with this scheme of yours." Shaking her head, Candace added, "Boy, I am not about to sign Stone's name to anything. Your father is not going to strangle me."

"Why would I want to strangle you?"

Candace glanced over her shoulder at Stone, then back at Korey. "I knew this wasn't going to work," she muttered almost to herself.

Strolling into the room, Stone asked, "Son, what's going on?"

Korey explained his plan to give his mother a wonderful Mother's Day sponsored by the *Alonzo Clark Morning Show*. "She's one of the winners. They called her a couple of days ago."

Stone wondered why Kree never bothered to mention it to him.

"And so now you want me to write in for a date with your mother? Is that what you're suggesting?"

Korey nodded. "The letter has already been done. We just need you to read it and sign it so that we can put it into the mail."

Stone seemed to be considering the idea.

"It's just one date," Candace emphasized. "Kree needs to get out of the house and just have some fun for one evening."

"I'll do it, but, son, this may not work out the way you've planned it. I'm sure other men will be writing in as well."

"You know Kree—she knows you. My sister will feel most comfortable with someone she knows and trusts. We really need your help, Stone."

"Dad, do you want Mom meeting some man and going on a date with him? What if she starts to like him?"

Stone took the letter from his son and read it. When he was done, he glanced at Candace and then his son. "You really think this is going to work?" he asked them.

"Yes," they replied in unison.

Without saying a word, he took the pen Korey held out to him and signed the letter.

Six

Kree drove Candace to the Bridal Boutique to have her wedding gown fitted. Since Charles's death a little over a month before, this upcoming wedding gave her something to which to look forward.

They parked and strolled into the store. Kree immediately felt a sense of sadness standing in the midst of mountains of white and ivory lace, tulle, silk, and taffeta. She turned around slowly, gazing at the various designs—styles for every little girl's dream wedding.

Candace had gone to put on her dress. Kree picked up a nearby gown and held it up to her, enjoying the feel of the fabric against her.

"That would be gorgeous on you," the salesperson complimented.

Putting the dress back, Kree shook her head. "I'm not getting married. It's very pretty though." Hearing movement behind her, she turned around.

Kree stood there eyeing her sister in her wedding gown, embroidered Shantung with beaded trim and a detachable semi-Cathedral train. The V-neck neckline and empire waist were very flattering. "You look so beautiful. Mama would be so proud of you."

"I wish she could be here."

"She is . . . in our hearts."

"Sometimes I have trouble remembering her voice. I miss her so much though."

Kree heard the pain in her sister's voice. "You sound a lot like Mama."

"I do?"

Kree nodded. "If my eyes are closed and you say something, it's like her talking. There have been times I've expected to turn around and find her standing there. She was a great mother."

"You are too. Kree, I wouldn't be the person I am if it weren't for you. You even managed to keep Mama alive for Charles and me through photo albums and stories of our childhood. For someone so young, I think you did a wonderful job. I hope I'm half the mother you are."

Fighting tears, Kree embraced Candace. "You're going to be a wonderful mother when the time comes."

"My only regret is that you lost your husband in the process. Kree, I'm sorry we broke up your marriage."

"Candace, you didn't break up my marriage. Stone and I did that."

"It was because of Charles and me," Candace insisted. "Mostly Charles, I know. I just want you to know how grateful I am to you. I hope to repay you one day for all you've done."

"I love you, Candace, and I'm going to miss you so much. I don't know what I'm going to do in that big house by myself."

"Maybe you won't be alone," she hinted.

"I know you don't think that Stone is going to allow Korey to move in with me?"

"I think maybe you two will be able to work something out. You and Stone seem to be getting closer more and more each day."

"Korey's fourteen. It may be better to leave things just the way they are. Uprooting him might cause some problems. As far as Stone and me—we're just friends."

"Kree, have you ever told Stone how you feel about him?"

She shook her head. "There never seemed like a right time. I've had to accept that maybe our life together is really over."

"I don't believe that."

"Stone's never said anything."

"He's never married again."

"I thought at one time he was going to say something but Myles was in my life."

Candace gave a short laugh. "Stone couldn't stand Myles. I think he was afraid he was losing you to him."

Kree shook her head sadly. "Myles was a big jerk. I don't know what I ever saw in him. I should have gotten the hint when he tried to take me to bed on the second date. He was only after sex and money."

"You were trying to forget Stone. He was dating that Angela person back then and you thought he was going to marry her. Myles was nothing more than a rebound for you."

"Angela made a point of coming to my house to tell me they were getting married."

"She just said it to hurt you, Kree. Stone never had any intentions of marrying her. I told you that."

"I didn't know what to believe back then. He seemed to really care for her, Candace."

"He liked her," she admitted. "But I think that's all there was to it."

"They were together for five years. He didn't just like her. There was more to it." Although it hurt Kree to admit it, she had to—Stone had loved another woman.

"He didn't marry her."

Kree put the palm of her hand on her face. "Korey didn't like Angela. He would never tell me why."

"I didn't like her either," Candace admitted. "Whenever Stone wasn't around, she was an entirely different person."

"I can believe that. Angela definitely didn't like me. The woman nearly had a stroke each time I showed up at the house to pick up Korey. I was afraid Stone was going to let her move in she was there so much."

"She tried to move in but Stone wouldn't let her. He felt that would set a bad example for Korey. Stone wouldn't even let her spend the night unless Korey was at our house."

"I know. I appreciate his discretion."

"He's really a good man."

"So is Trey. I'm very happy for you, Candace. I want nothing more for you than a long, happy marriage."

"It's my prayer also. Trey and I are the best of friends and I love him dearly. I want to be a good wife to him."

"You will be," Kree assured her. "Better than I was to Stone."

"There you go again. Stop thinking like that."

"Candace, I can't help it. I don't regret having you and Charles with me. I just wish I'd handled my marriage better. It's hard to explain. . . ."

"I know what you mean. You love Stone and now you wish you'd fought harder for the marriage. It's not too late, you know."

"We're divorced, Candace. It's way too late."

"You can always talk to him. You both have matured and you're both in much better places now—sometimes we have to part just to grow."

Smiling, Kree said, "You're definitely a bride-to-be. You are filled with the happily ever after, love conquers all syndrome."

"There's nothing wrong with that."

"No, there isn't." Kree embraced her sister once more. "My prayer for you is that happily ever after is just that."

~

Kree was pampered and treated like a queen at Soigné European Day Spa. Her body tingled and glowed from the aroma steam sauna, the salt aloe bath, the Swedish body massage, and the European facial.

After the paraffin pedicures, Kree decided to invest in lots of open sandals for the warm weather. She felt good from head to toe, having had a shampoo moisturizing, protein-steam-conditioning hair and scalp treatment, cut and hair design. All of this was complemented by a champagne lunch.

Scrutinizing her reflection, Kree had to admit she'd never looked so good. The subtle colors in her makeup brought out her eyes and high cheekbones.

"Will you come home with me?" she asked the makeup artist. "I'd like to look like this every day."

"I'll show you what I did."

"Really?"

"Sure. It's something you can do at home. Just remember the focal point of your makeover is your eyebrows."

Kree wasn't much for wearing makeup but seeing the way she looked now, she decided to do so more often. She paid attention to what the woman was saying.

She hadn't told Stone about her date or the makeover. Kree wondered what he would say when he found out. She was a little surprised that Korey hadn't said anything about it to his father. Deep down she hoped he would and that Stone would be jealous.

Kree sighed softly. She was going on a blind date in a few hours. Stone didn't even know what was going on. Another thought occurred to her. Maybe he did know but just didn't care one way or the other.

She needed to find a way to get Stone out of her system. He was never coming back to her. As much as Kree wanted to forget about him and move on with her life, she couldn't. Her heart was holding her back.

~

Stone found his phone flashing when he arrived home from work. He checked his voice mail and discovered that his mother had called. He was due to meet Kree for their date in a couple of hours, so he debated whether to check his messages now or wait until later.

His mother sounded agitated, however. Stone called her back. "I just got the message that you called. Is something wrong?"

"Did you know your sister had a baby?"

"No. But then Janine and I don't talk much since I wouldn't give her money for drugs the last time she called. That was almost a year ago."

"Your cousin Leanne called and said Janine's in Virginia. She gave birth to a baby girl and then left the hospital. Nobody knows where she is. Janine left a note requesting that the baby be put up for adoption."

"What?"

"She's giving the baby up for adoption. That girl has lost her mind. I'm going up to Virginia and have a talking-to with Janine. No blood of mine is going to be thrown away like that. I'll bring the child home and raise her myself if I have to."

"Mom, are you sure you want to raise another child?"

"That baby is not going to be put up for adoption."

They talked a few minutes more before Stone ended the call. Taking off his clothes, he headed straight to the shower.

Stone was in shock over the news of his twenty-one-year-old sister having a child. Janine had had a drug problem since she was eighteen. He agreed with his mother though—he didn't agree with blood relatives being given away for adoption.

Troubled, he showered quickly and then climbed out of the tub and dried off. How could Janine do this? He was of a mind to drive to Virginia to shake some sense into his sister. Janine was sick, he reminded himself. She didn't need a child right now, but the baby was here.

Seven

"I have to admit that I'm nervous," Kree said into the receiver. "I love my new look, however." She couldn't believe she was actually talking to Alonzo Clark. He was her favorite morning disc jockey. The interview was being taped and would air the very next day.

"Did you have any idea your son had written in to the show?"

"Not at all. This came as a complete surprise to me." Smiling at her son, she added, "I appreciate it though. Korey has always been very thoughtful. I don't know what I would ever do without him."

"In his letter he stated that you also raised two of your siblings. I'm very impressed."

"I was afraid that my brother and sister would be separated, and I didn't want that. It was hard enough losing our parents. I didn't want us to lose one another also."

They talked for a few minutes more and the interview ended. A local reporter would be arriving a few hours before her date to do another one. Kree wasn't comfortable with all the attention but it didn't help that she was so nervous.

The next couple of hours flew by and it was soon time for her to get ready. Kree went upstairs to change.

The simple black dress with web straps she had bought during her shopping spree made Kree feel sexy.

"You look great," Candace announced from the doorway. "I love that dress on you."

"I like it too."

The doorbell sounded.

"You finish getting ready, Kree. I'll answer the door." Candace turned on her heel and rushed off.

Kree studied her reflection in the mirror. "Please don't let me make a fool of myself tonight," she prayed.

She could hear her sister and another woman laughing and talking in the den. Kree assumed the reporter had arrived. She ran her fingers through her hair one more time and then stepped into a pair of black strappy sandals before leaving her bedroom.

"Hello," she greeted. "I'm Kree Mansfield."

After the introductions were made, Kree sat down and answered the questions thrown by the reporter.

The clock in the hallway chimed, announcing seven o'clock. Kree started to tremble. It was time for them to leave for the restaurant where she would meet her blind date.

"Nervous?" the reporter asked.

She nodded. "I hate blind dates."

The reporter laughed. "I understand. I've had my share. This time things may be different though."

"I doubt that," Kree muttered softly.

"I'll be here when you get back," Candace promised. "Have a good time."

"I'm going to try."

Kree got into her car and pulled out of the garage. The reporter got into her car and pulled off. They were heading to Gregory's.

When they arrived, Kree resisted the urge to stay in the car and just forget about the evening. "I can do this," she mumbled to herself. Taking a deep breath and exhaling slowly, Kree climbed out of her automobile and straightened her dress.

She stopped right before she entered the restaurant and took another deep breath. "Okay, I'm ready." Her date had arranged for them to have a private dinner away from the other dining guests.

She walked inside and came eye to eye with her ex-husband. "Stone! What are you doing here?"

Handing her a single red rose, he announced, "I'm your date."

Kree placed a hand on her mouth. She wanted to burst into tears of happiness, but didn't want to ruin her makeup. "I don't believe this. Why didn't you tell me?" She glanced over at the reporter. "You knew?"

The woman nodded with a smile.

Stone laughed. "Then it wouldn't have been a surprise, silly."

She was weak with relief. Kree had been dreading meeting her date for the evening, but now that Stone was there, she felt like everything was going to be perfect. Maybe this was the push they needed.

"I'm so glad it's you," she whispered. "I wasn't looking forward to making conversation with a stranger. Having someone following us around is bad enough."

"You really look beautiful, Kree. I mean you always look beautiful, but . . ." He seemed to be struggling for the right words.

"Thank you for saying that."

"I mean it. You look wonderful. You'd better watch out. You're going to turn a lot of heads tonight. If I'm not careful, I could lose you."

She grinned.

"You know what I mean."

"I'm beginning to think you're just as nervous as I was earlier." Kree settled back in her chair, preparing to enjoy the evening. This night was the beginning of a dream come true for her.

~

Stone was mesmerized. He struggled to take his eyes off his ex-wife. Kree was practically glowing.

The reporter was saying something to him, but Stone had no idea what. Turning his attention away from Kree, he said, "I'm sorry. What did you say?"

"What do you think?"

"Kree's always been beautiful, but tonight . . ." He smiled. "I'm speechless." He felt like a silly young boy.

He sat down beside Kree as they talked about how they met and fell in love. Stone kept stealing glances at his ex-wife. She looked exquisite and his heart was doing flips. *This is the woman I want to spend the rest of my life with,* he confessed silently.

". . . we grew apart and divorced," Stone heard Kree saying. Right before the divorce was final they had agreed not to disclose details about why their marriage ended. Neither of them wanted to air their private lives any more than necessary.

"Kree is the love of my life," Stone announced. "She's also my best friend. I thank God we have been able to remain close."

Kree seemed surprised by his words but she retained her composure. Finally, she said, "I feel the same way."

The waiter arrived to take their orders. They continued the interview until the food arrived.

"Well, this is where I leave. The interview is done. Thanks for being such good sports," the reporter said. "Enjoy the rest of your evening."

"I heard that Alonzo Clark went on a date with one of the winners," Stone announced.

Kree looked up from her plate. "Really?"

Stone nodded. "I'm glad it wasn't you," he admitted.

"Why?" She hid her smile behind her hand.

"I would have had to boycott his morning show."

She laughed. "You admit you have a jealous streak?"

"Okay. I admit it. I'm glad I'm your date."

"For the record, I'm glad you're my date also. I don't think I'd be comfortable with a stranger."

"You really look beautiful, Kree."

"You keep saying that. I'm not complaining, mind you. I love hearing it." He laughed suddenly.

"What is it?"

"We're acting like young kids on a first date."

Kree smiled. "Well, it has been a long time. Although we're around each other, it's not been like this."

~

Kree hadn't wanted the night to end. She couldn't remember the last time Stone had shown so much interest in her. Tonight he reminded her of the way it was in the beginning.

Candace knocked on her door. "I've been waiting up to hear how things went."

"You and Korey set this up, didn't you?"

Feigning innocence, her sister answered, "We had nothing to do with you and Stone winning the contest. That was Alonzo Clark and his staff."

"Tonight being with Stone was just like old times. It couldn't have been more perfect." Kree couldn't stop smiling. "I haven't been this giddy in a long time."

"Korey said all along this would work but I have to admit, I was a little bit skeptical. Seeing the big grin on your face now . . . I think your son was right. You and Stone both needed this night."

"I think so too. I just hope he feels the same way. Stone could hardly take his eyes off me tonight. All through dinner he just kept staring at me and telling me how beautiful I looked."

"You do look beautiful, Kree. And happy."

She stood in front of Candace. "Would you unzip me please?"

Her sister did as she requested.

Kree took off the dress and slipped on a faded T-shirt and a pair of men's pajama bottoms. "I didn't want the evening to end. I love Stone so much, Candace."

"He still loves you too."

"You really think so?"

"I do."

"Do you think I can get him back?"

Candace nodded. "Tonight's a good start. Now all you have to do is ask him out on a second date."

"I don't know if I can do that."

"You want your man back, don't you?"

"You know I do. I just—"

"You'll do whatever you have to do, Kree. If you want Stone back as much as you say you do."

Her sister's words were still imprinted in her mind long after Candace left the room. Kree stared into the mirror for a few minutes before removing her makeup. Stone had really liked her new look and so did she. She was glad that she'd gone out and purchased all the colors the makeup artist used on her. Tomorrow, Kree would bravely attempt to duplicate the magic.

Eight

The next day Stone called his mother to check on Janine since finding out about the baby. His sister had been located and placed in a drug rehabilitation center. He prayed she would get some help this time.

"She's going in rehab but she don't want that baby," his mother announced. "I can't change her mind."

"Janine doesn't know what she's doing," Stone uttered in anger. "If she gives this baby up, she'll regret it later."

His mother disagreed. "I don't think so. She's not the mother type, Stone. She'll have babies and just drop them wherever she can or throw 'em away. I don't even believe that this is her first pregnancy."

"How could she do this?" Stone steamed over the idea of Janine just abandoning her baby.

"I keep asking myself that."

"How is the baby?"

"She's fine. And so beautiful. Stone, you've got to see her. I named her India."

"You've always liked that name." He recalled her suggesting the name when Kree was pregnant with Korey.

"I finally got my India," his mother mumbled almost to herself.

"I've been thinking about something, Mom. Maybe I should take the baby—you know, adopt her." He could hardly believe the words that had come out of his mouth.

"Are you sure, Stone?"

"She needs someone. I know you love her, but, Mom, you're not as young as you used to be. Your blood pressure's high. . . ."

"Don't count me out yet. Stone, what are you going to do with a small baby? You have Korey and no wife. India's going to need a lot of care. She's a crack baby."

"Korey is no problem and as for a wife . . . well, you never know. Things may change."

"Is there something I should know? You're not back with that Angela, are you?"

He could hear the displeasure in his mother's voice and laughed. "No, that's not it at all."

"Humph," she grumbled. "What does Kree have to say about this?"

"There's no other woman, Mom," Stone reassured her. "Kree *is* the only one I want. I don't think we should have gotten a divorce but I couldn't see it before. I was so angry back then."

"You were scared. You thought you were going to lose your son."

"But that's no excuse. I was wrong to blame Kree. Charles was a teenager, and I should have been a little more forgiving."

"You and Kree are long past that, Stone. You can't undo what's happened."

"I know that."

"By the way, how did your date go?"

Stone was surprised by her question. "How did you know about that?" His mother didn't listen to anything other than gospel music.

"Korey told me. You know you don't tell me anything. I have to find things out third hand."

He laughed. "We had a great time. It reminded me of how things used to be between us."

"That's wonderful. Do you think she wants you back?"

"I believe we're on the same track."

"Lord knows, it's about time."

He broke into a short laugh. "I'm driving down to Charlotte today. I want to spend some time with you." Stone planned to take her to dinner and give her the gift he'd bought for Mother's Day. He had originally planned to spend Sunday with her but since his date with Kree, Stone wanted to stay in Raleigh.

"Korey coming with you?"

"Yes. We'll be there before nightfall. We're not going to stay over till Sunday though. We're planning something special for Kree on Mother's Day."

"What?"

"I'll tell you when I get there." Stone ended the call and went in search of his son. The drive to Charlotte would do him some good because he had a lot to consider.

~

Stone wondered how Kree would feel about another child. Before their marriage went sour, she'd always talked of having another baby, but now she might feel differently.

"Did you and Mom have fun?" Korey asked, cutting into his father's thoughts. They were in the car and on the way to Charlotte.

"We did. We had a real nice evening."

"I'm glad."

"Thank you for setting this up, son. I probably wouldn't have done it on my own."

"I'm glad you're not mad at me. I just wanted you and Mom to have a good time."

"And you were hoping something more would come out of it, too."

"Yes, sir. You and Mom belong together."

Stone smiled.

"Don't you think so?"

Stone stole a glance at his arm. "Your mother and I will always care about each other, Korey. We just may not be able to live together."

"I know. I believe it would be different for you and Mom. You broke up because of me."

"What are you talking about, son?"

"You and Mom got divorced because I almost died. Uncle Charles didn't mean to hurt me, Dad. And it wasn't Mom's fault."

"Korey, where did you get this stuff from?"

"I heard you and Mom arguing about it a long time ago."

Stone didn't want to give his son false hope. "I'm sorry about that. It's really not that simple, however. Your mother and I had a lot of problems back then. We weren't communicating and things were very stressful. We've made peace with the past, so don't worry about that."

"Dad, do you still love Mom?"

"I will always care for her."

"But do you love her?" Korey pushed.

"Yes, I do. Nothing will ever change that." Stone glanced down at his watch. "Are you packed and ready?"

"Yes, sir. I can't wait to see Grandma's face when she opens her present. She's going to love that Bible."

"She needed one with the large print. Her eyes are not getting any better."

"Grandma seems real mad at Janine because she don't want the baby."

"It's not so much that she's mad at her," Stone explained to his son. "She's hurt and very disappointed."

Inclining his head, Korey questioned, "How do you feel about her?"

"I love my sister, son. I'm disappointed in Janine but I'll never stop loving her. I want to help her get off drugs and stay off them."

"I don't know why anyone would do drugs."

Shaking his head, Stone responded, "I don't either. No matter how hard we try, there are just some people we can't help." Charles stumbled into his thoughts, troubling him. The truth was that he felt he'd failed his brother-in-law in some way and the guilt haunted him.

~

Succulent smells greeted Kree when she entered her house.

"What's all this?" she asked. "I just went to church—I wasn't gone that long. How did you three do all this so fast?" Kree walked into the dining room, which had been transformed into an exotic paradise. "It looks beautiful in here."

"I'm glad you like it," Korey replied. "Candace and Dad did all the work. They take directions well. We have your favorite—pineapple chicken."

Kree broke into a smile. "Who cooked?"

"I did," Stone announced proudly. "Candace helped but I did most of the work."

"You actually cooked the pineapple chicken?"

"As I said earlier, Candace helped." Stone broke into laughter. "Okay, Candace did the chicken and I did everything else."

"Everything?"

"Candace helped with . . ." Stone's voice died as Korey and Candace howled with laughter with Kree joining in.

"We want you to just take a seat, big sister, because today is your day. We're not going to let you do a thing."

"You guys are spoiling me."

"You deserve it," Candace said. "You're a great mother, Kree."

The memory of her brother and how he lived brought tears to her eyes. "I don't know about that. If I'd been a better one, maybe Charles would still be alive," Kree murmured softly.

Stone wrapped his arms around her.

"I miss him so much, Stone."

"I know you do. I miss Charles too. We all do."

"I would give anything to have one more day with him. There's so much I want to say to him—things I should've said, but now it's too late. Charles is gone."

"He's with Mom and Dad now," Candace said. "And he's found peace."

"It doesn't make me feel better. He was too young to die." Kree wiped away her tears.

"It's going to be all right, baby," Stone murmured.

Kree hugged him tightly. She didn't want to let go.

After a while, she said, "I'm sorry. I didn't mean to put a damper on the celebration. I just couldn't help thinking about Charles."

Stone gave her an understanding smile. "He's on all of our minds. Charles has been on my mind a lot lately as well."

Kree wasn't surprised by his admission. She knew that deep down Stone had loved her brother.

"So, are we ready to eat?" Candace inquired.

Kree nodded. She was too emotional to speak at the moment.

Stone took her by the hand and led her to the table. His touch sent tingles down her spine and made her heart pound faster. He held out a chair for her. When Kree was seated, he walked around and took the seat across from her.

Candace and Korey joined them at the table.

Kree bit back a smile when her son offered the blessing of the food. She was so proud of him. Stone had done a wonderful job of raising him.

"Where's Trey?" Kree asked her sister.

"He's with his mother. Trey and his brother took her out to dinner. She's still not over losing Trey's father." Candace poured a glass of tea and handed it to Korey. She poured another one and offered it to Kree. "He's coming by later this evening." Glancing over at Stone, she inquired, "Would you like some tea?"

"No, thank you. The water's fine for me."

Kree buttered a roll. "Korey told me you guys went down to Charlotte to see your mother." She met his gaze. "How is she doing?"

"She's fine. She's on the warpath over Janine."

"Korey told me about the baby."

"She's a beauty. You know Mom named her India." Stone cut off a piece of chicken and stuck it into his mouth.

"She loves that name for some reason," Kree said in amusement. "I'm so glad Korey was a boy."

"Me too," Stone admitted. "I know how much you hate the name."

"I don't hate it. I just didn't want to name a child of mine India."

"I think it's pretty." Candace picked up her glass of iced tea. "It would really have to fit the child though."

Kree finished off her chicken. "I agree."

Conversation was cut to a minimum as they ate their dinner. Kree couldn't remember being this happy in a long time. The memory of this Mother's Day would stay with her forever.

Nine

Kree wiped away tears of joy as Candace came down the aisle on Stone's arm. She accepted the handkerchief Korey offered her. She had never seen her sister look so beautiful or so happy. Candace had always wanted a June wedding. It wasn't too hot or too bright. The day was perfect.

She couldn't help but recall her own wedding day. Her mother had cried throughout the entire ceremony. Kree smiled at the memory. She and her parents had been very close and she missed them.

Stone looked as handsome as ever in the black satin shawl jacket. Beneath it, he wore a white shirt with a mandarin collar and a zippered full-back vest in turquoise.

A few minutes later, Stone sat beside her and Kree stole a peek at him. She wondered if he was experiencing the same emotions. They had been spending a lot more time together since Mother's Day but hadn't gone out on another date. Stone would come over to her house or she would go to his.

During the ceremony, Kree found it hard to keep her emotions under control. Stone must have sensed it because he reached over and took her hand in his.

When the minister introduced the couple as Mr. and Mrs. Trey Baldwin, Kree jumped to her feet with the rest of the congregation and applauded. Stone surprised her by embracing her.

"Our girl's married," he whispered.

Kree was too emotional to speak.

They broke the hug and watched the wedding processional.

Outside the church, Kree sought her sister and new brother-in-law.

"Congratulations, Mr. and Mrs. Baldwin," she said.

Trey embraced her and planted a kiss on her cheek, followed by Candace.

"I'm so happy," Candace cried.

Kree smiled. "I know. You're practically glowing." She reached up to straighten the rhinestone comb in Candace's hair. "That's better," she murmured. "It was crooked. Trey probably moved it when he went to kiss you."

"Stone looks great, doesn't he?" Candace asked in a low voice.

"He's gorgeous in that tuxedo."

When the church was almost empty, the bridal party and the family returned for pictures. They headed to the hotel for the reception after the photo session.

Kree rode with Stone and Korey.

"She's beautiful," Stone said. "I'm glad to see Candace so happy."

"Me too."

As soon as they arrived at the hotel, Stone escorted Kree into the ballroom. Most of her relatives had already arrived and were seated. They joined Aunt Martha and another of her mother's sisters.

Stone greeted everyone at the table.

Korey joined his cousins at a table behind them.

Hors d'oeuvres were served while they waited for the bridal party to arrive.

"When do they leave for California?" Stone asked.

"In a couple of weeks. I'm going to hate to see her go."

"I have to admit that I'm going to miss Candace as well."

Kree glanced over at Stone. "How do you think Korey is going to handle her leaving? They're so close."

Stone shrugged. "I don't know. It's going to be hard in the beginning but I think he'll get through it. Besides he still has us."

"I'm sure he'll be thrilled at the news. Our poor son is probably sick of us, Stone."

"He still has his friends. Korey has more of a social life than we do. Let me change that—more than I do."

"What are you trying to say?"

Stone's face broke into a grin. "Nothing. Just that you may have a social life, that's all."

"Not me. I have it hard enough getting clients to call me." Kree burst into laughter. "I can't believe I sound so pathetic."

She gave Stone a slight nudge when he broke into a laugh. "It's not that funny." Kree tried to summon up the courage to ask Stone out on a date. Every time she tried to speak, it felt as if something were stuck in her throat and she couldn't get the words out. She took a sip of champagne and stole a peek at Stone.

He was watching her.

Nervous, Kree cast her eyes to her plate and played with her food. She couldn't believe she was acting like a nervous schoolgirl.

Aunt Martha excused herself from the table a few minutes later. "I need to make my rounds. Be back in a while." Pointing to her champagne, she said, "Don't let the waiters take this away."

Kree and Stone soon found themselves alone at the table.

"Was it something I said?" he joked.

She laughed. "I think they're plotting. They're giving us some time alone."

"I think so too." He took a bite of his chicken.

Kree took another sip of champagne. This was the perfect time to ask him. They were alone. It was now or never. . . .

"There's something I've been meaning to ask you," they said in unison. She and Stone both looked startled for a moment before bursting into laughter.

"What is it?" she asked.

"I was thinking about the other night. We had a good time, didn't we?" he said.

"Yes, we did."

"Why don't we do it again? Have dinner together?"

"Like a date?"

"Yes. I'm asking you out on a date."

"I'd love to have dinner with you, Stone." This day was not only the beginning for Candace—it was a beginning for Kree as well. She couldn't have been more pleased.

~

Stone arrived with roses for their date.

"They're beautiful," she murmured. Taking them in her arms, she inhaled their fragrance. "Give me a minute to put them in a vase. They're going to look wonderful on the dining room table."

He knew she'd always loved having fresh flowers grace her table. "We have time."

Five minutes later she had them arranged prettily in a crystal vase and brought them out of the kitchen. Stone watched her place them in the center. His body reacted to seeing her in the slinky dress she was wearing. Tonight she was playing the temptress, he thought.

A few minutes later, Kree grabbed her purse and they headed toward the door. Before reaching the car, however, Stone pulled her into his arms and kissed her, opening her mouth with his.

Kree gave in to the unleashed desires of his mouth against hers, reigniting the longing deep within. She ran her hand across Stone's shoulders, unaware of the currents shooting through him.

They pulled away slowly.

"I've been wanting to kiss you like that for a while," Stone confessed.

Kree felt the heat from their closeness. "I wanted it too."

"I guess we should be on our way."

She nodded, knowing full well that neither one of them wanted to leave. It would be a mistake to rush into sex, Kree reasoned. It was much too soon.

Their emotions settled down once they were seated at a corner table in Marco's. They'd placed their orders and were waiting for the food to arrive.

"It feels so strange not having Candace in the house. There are times I actually go to her room to talk to her. . . ." Kree waved her hand in dismissal. "But she's not there."

"I miss her too."

"It took me about a month to realize that Charles was really gone." Kree took a sip of her wine.

"Losing loved ones is not easy."

She nodded. "I know."

Their food arrived.

Kree sampled her pasta. "This is good." She pointed at his plate with her fork. "How is the salmon?"

"Great." Stone took another bite.

When they were halfway done with dinner, Stone spoke up. "I think we should talk about what happened before we came."

Kree agreed. "We should."

"We've been through a lot. There were times I didn't think we could get past some of the anger."

"Are you past it now?" Kree asked, ignoring the warning signs. Before they could move forward, she and Stone had to lay the past to rest.

"I will always hold Charles responsible for what he did."

"He never meant to hurt Korey."

Stone laid down his fork. "You always jump to his defense. Kree, Charles wasn't a saint. He—"

"I know that," she shot back angrily. "But he's dead now. Can't you just forgive him?" Kree couldn't hide her irritation. She'd assumed they were past all the blame.

"Will you calm down? I don't know how you can just dismiss the fact that your brother is the very reason our son is paralyzed. I don't hate Charles but I can't just forget what he's done to us. But the truth is that he ruined our marriage. If it hadn't been for him, we would probably still be married."

"He didn't ruin our marriage, Stone. We did that ourselves. I don't know how you can open your mouth to form those words."

"He was trouble."

"He was my brother and he needed me, Stone. Charles wasn't my idea of a good little boy either but love is unconditional. You should know that."

"I never said you shouldn't love your brother. I only meant that he needed the guidance of a firmer hand. You spoiled him and when he got into trouble, you let him hide behind your skirts."

"Then why didn't you teach him to be a man instead of just walking out on me?" Kree pushed away from the table. "I want to leave. I've suddenly lost my appetite."

"You always want to run away. Stop running, Kree. For once in your life be an adult."

"I don't have to sit here while you insult me. I'll take a taxi home." She stood and rushed off.

Ten

Stone was never going to forgive her or Charles for what happened to Korey. Kree's heart was heavy with sadness as that realization dawned on her. Tears rolled down her cheeks and she did nothing to stop them.

The house seemed so empty. Kree missed Candace. She missed Charles, her parents, Korey, and Stone. Over the years they'd worked hard to get past the hurt and anger, or so she'd thought. Now she wondered if it had all been a lie.

The phone rang but Kree refused to answer it. She didn't feel like talking to anyone. She just wanted to wallow in self-pity for the moment. The thought of losing Stone all over again caused her tears to flow harder. Her heart, still fragile from the first time, fell apart, broken. This time Kree didn't think she would ever recover.

She made her way to her bedroom. She climbed onto the bed and curled up in a fetal position, feeling utterly alone and miserable. Kree couldn't get Stone off her mind no matter how hard she tried.

She could not forgive herself for what happened; but she sought to find a way through Stone's love, though all of her dreams of them getting back together had been dashed because he couldn't escape the past.

How could fate be so cruel?

~

Stone muttered a string of curses. What he'd said to Kree had been uncalled for. He'd let anger get the best of him. He knew he'd hurt her by his words and now Stone wasn't sure if he could salvage the relationship they'd worked so hard to rebuild. Why couldn't he just bury the events of the past?

Kree had been right. Charles didn't break up their marriage. He'd been the one, Stone admitted sadly. She'd never wanted the divorce. Kree had pleaded with him to work on saving their marriage.

Through it all, his love for Kree never stopped. She was his life's partner and the only woman he wanted. "I've got to find a way to fix this," he muttered. Stone didn't even want to think of going forward without Kree. He certainly didn't want things to become as strained as they used to be.

Stone picked up the phone to call her. He changed his mind and hung up after the third ring. He couldn't talk to her over the telephone. Not about this. They needed to talk face-to-face.

He decided to walk the two blocks to Kree's house instead of driving.

"What are you doing here?" she snapped when she opened her door.

Stone could tell she'd been crying. "Can I come in?"

"We have nothing to say to each other."

"You're wrong," he interjected quickly before Kree could close the door in his face. He stuck his foot in the doorway. "We have to talk."

Kree didn't look convinced.

"I want to apologize for upsetting you last night."

"You were honest about your feelings. I can't really blame you for that."

"Please, can I come inside? I really don't want to have this discussion outside."

Kree opened the door wider and stepped aside.

"I was wrong about the things I said last night. The truth of the matter is that I don't blame you, Kree. I admit that I did in the beginning, but I don't anymore. I blame myself."

"What about Charles?"

"I still blame him for what happened to Korey. Charles brought a gun into our house against our wishes. Our son almost died because of it."

Stone sat down on the love seat while Kree took a seat on the couch, and he continued, "I can't blame your brother for the breakup of our marriage. I did that."

"We both did."

He shook his head. "You never wanted our marriage to end. I think I did it to punish you somehow. I was angry and immature." Stone's eyes rose to meet hers. "I was wrong, Kree. It's only recently that I fully understand what you must have gone through."

"How do you mean?"

"When I found out that Janine abandoned her child, I just couldn't see the baby being raised by anyone other than family. That child is a part of me."

"Stone, I hope you know that Charles loved Korey with all his heart. He could never forgive himself for what happened. He told me that the last time we talked. There was something else."

"What?"

"Charles was changing. According to Racine and Korey, he'd started attending church and studying the Bible. He was trying to become a better person. He told Racine that Korey was largely responsible for his wanting to make changes in his life. Charles was planning to marry Racine."

"I will always regret not having a chance to talk to him and straighten things out between us. Believe it or not, I loved Charles," Stone said quietly.

"I know. I've never doubted that."

"I can only hope that Charles knew it."

"I believe he did," Kree reassured him. "How are things going with the baby?"

"Mom wants to do what she can for India, but you know my mother's not able to raise another baby. On top of this, the baby was exposed to drugs in the womb and born addicted to crack cocaine."

Kree acknowledged, "I'd heard. Korey told me and I think it's such a shame. I thought Janine had gotten off the drugs a while back."

"She did. But that didn't last long."

Settling back against the cushions, Kree asked, "The baby . . . is she okay? Does she have any medical problems?"

"Mom says India does a lot more crying than most babies and it's hard to console her. She says it's like she doesn't want to be touched. India seems to enjoy being bathed though."

"The poor little baby," Kree murmured softly. She'd never seen a baby addicted to crack but she could only imagine that the infant needed special attention. "So what are you all going to do?"

"That's the other reason I wanted to talk to you. I'd like to take India and raise her as my daughter."

Stone's announcement astonished her. *"You?"*

"You don't think I can do it."

"You're a wonderful father. I'm sure you can do it. I'm just amazed that you'd even want to after all we went through. Caring for the baby is going to require a lot of work. I'm sure there are some long-term effects?"

"I've been thinking about that too. I wasn't very supportive back then and I'm sorry. You took on a great responsibility—I'm understanding that fact better now that I'm planning to bring India home with me."

"She's already got you wrapped around her finger, doesn't she?"

He nodded. "You should see her, Kree. She's such a beauty. She suffers from low birth weight and her head looks smaller than I've seen in most babies. She rubs her face against the crib sheet a lot so her nose is always red. To me, India cries different from other babies—it comes off real shrill and high-pitched."

"The first thing you need to do is set up an appointment with the doctor. It's important that you fully understand what you're going to be dealing with."

Stone nodded again. "I met with the pediatrician last week. He says that with an infant development program through two years of age, India can get caught up in physical coordination, language, and problem-solving skills."

"That's encouraging."

"I talked with him a long time because I wanted to know exactly what I was getting myself into. It's a real serious condition, Kree. When she gets older, he said, the slightest disruption could set off a temper tantrum. He says that with early interaction with other children, counseling, and tender loving care, India's chances to have a normal life can improve significantly."

Kree sensed he needed her approval. "You're doing the right thing, Stone."

"I'm glad to hear you say that. Kree, I want you to be her mother."

"Excuse me?"

"I want you and me to raise India. You've always said that you wanted another baby—maybe a little girl."

Kree was stunned speechless.

"It would mean seeing each other more and spending time together as a family. How would you feel about that?"

"We're not rushing into anything, right?"

"We'll take our time, Kree. Let's just try this out on a trial basis and see how things work."

"We're going to raise two children between two households?"

"It is my hope that we will eventually merge down to one. I still love you and I'm tired of being alone. I'm tired of being without you."

"You've never said this before."

"I've always told you that I care about you—you know that. Honey, I never stopped loving you."

"I feel the same way," Kree admitted.

"How do you feel about raising a baby? One with special needs?"

"I love babies. Despite the challenges ahead, I would want to raise India. She needs us, Stone. But what about Janine? What happens if she decides she wants to be a part of her daughter's life?"

"She doesn't want to be a mother right now—actually, she's in no condition to be one. When India is older, we can sit down with her and tell her the truth. Kree, I can't do this alone. India is going to need a mother, but I want you to take some time and think about this. This is a huge commitment."

She got up and walked around the coffee table to join Stone on the love seat. Taking his hand into hers, Kree replied, "I don't have to think about it. This feels so right and I want my family back. India is only going to make it better."

Eleven

Stone and Kree decided to take their son out to dinner. They waited until after the meal to make their announcement.

"Korey, we have something to tell you," Stone began. He reached over and covered Kree's hand with his own. "Your mom and I—"

His son cut him off. "You and Mom are getting back together?"

Kree burst into laughter. "I told you he would figure it out."

"That's great. I'm glad you two finally came to your senses."

"We knew you'd feel this way," Kree said.

"It's been my prayer for a long, long time. This time, I want you two to stay together."

Kree met Stone's gaze and smiled. "We want the same thing, sweetie. Your dad and I are going to do everything in our power to make it right this time. We're not going to rush into anything but we're not planning on dating long either."

"Can't you two just get married?" Korey questioned. "You already know everything about each other."

"We haven't been a couple for a long time," Stone replied. "We just want to take a few months to get used to the idea. Son, there's something else too. We want to have another baby."

Frowning, Korey asked, "You guys aren't too old for that?"

Stone grinned while Kree gave their son a playful pinch. "We're thinking about adoption. We would like to adopt India. How would you feel about a baby sister?"

Korey didn't hesitate with his response. "I've always wanted a little sister, so it's cool."

"Honey, are you sure?" Kree asked. "Having a baby in the house is not going to be easy. Babies require a lot of work—sick babies even more. India is going to need a lot of attention."

"I can handle it. I'll even help out where I can."

Kree's eyes filled with unshed tears. "You are such a sweetie. I'm so proud of you, Korey."

"Dad, you're going to have to work on her. Mom is getting mushier every day. She needs to be stopped."

"Don't worry, son. Your mother will soon be lavishing some of that affection on me and India."

"And I don't want to hear you complaining that I don't give you any attention," Kree warned.

"I don't ever have to worry about that," Korey shot back. "I know you're crazy about me."

They continued their light banter through dessert and all the way back home. Stone tried to convince Kree to spend the night with him.

"It's not like we weren't ever married. On top of that, you're my son's mother."

"We're not married now." Kree kissed him lightly on the lips. "We have to set a good example for our son."

"I can come back over here after he goes to bed," Stone offered. "I want to wake up next to you."

The heat of desire spread through Kree, threatening to weaken her resolve. "You're not making this easy on me."

"I love you, Kree. We have a lot of making up to do. Years of it."

She laughed. "I don't know. I think we should wait until our wedding night. Besides, there are still some things we need to work out before we take our relationship to that level. I really want to spend the rest of my life with you, so let's just slow it down a little bit. Okay?"

Sighing, Stone nodded in agreement.

"Let's have breakfast together," Kree suggested. "You come over around eight. Korey will be at computer camp, so we'll have the morning to ourselves."

"Sounds good." He leaned over and kissed her.

Kree closed her eyes to the feel of his lips on hers. He slid his arms around her waist, drawing her closer to him until she could feel the heat generating from their closeness.

They parted reluctantly.

"I'd better get Korey home," he said in a hoarse whisper.

"I'll see you in the morning." Through her window, Kree waved and watched as they pulled out of the driveway and drove away. She'd wanted nothing more than to have Stone make love to her, but this time everything had to be perfect. If their relationship did indeed lead to marriage, she didn't want another divorce. She wanted happily ever after.

After changing for bed, Kree made a phone call to Candace. California's time zone was three hours behind, so it was still early on the West Coast. Her sister answered on the third ring, and Kree went straight to the point.

"Candace, I've got something to tell you."

"What is it?"

"Stone and I are back together."

Kree heard her sister squeal with delight on the other end of the receiver and she burst into laughter. "I think you and Korey are happier than me and Stone."

"I don't know about that, but we are thrilled. It's about time you two got back together."

"I can't agree with you more. This is something I've wanted for years. I wish the divorce never happened in the first place."

"Maybe it was a good thing, Kree. It forced you and Stone to grow up."

"But I think we would have done that anyway."

"Stone was your world. When Mama and Daddy died, Charles and I became your world. I don't think you'd be as independent as you are if you'd stayed with him."

Kree gave this some thought. "You may be right."

"I'm very happy for you, sis."

"Stone and I are planning to raise India," Kree announced.

"Janine's daughter?"

"Yes. We're going to adopt her."

"That's wonderful. You always wanted another baby." Candace paused a moment before asking, "Now how does Stone's mom feel about it? I know she loves that baby and she's had her since the day she was born."

"Stone says that she's willing to let us raise India. She just wants us to be sure we're going to be together. We're as sure as anyone can be."

Kree and Candace spent the next ten minutes talking about babies. She hung up and crawled into bed, reading until she fell asleep.

~

Stone and Korey drove down to Charlotte the following weekend, taking Kree with them. Stone wanted her to meet India.

"Hey, Mom, I brought you some company," he called out. Stone had called his mother to let her know about his impending visit but left out the fact that Kree would be joining him and Korey. He wanted to surprise her.

Waverly Mansfield grinned when she saw Kree. She held her arms open and said, "Honey, it's so good to see you."

Kree embraced her former mother-in-law. The two had remained friends throughout the years. "It's good to see you too, Mother Mansfield."

"Hey, Grandma," Korey greeted.

Hugging her grandson, Waverly asked, "What are you up to? You staying out of trouble?"

"Always."

Turning to Kree, she said, "I ought to take out a belt and spank you. You haven't called me in almost a year."

"I'm so sorry. Most of my time was consumed with Candace and her wedding; then Charles died. . . ."

"Honey, you don't have to tell me. I understand."

"I'm sorry you couldn't make it to the wedding. It was beautiful."

"I hate that I missed it. Stone showed me some pictures. Candace sure was a pretty bride. My blood pressure was sky-high and I couldn't do nothing. My gout was bothering me too."

"That's why you have to take it easy."

"I'm trying, Kree. It's hard sometimes. I've got the baby and then I'm in the choir at church . . . then there's Bible study. I can't just sit still."

"I've heard so much about this baby. I can't wait to meet her."

"Well, y'all go on and have a seat. I'll bring India out." Waverly ambled toward the hallway. "She was up most of last night. Now she trying to sleep the day away."

Kree leaned over and whispered, "Your mother looks so tired."

Stone agreed. "She's not able to do this. Mom will try and find a way to raise India, but it's already taking a toll on her health. She's raised her own children and one other grandchild. It's time for her to take it easy."

"How do you think she'll feel about us raising India?"

"She's fine with it. Mom knows we'll be good parents."

Waverly brought out the baby. "She's just waking up." She handed her to Kree.

"Oh my goodness," she murmured softly. "She's so beautiful." Kree held the infant close to her heart, inhaling her baby scent. "I haven't held such a tiny baby in a long time."

"She's small but she's a fighter."

"Hello, cutie," Kree uttered. "How are you? Is that a smile?"

Stone smiled. Kree loved babies and she was a good mother. Even after their marriage ended and he took custody of Korey, she refused to be too far away from her son.

Kree had insisted on being included in every aspect of his recovery back then—even when they weren't on speaking terms. She had always put Korey before everything. Kree had done the same thing for Candace and Charles. It was one of the reasons she worked mainly at home, going in to the office only when necessary.

He had been so selfish back then, Stone admitted. Perhaps they would still be together had he not acted so foolishly back then. At the time, all he wanted to do was protect his son. Stone wouldn't have survived if Korey had died back then. He couldn't understand how Janine could just abandon her child, but on the other hand she had made what was probably the most mature decision she'd ever made in life.

Waverly allowed Kree to give India her bottle. "I could get used to this," Kree said.

Stone's eyes filled with amusement. "What about changing diapers, cleaning spills, and all the other stuff that comes with babies?"

Shaking her head, Kree replied, "I don't mind it. I love children. They just grow up much too fast."

Stone nodded in agreement.

Korey played with the baby while the adults talked.

"Are y'all sure you want to take on this responsibility?" Waverly asked. "This baby requires a lot of tender loving care."

"We're prepared to give her everything she needs, Mom. Kree and I intend to raise India as our own daughter. She will get the best medical care and all the love and attention we can give. Raising a special-needs child is not new to us."

"I know that you and Kree will be good parents," Waverly assured them. "I just want you two to pray about this. You're just starting your lives again as a couple."

Kree spoke up. "Stone and I are committed to India. No matter what happens between us, we will never forsake her. We're a family. However, I think this time we're going to get it right."

"Till death do us part," Stone added with a smile.

Waverly nodded in approval.

~

The summer months merged into one another and the tree leaves had changed colors, falling to the ground in protest of the fall season. Stone and Kree had started adoption proceedings for India.

The infant was six months old and had been with Stone and Kree for four months. Stone's mother traveled to Raleigh whenever her health permitted to help with the baby. Kree also had a part-time nanny.

The week before Thanksgiving, Stone and Kree sat in her den planning the menu for their holiday dinner.

"Kree, I've been thinking about something." He laid the sleeping baby in her playpen. Walking back over to the couch, he said, "I need to talk to you."

She glanced up from her notes. "What's on your mind?"

"You are," Stone stated. "I don't know about you but I'm ready to take the next step in our relationship. I want my family under one roof."

"So what exactly are you saying?" Nothing could have prepared Kree for his admission. She'd just assumed he would wait until Christmas or Valentine's Day although she'd been dreaming about it for months now.

Taking her hand in his, Stone confirmed his feelings for her. "I'm saying I want you to marry me for the second and final time." Staring into her eyes, he asked, "Will you marry me, Kree?"

"Yes. I want to marry you more than anything."

Stone pulled a tiny box out of his pocket. He opened it to reveal a diamond engagement ring.

"It's beautiful," she murmured. Tears sprang to her eyes as Stone placed the ring on her finger.

"I don't want to wait too long before we get married."

"I don't either. I don't want anything really fancy, Stone. We did all that the first time. We can just go to the justice of the peace and get married."

"No, I want more than that. Just a small ceremony at church. There's a lot to do. I'd like to be married before the end of the year. What do you think about New Year's Eve?"

"Let's do it New Year's Day," Kree countered. "It represents a new beginning."

"I'm fine with that. We also need to place both of our houses for sale so that we can get the one we really want."

Kree frowned. "What are you talking about?"

"Remember the house on Martin that we used to drive by every weekend just to look at it and fantasize about living there?"

"You mean the ranch house with the huge yard? That house has to be three or four thousand square feet."

"Thirty-five hundred to be exact. Five bedrooms and a huge recreational room that can be converted into a home office."

"Is it on the market?"

Stone nodded. "You've got to see the kitchen. It's exactly the way you envisioned it."

"I can't believe it. Our dream house is finally for sale." Kree had fantasized about owning that house for years.

"I called the owner and made an appointment. We can have Korey watch the baby while we take a tour of the house tomorrow morning. If you still want it, we can make an offer."

Kree reached over to embrace him. "I love you, Stone."

"I love you too, honey."

The couple worked on plans for their wedding the rest of the evening. When India woke up, Stone gave her a bottle and changed her. Together, he and Kree put the baby to bed.

Twelve

"I have something to tell you all," Candace stated after everyone gathered in the den after Stone and Kree's rehearsal dinner. She and Trey had arrived the day before for the wedding. Wrapping her arms around her husband, she announced, "I'm pregnant. I'm going to have a baby."

"That's wonderful news." Kree jumped up and hugged her sister. "I'm so happy for you." She embraced Trey next. "Congratulations."

"If it's a boy, we're going to name him Charles Korey Baldwin."

"I like it," Korey announced.

"So do I," Kree agreed. She and Candace hugged again.

When Aunt Martha strolled into the room carrying India, Candace teased, "I see you guys didn't bother to wait for the marriage before you brought another baby into the house."

Kree bubbled with laughter. "Our baby didn't come the traditional way though."

"I'm so happy you two are finally getting back together," Aunt Martha interjected. "I'd been telling y'all to do that for years."

Stone and Kree burst into laughter.

"That seems to be the consensus of everyone." Stone wrapped an arm around his future wife. "I hate that it took us so long to see it."

"Speak for yourself. I knew it years ago."

He meet Kree's gaze. "All right. It was me. If Kree had had her way, we never would have gotten divorced. I can admit when I'm wrong."

"You're a good man, Stone. My niece is a very lucky woman," Aunt Martha said.

"Thank you for saying that, Aunt Martha. The truth is that I'm a lucky man. It takes a special woman to go through everything Kree has and emerge like she has. She's loving, forgiving . . ." Stone broke into a big smile. "And downright cute."

As the year drew to a close and the new one began, one by one, their family drifted off to bed until Stone and Kree were the only ones left up. They sat cuddled up on the sofa watching a movie. When it ended, Stone whispered, "You should go to bed, honey. You look tired."

"I am," Kree admitted. "I'm exhausted."

"The wedding's tomorrow, so after that, everything will return to normal."

"Normal," she murmured softly. "I can't remember what that feels like. The past few weeks have been a whirlwind."

"Yeah," he agreed. "We've had a lot to do in a short time, but I think we pulled it off. Everyone is going to have a good time tomorrow." Stone leaned over and kissed her. "It's late. I should go home. We both need to get some sleep for the big day. Walk me to the door."

Yawning, Kree stood and followed Stone.

In the doorway, he said, "I'll see you at the church."

Placing a hand on Stone's cheek, Kree said, "Thank you for coming back into my life. It was so empty without you."

"Thank you for allowing me to return. I certainly didn't deserve another chance—not after the way I treated you."

"Whatever happened in the past is gone tonight, Stone. Tomorrow is a new beginning for our family."

ABOUT THE AUTHOR

Jacquelin Thomas is the author of more than twelve novels and two novellas in print. She lives in North Carolina with her family and is busy at work on another project.

A Mother
For Scott

Karen White-Owens

ACKNOWLEDGMENTS

To my editor, Chandra Sparks Taylor, thank you for your editorial input. I'd like to thank my critique group, Natalie Dunbar, Kimberley White, and Angela Patrick Wynn for their support and Deborah Flournoy and Diane Perttola for their first read.

Thanks to my mother-in-law, Grace Booker Rose, and her sister Jean Crittendon for their solid support and help.

To Ellen and Helen Jones, thank you for the wonderful book-signing party.

One

"It's the top of the third and the score is two to one. The Blue Jays are up to bat. The Tigers are ahead by one," famed Tiger baseball announcer Ernie Harwell drolled from the black digital clock radio perched at the back of Ashleigh Davis's desk. She sighed, hoping the Tigers would be able to maintain their lead throughout the game as she erased the day's sixth-grade reading assignment from the blackboard and replaced it with Wednesday's math review.

Tucking the eraser on the lip of the blackboard, Ashleigh retrieved a cotton handkerchief from her oatmeal-colored Dockers, adjusted her raspberry sweater, then wiped the residue chalk dust from her fingertips. Returning to her desk, she swept a mass of caps, balls, and handheld computer games she had collected from her students during the day into the bottom drawer. At the next parent-teacher conference, she'd return the items.

Examining the confiscated items, Ashleigh shook her head. It amazed her how children got out of the house each morning with so many expensive toys in their book bags.

"Stewart is at the plate, taking a few practice swings, waiting for the pitch," a second announcer said. "Ernie, I don't think we're going to finish this game. There are storm clouds hanging over Comerica Park like a hungry tiger ready to pounce."

Ashleigh glanced out the window, silently agreeing while toying with the accordion metal band of her watch, stretching it away from her wrist. She contemplated the gray rain clouds in the March sky and muttered, "I'm not liking this. Not liking this at all."

Gnawing on the edge of her lip, she considered the two children playing instead of doing their homework. Ashleigh took a second glance out the window and came to a decision. "Eve, Scott, get your stuff together. We're going home before it rains," she directed, snapping off her radio.

"Ma, what about Scott?" Six-year-old Eve rose from her chair, pulled her book bag from under the desk, and gazed with wide-eye innocence at Ashleigh.

"Yeah, what about me, Miss Davis?" Scott asked in a worried voice. "If I'm not here or in Latchkey, my dad won't know where to find me."

"Latchkey is closed for the day. You're coming home with us." Ashleigh gave Scott a reassuring smile as she strolled toward him. A rush of warm, loving feelings surged through her when the beginning of a smile tipped the corners of his mouth. "We're going to call Mr. Harris and tell him that we're leaving before the storm," Ashleigh explained, removing her cell phone from the holster at her waist and handing it to Scott. "Your dad can pick you up at our house. Okay?"

A big smile of approval lightened his face. "That's tight."

She giggled, hugging him close. "If you say so."

Tall for an eleven-year-old, Scott had smooth, milk-chocolate skin, a round, open face, and long, thick eyelashes that shielded his soft brown eyes. His soulful gaze displayed all the heartbreaking pain he'd suffered in the short time he'd been on earth.

That's what drew Ashleigh to him. It broke her heart when she realized how much Scotty had suffered. And the need to protect him, reduce his pain, and offer him a measure of comfort was part of the reason she spent so much time with him.

As he shoved his homework inside his book bag, Scott's brow crinkled above worried soft, brown eyes. "I'm not sure my dad remembers how to get to your house."

"I've got it covered," she assured him, glancing across the room to make sure Eve was okay. "Don't hang up once you've finished talking to him. I'll make sure he has our address and directions."

Scott's eyebrows drew together while he considered her words, before he nodded, then punched in the telephone number. After a few rings, Scott spoke into the phone. "Hi, Dad. I'm at school with Miss Davis but she's going home because it looks like it's going to rain."

A lost, almost abandoned expression clouded Scott's brown face while he plucked at the plastic fastener on his navy and gray book bag. He handed the phone back to Ashleigh and said, "Voice mail."

"Hello, Mr. Harris, I'm leaving the school now. You can pick up Scotty at my house. Call me at 313-555-3334." She switched off the phone and returned it to her holster, glancing at Scott.

"Everything's okay," Ashleigh assured him. "Once he picks up his messages, he'll know where to find you." She understood Mr. Harris's position; as a busy attorney with a thriving practice, his time was not always his own. As a single parent herself, how could she not? But what if something happened to Scotty, how would the school get in touch with him if it was so difficult to reach him?

Ashleigh gave Mr. Harris a lot of slack. The law stated that if parents were more than a half hour late arriving to pick up their children, the school was obligated to notify the police. But she never called. Many afternoons she waited with Scotty for Mr. Harris's arrival.

Sometimes Ashleigh found it difficult to maintain a neutral attitude about the children in her care. She really liked Scotty and wanted him to be happy. Since his mother's death last year, his father had refused to give Scott the time he needed to recover. She tried to fill that void, offer Scott a tiny portion of the love he'd grown to expect from his mother. And in some ways, she felt confident that she'd helped him. Unfortunately, she understood that nothing replaced a mother's love.

Ashleigh scooted down next to Scott and asked, "Why is it so hot after a baseball game?"

Scott shrugged. "I don't know."

"Because all the fans have left."

He laughed.

"Good. That's what I wanted to see and hear. That smile on your face makes me happy. Don't worry." Ashleigh hugged him close and rubbed his cold arms below the short sleeves of his white oxford shirt. "Your dad will find you. Honest."

Eyes shut, Scott wrapped his arms around her and hugged her tightly. "Thank you, Miss Davis. You're the best."

"Well, you're welcome," she said, pleased by his compliment. Leaning close to Scotty's ear, she added, "Put your jacket on and then help Eve. She wants to be a big girl. Zippers give her a lot of trouble. If you can save her dignity by letting her believe she's doing it, I'd really appreciate it."

Scott winked back at Ashleigh. "I've got you."

"Thanks."

Fifteen minutes later Ashleigh gathered her small group together at the classroom door and asked, "Everybody zipped up? Do you have your book bags, lunch bags, and everything else?"

"Yeah, Ma," Eve said.

"Got everything," Scott said at the same time.

"Good. Let's go." After locking the door, Ashleigh led them down the corridor toward the school's entrance.

"Ma," Eve whined, tugging on the bottom edge of Ashleigh's jacket. "Ma, I left my gel pens in your room."

"Oh, Eve, we're ready to go home. Are you sure you don't have them with you?" she asked, digging inside Eve's book bag.

"No. Remember, you put them on your desk, so you wouldn't forget," Eve said, slipping the book bag on her back. "You promised to put them in your briefcase."

Bone-tired, Ashleigh shut her eyes and sighed. A mental image of the gel pens sitting on her desk flashed through her head. "Can't we leave them until tomorrow?"

"No. I don't want to lose them. Daddy gave them to me. Please, Ma, please." Tears gleamed in her eyes.

Ashleigh went stiff at the mention of her ex-husband. Professor William Davis had left them, their house, and his job for a sweet, young student from the university. Eve was unaware of the circumstances surrounding her father's exit from their life. She worshipped her father and didn't need to know.

"Well, we can't have that, can we?" Defeated, she placed her briefcase on the floor near the wall, dropped Eve's hand, fished her keys from her jacket pocket, and started for the door. "I'll get them. Scotty, stay with Eve and keep an eye on her. I'll be right back."

He touched Ashleigh's arm and volunteered, "I'll go."

"No. No. You stay here."

"You're tired, Miss Davis. I can do this for you." Scott took the key from her fingers and hurried down the hall.

Ashleigh watched him, thankful that he understood how worn out she truly felt. He unlocked the door, slipped inside the empty classroom, and flipped the light switch.

Preoccupied with making sure Scott got back without a hitch, Ashleigh stood with her back to the building entrance. Focused on her door, she failed to hear anything or anyone until a light touch at her elbow drew her attention.

Ashleigh gasped before spinning around to find Scott's father at her side.

With a hand at her chest, she muttered breathlessly, "Oh, Mr. Harris, you frightened the heck out of me. You shouldn't sneak up on people." Flustered, she pulled Eve against her.

Mr. Harris cleared his throat and straightened the knot of his tie. He asked in a deep bass voice that set her insides trembling, "Where's Scott?"

For a moment, she found speech impossible as she admired the delightful package that made up Dane Anthony Harris. He stood six feet four inches tall with the sleek, symmetrical lines of an athlete. His square jaw, goatee, and coffee-colored skin got her emotions churning. Yes, indeed, Mr. Harris presented a powerful package.

Dane Harris filled out his tailored business suit completely with the broadest shoulders she'd ever seen. His torso slimmed down to narrow hips and long powerful legs.

"Scott stepped back into the classroom to pick up something I forgot. He'll be right out." Those words were barely out of her mouth when Scott slipped from her classroom, locked the door, and hurried down the corridor with the gel pens in hand.

"I've got them, Miss Davis," he announced, handing the pens to her.

"Thank you."

Ashleigh deposited them inside Eve's book bag, but one slipped to the floor and rolled toward Dane. Chasing the runaway pen, she reached down to retrieve it at the same time Dane's finger wrapped around it.

As Dane offered the pen to Ashleigh and his hand brushed against hers, an electric shock swept through them both. He cleared his throat, then brushed his hand against the leg of his trousers.

"Thank you," Ashleigh uttered in a shy purr.

"You're welcome," Dane responded.

Scott stood between the adults, his eyes huge as his gaze swung from one to the other.

Clearing his throat a second time, Dane turned his attention to his son. "Scott," he barked, "why aren't you in Latchkey?"

Offended by his tone, Ashleigh jumped to Scott's defense. "Mr. Harris, Latchkey closed more than an hour ago."

He glanced at his watch. "Really? Someone always stays until I arrive. Why is he with you?"

"An emergency came up and Mrs. Reid needed to leave. She asked if I would stay until you arrived."

One dark brown eyebrow rose. "I'm sorry you were stuck with him. He should have called me."

"We did. Your voice mail kicked in."

Mr. Harris looked embarrassed for all of ten seconds. But any discomfort he displayed was quickly masked as he took another approach.

"Scott, I don't want you disturbing Mrs. Davis," he stated, wagging a finger at his son.

Again, Ashleigh stepped in, patting Scotty's shoulder. "On the contrary, I love having Scotty with me. He is helpful and never gives me a moment of trouble."

Dane Harris's eyes narrowed, but he said nothing. Instead, he pulled out his cell phone, turned it on, and tapped in a telephone number, all the while speaking to her. "Still, I don't want him causing trouble. I pay for Latchkey, and that's where he should be. Not traipsing up and down the corridor with you."

You insensitive fool, Ashleigh screamed in her head.

Scotty's face fell. His bottom lip quivered and he bit his lip. She lifted an arm to draw him against her, but stopped. Mr. Harris hated what he termed her "coddling" of his son. She might not be able to stop him from talking to his son any way he chose, but she could correct him when necessary.

Ashleigh gave Scott a reassuring smile. "It's all right, Mr. Harris. I like having your son around. He's a wonderful young man."

"Yes, he is." Pocketing the phone, Dane tented his hands together. "Mrs. Davis, I don't mean to appear so harsh. Since my wife died . . ." He paused, cleared his throat, then continued, "We have to learn to work together as a team. Scott and I must cope on our own. That's the only way we'll survive. Besides, I don't want him getting attached to you and when you or Scott move on he'll suffer another loss." Straightening his tie, Dane tried to smile. "Do you understand what I'm trying to say here?"

Yeah, I understand, Ashleigh thought. *You don't want anyone to get close to you or your son.*

~

"It's the bottom of the fifth and the Tigers need a few solid hits to pull this game out of the fire. The Blue Jays are ahead by three," the Tiger announcer said. The announcer's monotonous voice poured through the elaborate stereo system in Dane's Mercedes. Scott listened intently because Miss Davis loved baseball and the Tigers.

Scott sat quietly in the backseat watching the cars and scenery flash by as he and his dad headed to their Birmingham, Michigan, home. The soft *tap, tap, tap* from the rain closeted them in a warm cocoon of wet wonder as they sped along Telegraph Road. Scott didn't want to go home. That house hadn't felt like home since his mother died. The rooms were empty and nobody talked to him.

When his class had done the geology retreat, some of the kids had spent the night at Miss Davis's house before leaving for Howell. Miss Davis's house felt so different. It smelled like cookies. All the kids and Miss Davis snuggled on the sofa in the family room and watched videos and he'd felt like a part of a family again.

He wished Miss Davis and Eve could come and live with him and his dad. Make their house better, a home. She'd chase away the loneliness that filled him to the top each time he remembered his mother.

Scott missed his mother. His bottom lip quivered. He bowed his head as he tried to keep from crying. His dad disapproved of tears. He focused on the game to take his mind off his mother.

"And the side went down in order. Three up and three away. The Tigers are behind by three going into the top of the sixth. Ahh, Ernie, it looks as if there's some activity going on in the Tiger bull pen. We might get a new pitcher for the next inning if the game isn't called because of rain."

Miss Davis would make a great mother for him. Her soft, encouraging touch and tone always made him feel better, no matter what the situation. It reminded him of his own mother when she read to him at night before he dropped off to sleep. Ever since his mom died, Miss Davis had been with him until his dad came to pick him up if he wasn't at Latchkey after school.

She was funny. Miss Davis always got him laughing with her jokes. Granted, she needed some practice and her jokes were lame. Maybe she could tell his dad one of them, make the frown disappear from his face, and make him laugh again.

Scott loved Miss Davis. And his dad liked her too. Scott could tell. Dad's voice always changed whenever she turned up. Plus, Dad cleared his throat like a hundred times. And he only did that when somebody made him feel real nervous.

Before his mother passed away, Dad was fun, teased and played with him all the time. But now, Dad had so much to do, taking care of the house and Scott and going to work. Dad wasn't the same person. Sometimes he was mean or stern, demanding that Scott make a daily contribution to the household, like picking up his room or unloading the dishwasher. Scott didn't mind, and he tried to help as much as he could, but he sure missed his mom. Mom had made Dad softer, happier.

Scott shut his eyes and Miss Davis's image appeared. She was real tall, close to his dad's size, and she stood proud like a queen. Her long black hair hung around her shoulders, soft and fluffy, and it felt like velvet and always smelled like strawberries. Her skin reminded him of cocoa with plenty of milk. And she spoke in a gentle tone that made the kids listen.

Looking through the rain-splattered windshield, Scott noticed the sun peeking through the clouds and a rainbow of red, yellow, and blue arched across the gray-blue sky. He shut his eyes and wished on the rainbow, praying low so that his father didn't hear him.

"Dear God," Scott began, "please make my dad happy again. It's been hard for him, taking care of me and missing my mom." A tear slipped down his cheek and he glanced at his dad to make sure he hadn't seen him before wiping it away with the back of his hand. "But if you can, please help him to find somebody to care about him the way my mom did.

"Please make Miss Davis and my dad fall in love with each other. Then they could get married and Miss Davis and Eve could come and live with us. And we all can be happy together."

Two

"Time to get up, Scott," Dad called from the doorway. "Come on. Move it or you're going to be late for school."

Scott opened one eye and immediately shut it against the sun beaming through his bedroom window. Turning on his side, he snuggled deeper into the blanket, ignoring his dad.

"I'm not going to tell you again," Dad warned. That warning note in his voice got Scott's attention.

Sighing, he flipped on his back, kicked the navy blanket toward the bottom of his bed, and said, "Okay. I'm up."

"Good." Dad turned on his heels and headed for the kitchen. "Come on. Get moving. Hurry up and take your shower. Breakfast will be on the table in about ten minutes. Don't forget to make your bed before you come down."

"Okay." As he swung his legs over the side of his race-car bed, the mouth-watering aroma of chocolate crept into his bedroom. *That's tight. Dad fixed cocoa*, he thought. *I love chocolate, especially cocoa.* "Hey, Dad, did the Tigers win last night?"

"No. Lost six to five."

"Man," Scott muttered. Miss Davis loved the Tigers. She would be sad.

Scott shut his eyes, yawned, and scratched his forehead. When he opened them, his gaze moved around his room and focused on a boy sitting at his desk. Scott was stunned; his head snapped back and his eyes widened. "Who are you?"

"Hey, dawg," the boy greeted, waving his free hand at Scott, the other holding a baseball mitt and ball. "I'm Tony," he explained, tossing the ball from his right hand into a mitt on his left.

Tony wore a Tigers baseball team white-and-blue-striped uniform and looked to be nine or ten. His round face was the color of milk chocolate and his huge almond-shaped eyes reminded Scott of Miss Davis, yet this kid's square jaw resembled Dad's.

Looking around the room, Scott tried to figure out what was going on. His window was closed. Had Dad let him in? And why hadn't Dad mentioned him? "How did you get in here?"

"Oh, I've been here awhile. Dawg, I'll tell you, you sleep really hard. And you snore too. I've been waiting for hours for you to wake up. It's about time. We've got things to do."

"Things to do?"

"Yep." Tony nodded, tossing the ball in the air and catching it with his mitt.

"Scott." Dad clapped his hands from the doorway. Scott jumped. "Move. I've got to be in court this morning."

"I-I-I," Scott stammered, pointing at the desk. "I was talking to Tony. Did you let him in?"

Dad glanced in the direction of the desk, then back at his son. His eyebrows dipped together in a confused frown. "Tony? What are you talking about? Who's Tony?"

"The boy sitting at my desk." Scott jabbed a finger at the desk. "Tony!"

Tony stood still as a statue. Baseball in hand, his eyes sparkled and his gaze bounced back and forth between Scott and his father.

Dad's mouth thinned with displeasure and his voice deepened to a disagreeable rumble. "Scott, don't play with me, boy. I don't have time for this." He started back down the hallway and called over his shoulder, "Get moving."

His harsh tone rang throughout the house. *Dad doesn't believe me,* Scott thought. Crushed, he turned to the other child and muttered in obvious disappointment, "Why didn't my dad see you? What's up with that?"

"Because he can't," Tony answered matter-of-factly.

"Can't? What do you mean? Why?" Scott waved a hand at him. "You're sitting right there."

"That's one of the rules. He can't see me. Most times grown-ups can't see us."

"Us? Rules? Whose rules? Who's us?" As Scott studied the boy's face for answers, he got scared. "Who are you? What . . . are . . . you?"

"Don't be afraid." He softened his voice to reassure Scott. "I'm your guardian angel."

Scott stared at Tony, then burst out laughing. "Yeah, sure. You think I'm stupid, don't you? Well, I'm not. Prove it."

"Okay." Tony shrugged and pointed at the dresser. "That's your mom, right?"

Scott nodded.

"Sweeeet." He focused on the picture of Scott's mom. A golden glow surrounded the silver frame. Without warning, it levitated off the surface unaided and floated across the room to Scott. It hovered in front of him for several seconds.

Flabbergasted, Scott's mouth fell open. His head spun from the photo to the boy and back again. He grabbed the photo, gazing into the smiling face of his mother as the consuming need to have her with him again overwhelmed him. He could almost smell his mother's perfume and feel her soft breath against his cheek when she kissed him good night.

I miss her so much, he thought. Tears burned his eyes and before he realized it, they slipped down his cheeks.

Trying to pull himself together, Scott felt a tap on his shoulder. Turning, he found Tony sitting on the edge of the bed next to him, a watchful expression in his eyes. *How did he get here?* Scott wondered.

A golden glow engulfed Tony's whole arm and after the light cleared, he unfisted his hand and a Kleenex tissue lay in his palm. "Here," he said in a gentle voice. "Clean your face."

Scott took the tissue and mopped away his tears.

"Satisfied?"

"Maybe," Scott answered, jumping up and moving around the bed to examine the younger boy. "I don't see any wings."

"Dawg, you're a hard sale. Get real. If I came down here with wings, you'd freak out."

"So what? I'm freaking now. You move things without touching them and pop all over the room without my seeing it. What other tricks can you do?"

"Some." Tony disappeared from the bed, then reappeared in the chair at the desk. "Is this enough proof for you?"

Forehead crinkled and mouth gaping open, Scott returned to the bed. He shoved one leg under him and turned to face this so-called angel. "Why are you here? What do you want?"

"Want?"

"Yeah, sure. In the movies, angels always come to do something. Unless they're here to take somebody back with them." Scott gasped, fear sweeping through him as the possibility became a certainty in his mind. He rose from the bed and took a tentative step toward the door and away from his intruder, ready to race down the hall to his dad. "Is that it? Are you here for my dad?"

"No." Tony sighed and shook his head. "Dawg, you've got some imagination. What have you been watching on TV? Too much *Touched by an Angel*."

Uncertain, Scott straddled the doorway. "What do you want?"

"Last night you said a prayer. Do you remember?"

Scott nodded, tilting his head to one side. "So?"

"I'm here to help you get it done."

"How do you think you're going to do that?" Skeptical, Scott raised his eyebrows.

"I've got some ideas." Tony gave Scott a half smile.

"Like what?"

Wagging a finger back and forth between them, he promised, "We'll work on this together. Go take your shower before your dad comes back in here and raises the roof. Then we'll talk about things on the way to school."

Tony had that part correct. Dad would have a fit if he didn't get a move on. Scott headed to his dresser, opened the drawer, and glanced back at Tony. A crinkled brow marred his face while he studied the boy. *An angel.* Scott shook his head, almost laughing at himself. This had to be a dream. He'd wake up soon enough and everything would be back to normal.

∼

"After the break, we'll return with stock prices at the close of business yesterday, weather, and sports." The articulate voice oozed from the car's digital-surround stereo system. Waiting for his father to take off, Scott leaned his forehead against the car window, allowing the coolness to seep into his skin.

"Buckle your seat belt," Dad commanded, watching him through the rearview mirror to make sure Scott complied with his wishes before setting off.

Tony popped into the seat next to Scott.

"What do you want?" Scott asked.

"I want to help you."

"With what?"

"What's that?" Dad eyed him from the rearview mirror. "Did you say something to me?"

"No, Dad."

His father turned, frowning at Scott. "Who are you talking to?"

"Nobody. I was thinking out loud," Scott explained, moving the book bag from his lap to the floor. "Talking to myself."

Frowning back at Scott, he said, "You're acting strange this morning. Are you feeling okay?"

"Yeah. I'm okay," he whispered, looking out the window.

Tony leaned close to Scott. "I told you he couldn't see or hear me. So, I'm going to talk for a minute and you just listen."

Scott eyed the other boy. He folded his arms across his chest, slumped down in his seat, and lowered his voice. "I don't want to listen to you. You could be bad and want me to do something wrong."

"Come on. I'm here to help you."

Shifting toward the other boy, Scott folded a leg under him and asked in a low, suspicious tone, "If you know so much, what did I wish for?"

"You want Miss Davis to be your mother."

How did he know that? Maybe he really is an angel. Embarrassed, Scott looked away.

"Hey, dawg, don't be ashamed." Tony gave Scott a playful punch on the shoulder. It felt like a soft caress of the wind. "It'll be okay. I have dreams and wishes of my own. Everybody does. We're going to make it happen."

"How can we? I know they like each other, but they always fuss and complain when they're in the same room. What can we do to get my dad with Miss Davis?"

Tony raised a finger and pointed at the dashboard. That golden glow of his engulfed it. "We do it like this." The digital dial jumped from station to station, catching a word here and a lyric to a song there as it skipped across the dial and stopped. Tony's full lips smiled in delight.

The voice of Alonzo Clark filled the small confines of the car. Scott's mother had always listened to this show when she took him to school each morning.

As he turned toward the backseat, Dad's face was scrunched up like a prune. He asked in a voice filled with surprise, "Did you see that, son? The radio went crazy." Dad snapped off the radio. But it popped back on.

Scott's eyes opened wide and his lips parted.

His father tapped the digital dial and the news again blasted through the car's speakers. Within seconds, the dial zipped back to the *Alonzo Clark Morning Show*. Dad repeated this act three times. Each time the dial flipped back to the morning show host.

"This car is going back to the dealer as soon as I get a free minute."

"This is Alonzo Clark and it's 7:28. Well, folks . . ." The voice on the radio drawled in its deep baritone voice coated with a southern twang. The Spinners sang "Sadie" in the background. "We all know Mother's Day is coming. And with that day comes all the great memories of what Mom sacrificed for us. I bet you all have great stories about your mother. How she worked two jobs, but always made it to your school play, or played chauffeur for your baseball team. We all have wonderful stories about our mothers. And I want to hear yours."

Scott turned to Tony with a question in his eyes.

"Shhhh." Tony put a quieting finger to his lips. "Just listen."

Alonzo Clark continued, "To honor mothers everywhere, we're having a contest. Boys and girls, young and old, I'm going to give you a chance to share why you think your mother is the best and deserves a shopping spree, a free makeover, and a night on the town." As he warmed to his topic, Alonzo's voice grew more animated with each word. "Write me a letter or send me an e-mail or fax about why your mother is the greatest. Send your letter to . . ."

Tony made whirling, writing motions with his hand, then wiggled a finger at the book bag on the floor. Scott yanked open his book bag and grabbed a pencil, jotting the address in his notebook.

Alonzo Clark intoned, "But that's not all. Fellas, you've got a part in this. We don't want you to feel left out. This is a win-win situation. Keep listening to my show. We're going to read those letters over the radio and we want you to choose some lucky mother to be your date for the evening and you can be included in her night on the town. Just listen and choose the letter that touches your heart. Remember, winners will be announced April first, so get your letter done and in the mail to me as soon as possible. We'll read the winning letters on the air and you gentlemen will have to convince the judges that you deserve to share Mother's Day with some beautiful, caring lady."

"Sweeeet." Tony smiled. "Now we have the way. All we need to do is find somebody to write the letter. Think about that and I'll check you later," he said and disappeared.

Three

Scott peeked around the corner, glancing into Miss Davis's doorway. She strolled across the room, sat in the chair behind her desk, and pulled a stack of papers from her briefcase. "Eve, get started on that assignment you have for Ms. Doherty. I want it completed before we head home."

"Okay." Eve removed papers from her book bag and took a seat near the back of the room.

Scott whispered, "Okay, Miss Davis is at her desk. What do we do next?"

Tony pushed his baseball cap to the crown of his head. "We've got to think about the rules for the contest. Alonzo Clark said the letter has to be written by the son or daughter about their mother. So . . ."

"That means it has to be Eve. She's the only one who can write the letter. How are we going to get her to do it? She may be little, but she's no dummy."

Tony shrugged. "We'll tell her the truth. Get her involved in what we're doing."

"I don't know." Scott scratched his head and answered slowly. "Maybe it'll work."

"Shhhhh," Tony warned, waving a hand at Scott. "Dawg, remember, you're the only one who can see me. Kids are looking at us. Don't talk so loud. Whisper. You don't want people to look at you like you're crazy."

Students passing through the halls were indeed staring at Scott. He turned his back to the crowd, lowered his voice a notch, and continued,

"Okay, okay." He nodded. "What are you going to say to her? You'll probably scare her."

"I won't scare her," Tony said with a wave of his hand.

"You promise?"

"Yeah."

Scott stuck his tongue in his jaw and eyed Tony. After a couple of minutes, he wagged a finger at the other boy and asked, "Wait a minute, can she see you? My dad didn't."

"It's different for kids. If I want her to see me, she can."

"I don't know," Scott muttered, shaking his head.

"Let me try. If I scare her, then we'll do something different. Okay?"

Scott didn't want anything bad to happen to Eve or Miss Davis. They always treated him well and included him in whatever they were doing. "Wait. I've got a better idea." He tapped his chest. "Eve knows me. I'll come with you."

"Sweeeet."

She sat at one of the round tables doing her homework. Shoving the baseball mitt under his arm, Tony entered the classroom with Scott on his heels. With a silent wave at Miss Davis, Scott followed Tony to Eve's table.

Eve looked up, curiosity on her chocolate face. "Hi, Scott."

"Hey, Eve." Scott stuck a finger in his guardian angel's direction. "This is Tony."

"Hi." She smiled shyly and waved. "You don't go here, do you?"

Tony grinned back at her and placed his baseball mitt and ball on the table. "Nah. I'm here with Scott."

Miss Davis looked up, studying them. After a few minutes, she returned to her work.

"Scott and I need your help."

Eve remained silent for a minute, then asked, "For what?"

"We want you to write a letter."

"What's it about?" She glanced from Scott to Tony.

"Miss Davis."

"Ma? Why?"

"We're trying to get your mom to go on a date with Scott's father."

"My ma stays home. She doesn't go out," Eve explained, fidgeting with her pencil.

"If you write the letter and she wins the contest, she has to go out." Tony scratched his ear. "You have friends, right?"

"Yeah."

"Have you ever thought your mom needs to have friends of her own?" Tony asked. "Don't you think your mother needs friends, like you and Scotty are friends?"

"Maybe. I don't know," Eve muttered and chewed on her yellow pencil.

"Think of it this way. Your mother's all alone. Remember when your dad lived with you, wasn't your mother happier?"

"Yes. Sometimes she cries. Ma hides it, but I know. I don't want her to be sad."

"If she wins the contest, maybe Scott's dad and your mother can be friends and go out. Do you think she'd like that?"

As she nodded slowly, Eve's brow wrinkled as she considered Tony's ideas. "Yeah. What kind of contest?"

"Mother's Day."

"That could be good. I don't have a present for Ma."

Tony nodded. "See? Told you it could be a good thing."

"This could be her present."

"This guy on the radio wants kids to write in and tell him why their mother should have a shopping spree, a makeover, and an evening out."

Eve caught the tip of her tongue between her small teeth and nodded. "What does it have to say?"

"Tell all the good things about your mother and why you think she needs a night out on the town. If you want, Scott and I can help you."

"Okay. I'm not a good writer," Eve confessed. "I'm only six."

"That's all right."

Scott removed a sheet of paper from his notebook and slid it in front of Eve. "We'll work on it together."

Miss Davis glanced up at their table. "You guys okay?"

"Yes, Miss Davis."

"Yeah, Ma," Eve responded.

"What's next?" Scott asked, flipping to the page with the radio station's address.

"We need to get Miss Davis and your dad together whenever we can," Tony explained, lifting his baseball cap from his head and repositioning it in the exact same spot. "They need to get used to each other, so that they can start liking each other. Do you have any ideas?"

Grinning, Scott turned to Tony. "Yeah. I've got a good one."

~

From the school's playground bench, Ashleigh jumped up and clapped loudly as the batter slid into first base. Baseball was her favorite sport and she always attended the school's games.

The hairs at the back of her neck stood tall, drawing her attention away from the game. Turning, she scanned the audience. Her pulse quickened when she caught sight of Scott's father making his way through the stands toward her.

For the hundredth time, Ashleigh wished things were different for her and Dane. Perhaps she should invite him and Scott over for dinner or suggest they get together for an outing with their children. But Dane had made it clear that he did not want Scott to get too attached to her.

Watching him approach from the corner of her eye, she thought Dane looked as handsome as he normally did, but a tiny bit out of place, strolling through the stands in a dark gray business suit. His gaze locked with hers, making her heart accelerate. She fidgeted with the accordion band of her watch, stretching it away from her wrist.

Stopping in front of her, he removed his sunglasses and slipped them into the breast pocket of his jacket.

"How are you, Mr. Harris?"

He cleared his throat and answered, "Fine. And it's Dane. Call me Dane."

"Dane it is, and I'm Ashleigh."

"Like *Gone with the Wind?*" he muttered, eyebrows arched.

"That's me." She jumped to her feet and yelled, "Go for it, Jamal. Hit that ball out of the park."

"Interesting. I didn't know you enjoyed sports."

She laughed, returning to her seat. "I love all sports, especially baseball. Besides, look at me. I'm six feet tall." Her heart almost stopped when he did a slow, precise perusal of her slender frame. She felt as if warm ginger ale were pumping through her veins.

"That you are," he whispered in that deep bass voice.

"Mmm," she muttered, fighting to regain her composure. "I went to school on a basketball scholarship."

"Well, you're not alone. I went to school on a scholarship too. But football instead of basketball." He pointed at the empty spot next to her. "Do you mind?"

"Not at all," Ashleigh admitted eagerly, flushing under her skin. *Oh, Ashleigh, calm your jets. He doesn't even see you,* she thought, moving across the bench and making room for him. "Help yourself."

"Where did you go to school?" Dane asked, sliding in beside her. The subtle fragrance of his cologne and the deep bass of his voice made her heart flutter. It took her a few seconds to connect his words.

"Eastern Michigan. How about you?"

"University of Michigan."

Nodding approvingly, Ashleigh said, "That's a great school."

"Yeah, I was lucky. I'm sure Eastern was the perfect school for you. It's one of the best universities for educators we have in the state."

"True. I'm proud to be an alumna."

Dane checked his watch and said, "I know I'm a little late. Court held me up. What inning are they in?" He shrugged out of his jacket and dropped it carelessly onto the bench beside him. His tie followed the jacket and he rolled up the sleeves of his shirt.

"Second."

"Has Scott had his turn at bat?"

Ashleigh removed the cap from her Gatorade and took a long drink. "No. His turn comes up in the next inning."

"You didn't want to turn pro after you finished college?" Dane asked, perching his sunglasses on his nose.

"No, thank you."

"Why not?"

"I'd had enough. I wanted to teach."

"Maybe you should have thought of another sport. You're tall. How about boxing?" Hands balled into fists, he weaved back and forth like a boxer.

"No, thank you."

"Why not? Are you afraid to get that beautiful face of yours hit?"

Ashleigh was ready with a comeback but when he mentioned beautiful and her in the same breath, her mouth snapped shut without uttering a word. *He thinks I'm beautiful,* she thought, holding those words close to her heart. "No." She coughed in the middle of her emotional revelation. Ashleigh pointed to home plate and said, "Look, there's Scott."

Dane rose, cupped his hands around his mouth, and yelled, "Come on, Scott."

Scott searched the bleachers and found his father and Miss Harris together. He broke into a wide, silly grin and waved at the pair.

"He saw you," Ashleigh said, waving at Scott. "Look, he's all teeth. I think he's happy to see you here."

Dane sat, grinned back at her, and admitted, "I'm excited to be here."

Scott stepped up to the plate and Dane and Ashleigh leaned forward, waiting for the first pitch to be thrown. The ball zipped over the plate.

"Strike one," cried the umpire.

"Ohhh!" they muttered in unison.

"Get the umpire out of there," Dane muttered. "That pitch was wide."

She cupped her hands over her mouth and yelled, "Come on, Scott. You can do it."

He stood ready for the pitch, but the ball flew by him.

"Strike two," the umpire bellowed as his arm swept into the air.

Ashleigh took a deep breath and let it out slowly. She crossed her fingers and offered a silent prayer. *Please don't let Scott strike out. It would tear him apart if this happened in front of his father.*

From their seat on the bench, Ashleigh noticed how Scott kept stealing glimpses at his father. *Come on, you can do it*, she chanted in her head. *You can do it.*

Three more pitches flew by and now the count was three balls, two strikes. Gathering all her strength to keep her nerves in check, Ashleigh waited for the payoff pitch. Tension mounted as Scott prepared for the final pitch with a few practice swings.

Unconsciously, Ashleigh's hand crept over Dane's arm. She felt the muscles ripple in reaction to her soft touch, but he didn't pull away. Turning to him, Ashleigh noted the spark of surprise in his eyes.

The pitcher released the ball. It moved toward the plate and Ashleigh squeezed Dane's hand. Scott's bat connected with the ball and it flew between the shortstop and second base.

Jumping to her feet, Ashleigh yelled, "Yes! I knew he could do it."

Dane beat Ashleigh off the bench by a split second as he cheered his son's two-base hit.

As the crowd died down, their hands dropped away. Embarrassed, Ashleigh refused to look Dane in the face.

Dane cleared his throat and picked up his suit jacket, then dropped it back on the bench. "I think I got a little carried away there."

"Me too," she muttered and sat down on the bench.

From his position at second base, Scott glanced into the stands. He saw his father and Miss Davis cheering and his heart swelled with love and pride. On the bench behind his father and Miss Davis, he saw Tony. His favorite guardian angel saluted him with a tip of his baseball mitt.

Scott grinned. "That's tight."

Tony said he could bring them together, and he had. Maybe this Mother's Day thing would work. After all, how could it fail when he had his own friendly neighborhood angel to make things turn out right?

Four

"Piece of junk," Dane said, punching black button after black button on the radio console. "The dial won't budge from this station. I can't believe I paid all this money and we're reduced to a steady diet of Alonzo Clark."

Scott sat quietly in the backseat, watching the war of the radio. His father had fought the battle for radio supremacy for more than a week. Each morning, Scott got in the backseat of the car and waited while his father fussed with the radio and complained about missing his morning news.

"There's got to be a way around this radio problem," Dane mumbled, removing a CD from its jewel case and popping it into the player. It hummed for a minute and Scott noticed the now-familiar gold light engulfing the console. The CD jumped out of the player and hung on the edge of the unit, mocking Dad like a kid sticking out his tongue. Dad's eyebrows bunched together and he muttered under his breath, shoving the CD back into the player.

Music filled the car, then stopped. Silence replaced Kurt Whalum's sax. Suddenly, songs and music spun together in hyperspeed, skipping a track here, skipping a track there until it reached the end of the CD. The player hummed for about thirty seconds; then the disc shot across the car, smacked the leather seat beside Scott, and sank to the floor.

Dad's eyes grew so large, Scott thought they might pop out of his head.

"This thing is crazy." Patience shot, he snapped abruptly, "I've got to get this radio fixed. I hate doing without my morning news."

Scott picked up the CD and handed it to his father, who returned it to the case before he turned the key in the ignition. As he navigated out of the drive and down the street, silence filled the car.

Tony popped into the seat next to Scott, turned to him with a big cheesy grin on his face, and laughed out loud. His shoulders shook and he held his stomach as if it hurt. Carefully covering his mouth with his hand so that his dad didn't see him, Scott chuckled softly.

Well, there were cool things about being invisible, Scott thought. You could laugh at anything and everything, and no one was the wiser.

"Well, folks, welcome back to the morning show," drolled Alonzo Clark. "We've narrowed our search to three letters. And, fellas, believe me, it's going to be difficult for you to choose one special mother to spend your evening on the town with."

Scott and Tony leaned toward, barely breathing, as they waited for Alonzo Clark to continue.

"I'm going to read the first letter and then we'll take a break. To minimize any confusion, we won't release the names of our winners until everyone has been notified. Ready? Here we go, folks. This letter comes from a little lady in Dee-troit."

The letter rattled in Alonzo Clark's hands.

"She writes: 'My ma is special because she loves all kids. She loves me first and then gives all of her extra love to the kids in the school where she works. Once, when one of the boys at the school's mother got sick, she stayed with him until his daddy came to get him. She does everything with love. But she never asks for anything for herself. Now, I think it's time for her to have some fun.' "

Tony turned to Scott with a grin on his face. He winked at Scott and whispered, "I told you she'd win."

"Did you do that?" Scott asked.

Tony shook his head. "The letter was good. I knew she'd win."

"Now that we've all heard what this little lady has to say about her mother," Alonzo Clark said, "it's time for the fellas in the metro Detroit area to get into the act. So that you'll have a chance to hear each special mother's letter and make an educated choice from the group, we're going to read them over the next three days. If one of our letters touches your heart, send in a letter explaining why you think you should be part of this mother's special day."

"Sweeeet." Tony turned to Scott with a big grin on his face. "It's time for us to get into the act."

"How?"

"You're going to write a letter for him." Tony tilted his head toward Dad.

"Send your letters to the same address," Alonzo Clark said and gave the address again. "And, fellas, hurry. We're only giving you a week to get everything in. The winners will be announced April first. So make your choice and follow through."

"What do we do?" Scott whispered with a hand over his mouth while watching his father.

"Did you say something to me, son?" his father asked from the front seat.

"No, Dad. Just talking to myself."

Silence followed; then Dad asked, "Is there anything you need to talk to me about?"

"No."

"I don't want you to think that I won't listen." His father adjusted the rearview mirror so that he could look at Scott. "Because I will."

"I know."

His father searched Scott's face, then returned his attention to the road.

Tony tossed the ball from his left hand into the mitt on his right. "When we get to school, we'll find a spot and write the letter."

"Okay," Scott whispered back.

"Don't forget to talk about how Miss Davis helped you when your mother got sick."

Scott nodded.

"And how she always stays until your father comes to pick you up no matter how late it is and helps you with your homework."

"Okay."

"What about how she always comes to your baseball games and cheers for you?"

"I will," Scott repeated.

Grinning, Tony said, "Sorry, dawg. I don't want you to forget anything. This is important."

"Yeah, I know. What about the letter? It won't look like my dad wrote it," Scott whispered out of the side of his mouth, watching his father.

"Don't worry. The biggest part of the letter will be from the computer."

Scott thought about it for a minute and nodded. "That's tight. But what about Dad's name at the bottom? How will we get that? I don't know how to do that. If I could copy it, he'd never see any of my science papers from Mr. Winters."

"Don't worry, I've got a plan."

"Like what?"

"I'll show you when the time is right. Dawg, you just think about what you want to say and leave the rest to me." Tony disappeared without another word.

Scott squirmed around in his seat, found a comfortable spot, and shut his eyes. Whenever Tony said to leave the rest to him, he complied. So far, their plan had been working.

~

At the light tap on her door, Ashleigh looked up from grading papers. She drew in a deep, calming breath, rose from her chair, and called, "Come in."

Dane Harris stuck his head inside the room and smiled.

Since the baseball game, each time Dane picked up Scott, he spent a few minutes talking with Ashleigh and she looked forward to that time alone.

During their talks, she'd learned many things about Dane, although he didn't realize it. He had expressed some of his feelings of loss after his wife's death and being responsible for his eleven-year-old son. She'd sympathized with him and offered advice about raising children as a single parent.

"Hello, Ashleigh," he greeted in the husky, bass voice that made her melt like an ice cube.

"Hi, Dane," Ashleigh responded in what she hoped was her normal voice. She waved him into the room. "Come on in."

He moved inside the room and shut the door behind him. Crossing the floor, his sure steps echoed off the empty classroom walls.

"Thanks for dropping by, Dane," Ashleigh said. Extending her hand she shook his as a sweet wave of sensations assaulted her. *Stop this now,* she chastised herself. *This is serious business.* Chances were Dane wouldn't like what she planned to say.

He took the seat in front of her desk, unbuttoned his jacket, and cleared his throat. "Well, you made it sound urgent. I responded accordingly."

She took her seat behind her desk, slipping into professional mode. Closely watching Dane before speaking, Ashleigh hoped he'd take her suggestions the right way. This was about Scott and making certain he was fine. Dane should be informed of anything involving his son.

"Ashleigh?"

"I'm sorry." She fidgeted with the pencils on her desk. "This is difficult for me."

Eyebrows drawn together, he asked, "How so?"

"It's not my goal to cause trouble."

"Well, now I am intrigued. What's going on?"

"I've been very concerned about Scotty. Recently, he's gotten into the habit of talking to himself."

Dane leaned forward, but stayed silent. His eyebrows formed a straight line across his forehead while his unblinking stare made Ashleigh nervous.

She twisted her hands together under her desk, but plunged ahead. "Wednesday, he sat near an hour talking to something or someone. Each time I question him, he shrugs and gives me the same answer, 'just talking to myself.' Normally, I wouldn't have worried about it. But, Scotty's life has been turned upside down in the past year and I think it's time to consider what might be going through his head."

Dane drew in a deep breath and let it out slowly, leaning back in his chair. "True, things haven't been easy for him, or me. But I think we're dealing pretty well considering our lives changed overnight."

"You may be dealing, but I think there's more going on inside Scott. He lost his mother, his caregiver, and I believe he's experiencing grief that he didn't display at the time of her death. I'm not a psychologist or counselor, I'm just a teacher who's concerned about a student in her care."

"You're right. You're no psychologist."

"Pardon?" she asked, feeling the first wave of animosity from him. Ashleigh knew Dane might reject her observation, but she had to try and make him understand for Scotty's sake.

He cleared his throat. "I know your heart is in the right place, but, could you be making too much of things?"

"No. I've gotten to know your son, and I'm convinced that there is something going on and you, me, or someone, maybe a professional, needs to talk with Scotty."

"We've talked before about your role in Scott's life." Dane's eyes dulled as he linked his fingers together. "I appreciate your help. But I don't believe it's a problem and it's certainly not yours. Scott will be fine. He needs a little time to readjust his thinking, that's all."

"What if you're wrong?" Ashleigh challenged. "What if he needs some help that you can't provide? What are you going to do?"

"Take care of it," Dane answered in a clipped, leave-this-alone tone.

I'm going to ignore you, she thought, pressing ahead. "That's not all. Teachers and students have come to me asking what's going on with your son. I wouldn't bother you with this if I felt it was a trivial matter. But I don't believe that. I'm concerned and want you to be aware of what's going on with Scott."

"Are you trying to say that you believe my son has a mental problem?"

"Not at all. What I'm saying is maybe, just maybe, we need to put more time in with Scotty."

"We? I don't recall there being a we."

"I disagree." Ashleigh placed her hand on her bosom. "I'm Scotty's teacher and I see him five out of seven days a week. And I care about what happens to him."

"Maybe you're too close to the situation." Placing a hand under his chin, he explained, "I've been worried about Scott getting too close to you. I should be concerned about your attachment to him."

"Dane—" She licked her dry lips. "I'm not the enemy. Part of my job is to make you aware of what I've observed. I'm not accusing or pointing fingers, all I'm saying is you should take a closer look at Scotty and his behavior."

"It's Scott."

"I'm sorry?"

"My son's name is Scott. S-c-o-t-t," he spelled. "Scott."

"I'm sorry. It's a nickname I have for him. It didn't mean anything."

Face closed and arms folded across the broad expanse of his chest, Dane asked, "What is your recommendation, Mrs. Davis?"

It's Mrs. Davis now. I must have hit a nerve. As long as it got Scotty what he needed, it could stay Mrs. Davis.

"I believe *Scott,*" she emphasized, "needs you. Your time and your attention focused squarely and completely on him. Nothing or no one else."

"I assure you, Scott gets all the attention he needs."

Oh, you're getting ready to blow every chance you might have with this man. If, in fact, you ever had any. But it's got to be done. Holding his gaze with her own, she stated in a clear, firm voice, "I'm sorry, I disagree with you."

Dane stiffened as straight as a broomstick. He rose, planted his hands on the desktop, and spoke in a voice filled with disdain. "You disagree. Who gave you that right?"

"The fact that I stay late four out of five nights a week, waiting until you arrive to pick up Scott, gives me some insight into yours and Scotty's relationship. Work seems to be a bigger part of your life and Scotty doesn't get as much attention as he may need. All I'm trying to do is make you consider Scotty's needs."

Standing, he buttoned his suit jacket. "You don't know anything about my family and not much more about my son. Stick to what you're paid to do. Teach Scott and leave the parenting to me."

"Dane . . ." Ashleigh paused. "Mr. Harris, please listen."

Strolling across the room, he threw over his shoulder, "Good evening, Mrs. Davis."

Five

Ashleigh folded the sheet of elegant stationery and returned it to its embossed envelope, dropping it on the hall table as she passed it. Turning into her kitchen with the telephone glued to her ear, she headed for the stove and lifted the lid from the pot. The aroma of cumin and tomato filled the room. She stirred the simmering chili before returning the lid.

"Thank you," Ashleigh said into the telephone, listening to the woman on the other end. "Where did the information come from?" In the family room, she sank into the burgundy-, beige-, and green-striped sofa and tucked her bare feet under her. "I would like to read it for myself. Send me a copy of the letter, please. Thanks again. Good-bye."

Disconnecting the call, Ashleigh placed the telephone on the coffee table, picked up the remote for the surround sound system, and tapped the CD button. The room filled with classic soul from Prince.

Ashleigh had no intentions of making a spectacle of herself on the Alonzo Clark show. Whatever her daughter had cooked up, she planned to put an end to it here and now. "Eve," she called.

When she received the first voice mail, explaining how she had won the contest, Ashleigh assumed it was all a mistake that would be rectified without her intervention. Then the letter had arrived addressed to her, detailing her itinerary for the Mother's Day makeover, shopping spree, and blind date. That pushed her to the telephone and a call to find out the truth.

How had Eve learned about the contest, written a letter to a show that they never listened to, and won? Ashleigh shook her head, baffled by the lengths her daughter had gone to. For goodness' sake, she was only six years old. Someone must have helped her, told her about the show and what to say in the letter.

Eve scurried down the stairs and made her way to the back of the house. She stopped outside the family room, peeped around the corner, and caught sight of her mother. "Hi, Ma."

She beckoned with a wave of her hand. "Come on in."

Reluctantly, Eve trudged into the room on feet that seemed stuck to the floor. Head hung and a Powerpuff Girls Game Boy in her hand, she gazed at her mother, then quickly looked away.

"I just got off the telephone with someone from the Alonzo Clark show. I want to hear your side of the story. Tell me what you did." She intertwined her fingers and let them hang between her open legs.

Eve's eyes grew large. She took a step back. "I-I-I," she stammered, gazing at the forest-green carpet.

"Come on," Ashleigh said in a voice that demanded the truth. "Tell me. I want to hear it from you."

"It was supposed to be a surprise. A gift. I wanted to buy you a present for Mother's Day. Make you happy. But I didn't have any money." Fidgeting with the toy, she explained in a weak, almost pleading tone. "I heard about the contest and I wrote a letter so that you could win. I wanted you to have fun."

"Eve, what makes you think I'm unhappy?"

"Because Daddy's gone. You don't have anybody to have fun with. Mommy, I don't want you to be sad. I hear you crying sometimes after you think I'm asleep. And you're all alone."

"Sweetheart, I'm fine. I have you. And I love you more than anything else in my life. Sometimes I cry because . . ." She paused, at a loss to explain to Eve. "It's a good way to make yourself feel better. Do you understand?"

Eve's face scrunched up and her lips moved although no words came out. Finally, she answered, "A little."

"Believe me."

"Do you miss Daddy?"

That question almost made Ashleigh's heart stop in her chest. "Little bit," she admitted, feeling the bitter edge of pain and regret. Yes, she missed having a partner, someone with whom to share the good and bad of her day. It would be wonderful to have a man to hold her and make love with at night. But she didn't miss Bill's constant criticism and nagging. No, she didn't miss him at all.

An image of Dane Harris filled her head. For the hundredth time Ashleigh considered how things could be if they were open to each other. She shook his image from her head. *No*, she thought, *he's not the man for me.* Dane had made that very clear.

At some point in the future, she planned to venture into the world of dating and relationships again. But for now, Bill's betrayal kept her satisfied at home with her daughter.

Watching Eve, Ashleigh wondered if her child felt the absence of her father much more than Ashleigh imagined. Or was she harboring guilt over the breakup of her parents' marriage? Did she feel responsible? Did she believe her father left because of her?

"Sweetheart, you don't think your daddy left because he was mad at you, do you?" Ashleigh captured Eve's small hand. "Your daddy loves you. You know that, don't you?"

Eve stood silently before her mother, digging her bare toes into the carpet. Her silence was confirmation enough.

"Your father wanted a new life. It had nothing to do with either one of us. He wasn't mad at you. Believe me."

"Okay."

"Are you sure?" Ashleigh coaxed, giving Eve's hand a little shake to make her look at her. "I don't want you to think like that."

"Okay."

"Don't say what you think I want to hear. Tell me how you feel."

"Daddy and you yelled a lot before he left."

"Yes, we did."

"Sometimes you fussed about me."

What do you say to a six-year-old about her father? Ashleigh scratched the side of her neck and tried to think up a way to explain Bill's wanderlust. "How do you know that?"

"I heard you. And you cried when Daddy yelled."

"I'm sorry you heard us. That was not for your ears. What I want you to understand is that we both love you. Even though we can't live together anymore, our love for you hasn't changed. Okay?"

"Okay."

Expecting Eve to elaborate, Ashleigh waited. When nothing came, she decided to push ahead. "Now, young lady, let's talk about the contest."

"Did you win, Ma?"

"Mmm-hmm. I did."

Eve balled her hand into a fist and jerked down, yelling, "Yes!"

"You wrote a powerful letter, young lady. How did you come up with that?"

"I didn't want you to be alone anymore." She took a step away from her mother. "I hate it when you cry."

"I'm not alone. I have you."

"But you don't have any friends older like you. No boyfriends to take you out. To make you laugh. Please, Mommy, please go out for Mother's Day. It's your present. Please. Have a good time."

More lurked behind Eve's need to give her mother a present. Ashleigh sensed it all came down to Bill and his abandonment of them. So often children felt responsible for their parents' failure. Ashleigh didn't want that pain and guilt for her daughter.

If going on a blind date would put Eve's mind at ease and calm her fears, Ashleigh would do it. Even if the date turned out to be a jerk. After all it was only one date. Hopefully, she'd eliminate any fears Eve might harbor regarding her parents' mistakes.

"Okay, I'll go. But, little girl, I have some questions I need you to answer."

Eve launched herself at her mother, hugging and kissing her. "Thank you, Ma. Thank you. I want you to be happy."

"I am happy. Remember that. Now, it's your turn to tell Mommy some things. Who helped you? And don't try to cover up, because I know you didn't do this alone."

"I promised I wouldn't tell."

"Tell me. I'm not going to be angry, I want to know."

"Scotty."

Things began to come together in Ashleigh's mind. That's what they were doing the last couple of days, huddled together at the back of the room, giggling. They probably had been working on the letter. "Did you ask him to help you or did he ask you to do this?"

"He told me about the contest. Then said I should write a letter."

Ashleigh nodded. It all made sense now. Scotty always wanted to do things for her. She could see him trying to help Eve get a present for her.

She sat holding Eve in her arms. It was a wonderful gesture. She loved the idea of the makeover, but that's where she wanted the contest to end. Plus, she had no desire to share the evening with a man she'd never met.

~

"What do you mean I wrote a letter? I did not," Dane bellowed into the telephone. "Check your files. Obviously, you've been misinformed. Matter-of-fact, fax a copy of the letter, I want to see it for myself."

Swinging his legs off the end of his desk, he listened intently as the man on the other end of the line tried to explain how his name ended up on a list for a date on the Alonzo Clark show. Impatient, Dane cut him off, "Look, man. I don't listen to your show. And there's no way I'd enter a contest to have dinner with a woman I don't know. This is totally ridiculous," he muttered, slamming the telephone into its cradle.

For the past few weeks, he'd been reduced to a steady diet of the Alonzo Clark show. Now, the radio personality was invading his personal life.

He rose from his desk, shoved his hands into the pockets of his trousers, and paced the floor. Somehow, his name had been mixed up with someone else. That's the only explanation he could come up with.

The last thing he wanted was a blind date. There wasn't a snowball's chance in hell that he'd let himself be dragged into this farce with some strange woman. Now, if Ashleigh Davis was his date, he might give it a second thought. She was beautiful. But, not for him. Oh no. Besides, after that blowup they had in her office over Scott, she was probably plotting his demise.

Joyce, his legal secretary, stuck her head inside his office. "Is it safe to enter this domain?"

Dane chuckled, waving her inside. Joyce had been his confidante since he accepted an entry position at the law firm straight from college. "Come on in. I won't kill you. That's reserved for the idiots at that radio station."

"Did you get the situation straightened out?"

He perched on the edge of his desk, facing Joyce. "No. They still insist that I wrote a letter asking for a date. As if I would. Can you believe they have me down for dinner with some woman I've never met?"

"Really?" She dropped into a chair in front of his desk with a stack of files in her lap. She sifted through them, asking, "Did they tell you who she was?"

"No. I don't have a clue. They kept saying I'd have to talk with a lady named Bree Evans. She's handling the Mother's Day thing."

"So what's your next move?"

He cleared his throat and replied, "I don't know."

Crossing her legs and settling more comfortably in her chair, Joyce eyed him. "That doesn't sound like the Dane Anthony Harris I know. That lawyer's brain of yours is always working an angle. What's going on in your head?"

"Nothing. Everything. I don't know."

"Dane, Helen's dead," Joyce said in a quiet, but firm tone. "She's not coming back."

Dane flinched from the harshness of Joyce's words, suspecting that she wanted to jolt him back to her world. But, he wasn't ready. The bond between him and Helen was still firmly in place.

He shut his eyes and massaged his temple with two fingers. "I understand the cycle of life. I don't need you to explain it to me."

"No, you don't. Maybe you need to say it for yourself and accept it. I know you loved Helen. But she's gone."

"I've got a raging headache. Why don't you just cut through the bull and give me the facts?"

"It wouldn't hurt you to go out every once in a while."

"I go out."

"Yeah, I know. To company dinner parties when it's demanded of you. And you're always alone."

Dane swung around to stare at her.

"Oh yeah. I know what goes on. You get out all right," she said.

"Look, I have a son to raise." Pacing, he stopped and glanced out the window at the Canadian side of the Detroit River. "I don't have time for a lot of going out and partying and stuff."

"Helen was your love. I'm well aware of that fact. That doesn't mean you can't love again. There's a new someone in the world for you. Open your heart and you'll see."

"You think I can find all of this with a date from the Alonzo Clark show?"

She shrugged, placing the files on his desk. "Who knows? You have to take that first step to find out."

"Who indeed."

"I'm your friend, as well as your employee, Dane. You've been almost as dead as Helen for the past year. Do you think this is what she'd want for you? To mourn her loss forever? She enjoyed her life and she made you enjoy yours. Honor her memory by moving on."

"I can't think about this right now."

"Fine. Let's look at it in a different light. This is a great opportunity for the firm as a whole and you as an individual."

"Oh yeah? Explain how."

"The firm will get great publicity on a nationally syndicated show. You'll come off as an understanding guy who appreciates hardworking mothers." Joyce rose from her chair, picked up the remaining files, and started for the door. "Think about that before you call them back and decline," she said, slipping through the door.

Dane returned to his desk and practically fell into his chair. The envelope seemed to mock him as he sat, staring at it. He picked it up and turned it over.

Joyce always gave him grief along with a dose of the truth. Today wasn't any different. This time he planned to prove her wrong.

He'd loved Helen more than life itself. Her death almost did him in. Although Helen was gone, he had a full, enjoyable life. The practice was booming and his cases took up many hours of his day. Then there was Scott to care for. He didn't need anything else.

A surge of guilt swept through him as he thought of the horrible things he'd said to Ashleigh Davis. She had been right about Scott. He spent hours talking to himself. Maybe that's where his focus should be, not on this contest stuff.

Truthfully, he didn't see how going on this date would make things better. Help him to move on.

Tapping the embossed envelope on the edge of his desk, he'd decided to consider the offer. Take the time to think things through and make a decision after that.

To shut Joyce up, he might consider going on the blind date. That would show her that he was moving on with his life. That's what he'd do. Call the show and go out on the date. What harm could one little date do?

Six

A potpourri of soothing fragrances filled Calypso Spa as Ashleigh snuggled deeper into the gold and cream salon recliner. The manicurist massaged her feet, caressing each toe with revitalizing firmness. *I'm loving this,* Ashleigh thought, feeling like a wet noodle.

This contest thing may not have been what Ashleigh had in mind for Mother's Day, but she sure intended to enjoy the benefits. Eve deserved something special for orchestrating this present. Sunday morning, Ashleigh planned to get up early and prepare the biggest pancake breakfast for her daughter.

Heaven described the limo ride to Somerset Mall. When she compared the luxury of the stretch limo to her little compact, it felt as if she'd been riding on feathers.

Five hours later, she had emerged from Nordstrom's with a pantsuit, evening dress, shoes, and all the accessories. It had been years since she'd bought more than a garment or two at a time and never anything as frivolous or expensive as the clothing she'd chosen.

"Mrs. Davis, have you made your color selection for your nails?" the manicurist asked.

Ashleigh shook her head. "No."

"May I suggest this?" The manicurist displayed a blazing red bottle of nail polish for her to consider. "This would go perfectly with your skin tone."

Eyes large and round, Ashleigh considered the polish. Normally, she leaned toward quieter shades, staying in the shadows as opposed to center stage. But, this wasn't a day for lurking in the dark. For once she felt confident that she had the strength to hang with the big girls and stand in the limelight alongside them. "Mmm. I'm not sure," she said, eyeing the bottle.

"Oh, but it would be so beautiful with your outfit. Bring out the color of your skin and it goes so well with black or cream," insisted the manicurist.

What the hay? Ashleigh planned to enjoy this once-in-a-lifetime experience to the fullest. She threw caution to the wind and wiggled her fingers at the woman. "Let's try it."

While her nail polish dried, she relaxed in the leather recliner, waiting for the next phase of her makeover. She'd already had the body wrap and massage. Next on the agenda was her hair and makeup.

At the slight cough from the doorway, Ashleigh opened her eyes and found the spa's proprietor, Ms. Elise, waltzing into the room carrying a Nordstrom's garment bag. Ashleigh tossed her legs over the side of the recliner and returned to a sitting position.

"I must disturb you, Ms. Davis. We need you to make your wardrobe selection so the garment may be pressed and ready. Plus, it will help us decide how to prepare your makeup and hair. We pride ourselves on complete satisfaction. When you leave Calypso Spa, we want you to look and feel stunning."

She waited as Ms. Elise opened the bag and removed the cream double-breasted linen pantsuit. Professional looking and elegant described the garment. It struck the proper note between let's-have-fun and don't-go-too-far.

Then she turned her attention to *the dress*. With a hand to her cheek, she shook her head. How had she let the sales associate talk her into an item so revealing?

The hem of the midnight silk dress hit her upper thigh and curled around every curve like soap on skin. The low neckline cut across her chest, revealing the deep swell of her breasts.

With a garment in each hand, Ms. Elise asked, "Can you tell us which ensemble you've selected for tonight?"

Ashleigh studied each item. Her confidence didn't extend to the dress.

Pointing, she stated, "I'll stick with the pantsuit. The dress is not my norm. The pantsuit is a classic and can be dressed up or down depending on the occasion."

"I see." Ms. Elise considered the silk garment with an expert's eye. "Oh, this dress is gorgeous. And with your height you would look spectacular in it. Like a queen. Are you sure you don't want to reconsider?"

"Yes," Ashleigh answered with a firm shake of her head. Far too much of her body was laid bare in that dress. Better to wear the pantsuit. She didn't want her date to get the wrong impression. This dress would be saved for a special night.

"Very well." Ms. Elise sighed. "Such a shame. Oh well. I'm going to take your pantsuit into the back and have one of my assistants press it."

Relaxing in the recliner, Ashleigh pondered the evening ahead. Who was her mystery date? What would prompt a man to enter a contest like this? What would he expect from her?

With a startled shriek, Ms. Elise raced from the back room and stopped in front of Ashleigh. Shock and horror distorted her perfectly made up face. "Oh, Ms. Davis, I'm soooo sorry." She fretted, her hands wrung together in constant motion. "There's been an accident. Terrible, terrible accident. Please forgive my staff. No one seems to know how it happened."

"What's going on?"

"Your beautiful suit. Oh." Ms. Elise's eyes rolled up and she shook her head. "It's—it's ruined. The iron scorched the jacket. I'm so sorry. Please forgive us. And, of course we will replace the garment."

Ashleigh's face scrunched into a confused mask. "Scorched it?" She shook her head, trying to absorb Ms. Elise's explanation. "I don't understand. How did that happen?"

"We set the iron at the proper temperature, but somehow the dial shifted to a much hotter degree and when my assistant touched the iron to your jacket, poof." She tossed her hands in a wide circle. "It ruined the delicate fabric."

Stroking her brow with one finger, Ashleigh considered the situation. "What about the dress? Is it okay?"

"Fortunately, yes. My assistant decided to press the dress first and it's fine. Would you like to see it?"

"Yes. Thank you."

Hurrying to the back room, Ms. Elise called, "I'll be right back."

Ashleigh perched on the side of the recliner and waited. So much for her presenting a graceful, elegant persona. Such a shame, her brand-new outfit was ruined without her ever wearing it.

Ms. Elise returned minutes later with the dress in her hands. She displayed it, saying, "See? Perfect. It's ready for you to slip into."

Well, I don't have much of a choice, Ashleigh thought, eyeing the dress as fate took control of her wardrobe selection. Unless she wanted to wear the Dockers she had worn to the mall, the dress was her only option. This dress represented such a drastic change from her norm.

"Did your iron give out? Is that why it ruined the jacket?" Ashleigh asked, scratching the side of her neck while searching for a way to tone down the dress.

"No. The iron is fine. I have no explanation." Ms. Elise shrugged, then raised a thoughtful finger to her lips. "Although, my seven-year-old always plays in the back room and she keeps repeating a tale about this golden light she saw surrounding the iron seconds before it burned your garment. I don't know what she's talking about. I didn't see a thing. We must have misjudged the delicacy of the garment. I have no other answer."

Glancing at her watch, Ashleigh made a decision. "Well, it's too late to go back to Nordstrom's for another outfit. I'll have to wear the dress."

"Of course. The dress is ready." Ms. Elise offered a little formal bow. "I'm so sorry. So sorry. Select a day and come in. We'll purchase another garment of your choice. You have my word."

~

Dane Anthony Harris strolled into the radio station with a hand tucked inside his trouser pocket and all the confidence he had gained from his thirty-five years. Identifying himself at the security guard's station, he headed to the bank of elevators located in the west corridor of the building.

After years of appearing before members of the judicial system, he'd perfected his stolid face. His insides were a different story.

After days of playing telephone tag with Bree Evans, he was no closer to knowing who his date was. And that bugged him. Going on a blind date went against his idea of fun. Given a choice, he'd rather spend his free time at home working on a brief. How had Joyce convinced him to do this?

Joyce hadn't done anything. Dane knew why he was here. Pride. Stubborn, male pride that refused to let the issue rest drove him to accept the date. He wanted to show her that he was getting on with his life.

Stepping inside the elevator, he stood perfectly still as the doors closed and he waited for the contraption to reach the designated floor. He hoped he wouldn't regret this evening.

After announcing himself to the receptionist, he sank into a black leather sofa and waited. A tall blonde approached him with an outstretched hand and a clipboard in the other. "Hello, Mr. Harris. I'm Bree Evans. I'll be working with you tonight."

"What do you mean working with me? I'm just here for the Mother's Day date."

"Yes, you are." She offered him an empty smile as she led him across the lobby. "But, we're also going to have you and our lucky mother spend a few minutes on the air."

"Whoa!" Dane halted in his tracks. "Nothing in your letter discussed an interview or air time. Who decided this?"

"There's no need to be nervous." Bree placed a reassuring hand on his arm, urging him down the corridor. "It's only a five-to-ten-minute interview. Mr. Clark felt our listening audience would like to learn more about the people who won the contest."

"I didn't agree to this. And to be perfectly honest, I'm not sure this is the right thing to do." Pivoting on the heel of his shoes, Dane started back down the hall to the elevators, calling over his shoulder, "I'm sorry. This isn't for me. I'm not going to be used like a Jerry Springer wanna-be. Maybe you should call someone else in to be this woman's date. It's not going to be me."

Bree trailed behind him, chanting, "But . . . but . . ."

"Get someone else," he ordered, punching the elevator button.

As the doors opened, Kenny G's sax and a goddess emerged from the confines of the wood-paneled box. Dane's mouth dropped open as he watched this beautiful creature turn to him. Shock spread over her face.

Long, shapely legs encased in black hosiery led up to the hem of a black dress that caressed each curve. Dane's mind went blank. He continued his journey upward across a flat tummy, enticing breasts, the slope of her brown, creamy neck, and settled on her face. Stunned, he stood in front of her, gawking openmouthed.

I'll be damned, he thought. *Ashleigh Davis.* She looked absolutely gorgeous. He sure hoped she was his date. And if that was the case, he wasn't going anywhere.

Stepping back to allow her access to the lobby, he followed her like a lamb to the slaughter.

"Oh, Ms. Davis," Bree pronounced, taking Ashleigh's arm and leading her farther into the lobby. "Come in. You look wonderful! Simply beautiful! Please join us. Mr. Harris and I were going over the itinerary."

Dane stood back, admiring Ashleigh. His insides felt like a tight ball as he watched her move around the lobby on three-inch heels. *Come on, old boy, stop drooling like an adolescent. You've seen women before. Yeah, but not this woman. Not like this.* Not this temptress with the smooth coffee-colored skin that made his palms itch to run his finger across her cheek, made him control the desire to kiss her lips that were painted the color of wet strawberries.

Bree checked an item from her list. "Mr. Harris, this is Ms. Ashleigh Davis. Ashleigh Davis, Dane Harris."

"I know Mr. Harris. His son is one of my students."

"It's great that you guys know each other. Wow! This adds a different element to our evening, wouldn't you say?"

"Yeah, wow!" Ashleigh muttered.

Checking her clipboard, Bree said, "Well, let's get back to business. I was just explaining to Mr. Harris that we've set up a short air interview for you guys with Alonzo Clark. Although he doesn't broadcast from here, we're able to connect with him, and he'll be interviewing you for, say, five to ten minutes. The taped interview will air tomorrow during Alonzo's show. Our audience is excited to know more about you guys. Come this way."

Dane cupped Ashleigh's elbow and they followed the chatty blonde behind the receptionist station.

"Ms. Evans," the receptionist called.

"Yeeees," she sang.

The receptionist replied, "There's a call for you."

"I'll call them back."

"It's Alonzo Clark."

Sighing, Bree turned back to the lobby. "Excuse me. Put it through on my cell."

Dane moved closer to Ashleigh, plotting how he could get her alone so that he could offer an apology. Her floral scent filled his nostrils. Before he'd pulled a plan together, Ms. Evans returned.

Bree snapped shut her cell phone, composed her face, and explained, "I'm sorry about that. Change of plans. We're going to do a photo shoot first, then the interview."

Seven

Dane cleared his throat and tapped Ashleigh on the shoulder. Her bare skin felt like smooth chocolate pudding. The urge to run his hand along the slope of her neck and caress her cheek was strong, but he fought it. "Umm, Ashleigh, can we talk for a minute?" he asked, shoving his hands into his pockets to keep them from stroking her skin.

Ashleigh faced him. Her face a blank mask. "Don't you mean, Mrs. Davis?" she queried.

Humbled, Dane felt heat rise to the surface of his skin, and he glanced away. *Okay, she got me,* he thought. *But, I've got to make this right between us. This is her evening and she deserves to enjoy it.* He cleared his throat for the second time and drew closer. "Mrs. Davis, the last time we were together, you tried to help me and Scott."

Silent as the dead, Ashleigh linked her hands together and waited, offering no encouragement. Her unreadable stare bugged him. Where was the wonderful, compassionate woman who always listened to his explanations no matter how ridiculous they sounded?

"Since this is your evening and I'm tagging along we're sort of stuck with each other. I don't want you to feel uncomfortable."

Eyebrows lifted in a sign of disbelief, she muttered, "Isn't that sweet of you?"

Dane blew out a hot puff of air and rubbed his fingers back and forth across his chin. "Please understand," he begged, detaining her with a hand on her arm. "I wasn't—"

"Ummm, excuse me." Bree Evans glanced at Dane, then Ashleigh. "It's time for the publicity shots."

Ready to explode, Dane clenched his teeth and mentally reached for calm within himself. He swam through an ocean of frustration, but finally reached the level of calm he needed to proceed.

Standing, Ashleigh smoothed her hands down the front of her dress. "I'm ready."

"So am I," came Dane's response. He rose with unhurried grace.

"Great." Bree turned to a man shadowing her steps. The thin, shaggy-haired white man stepped forward in an ill-fitting gray polyester suit, holding a professional Nikon camera. "Ms. Davis and Mr. Harris, this is Gary Willis," she stated, placing a hand on Gary's shoulder. "He's one of our best photographers. I'm going to let him take over."

Gary nodded at them, glanced around the room, and pointed at the opposite end of the lobby. "Why don't we move over there? The lighting is better and we can use the station's call letters for our backdrop."

Dane and Ashleigh followed Gary's lead, allowing him to position them under the station's gold-plated call letters, then glanced through the camera lens. "I need you guys to move closer." He lowered the camera and let it rest against his chest by the straps, waving his hands together as if he were clapping.

Ashleigh's gaze swept over Dane and her lips pursed. She didn't want to be any closer to him than necessary.

"Come on, guys. Get closer," Gary muttered, an exasperated edge to his request. "Neither one of you has a contagious disease, do you?"

Ashleigh gave a quick shake of her head and glanced at Dane. He shook his head and slid a step closer.

Ashleigh made a particular note of the amount of space between them.

Oblivious of the tension between them, Gary instructed, "Mr. Harris, put your arm around Ms. Davis's shoulder."

Ashleigh's floral scent swayed back and forth under his nose as Dane complied with Gary's request. "Like this?" With one hand, Dane pulled her to his side, resting a hand on her shoulder. Her enticing supple frame brushed up against him. Unconsciously, he stroked the bare flesh under his hand. *I'm going to lose it if she keeps brushing up against me. I need to keep her still,* he thought.

Oh my, she thought. *What am I doing?* Her skin quivered under his fingers as she felt herself relax against his frame.

Gary gazed at them through the camera's lens. "Yes! That's it! Perfect! Now turn and look into each other's eyes and smile. Show the world you're enjoying yourselves."

Ashleigh leaned close to Dane as he drew her more firmly against his side. His clean, male scent made her giddy. She glanced into his face and felt her composure slip a notch more.

Blinding them, Gary snapped shot after shot. "How about a few single shots? Ms. Davis, can I take you first?"

"Sure," she answered, quickly moving away from Dane.

"Have a seat, Ms. Davis. I want a few shots with you sitting here." The photographer led her to the sofa and posed her, then fidgeted with his camera.

Dane watched Ashleigh's photo shoot from the opposite sofa. Although she smiled for Gary, Dane could tell that she wasn't comfortable with the whole session. Her hands were tightly locked together, displaying white knuckles. Gary lowered the camera, replaced the film, and motioned for Dane to take Ashleigh's place.

For the next thirty minutes, they continued through a series of photos. Ashleigh felt drained. She sat on the edge of the leather sofa and waited, trying to pull herself together before they did the radio interview.

Dane slipped into the space next to her. "As I was saying earlier, I wasn't angry at you—"

Clipboard in hand, Bree interrupted again, "Okay, folks, Mr. Clark's ready for your interview."

Annoyed, Dane stared hard at Bree. His displeasure slipped off her shoulders. He rose, helped Ashleigh to her feet, and tucked her hand into the crook of his arm.

Bree slipped into step beside Dane and Ashleigh. "I don't know if you're aware of this, but our photographer and reporter will be accompanying you for a small potion of your date."

He turned. "Accompanying us, Ms. Evans?"

"Ummm. Yes. Strictly for publicity. You won't even know they're there." She ushered them through the door to the studios. "We'd like photos and a story about your evening."

"And how much of our evening will they be part of?" Dane studied Ashleigh's silent profile, before focusing on the blonde.

Bree's hand fluttered over her clipboard. "Oh, just for an hour or so. I promise they won't disturb you. Really. Understand, we can't have such a high-profile event without our representative accompanying you."

Dane turned to Ashleigh. "What do you think?"

She shrugged. "It looks as if the choice has never truly been ours to make. We might as well scrape what fun we can from the evening."

~

"Good evening, folks. This is a special edition of the *Alonzo Clark Morning Show*. We're here with one pair of the winners of our Mother's Day contest. We have Ashleigh Davis and Dane Harris in the studio."

Ashleigh sat in the sound booth with a headset on her head while Dane claimed the chair next to her. She cut her eyes in his direction. Her stomach twisted and turned inside out, yet she couldn't deny the twinge of excitement over the prospect of spending an evening with Dane. She had always found him attractive, but so far life had conspired against their exploring the options.

"Ashleigh teaches at Gregory Middle School. Her specialties are math and science. And Dane is a partner in the law firm Williams, Jones and Harris in the motor city, Detroit, Michigan.

"We've just received some interesting news about our winners. They know each other from Ashleigh's school."

As usual Dane wore an expressionless mask that kept Ashleigh from guessing at his thoughts about the whole contest thing. For that matter, she didn't know what she felt.

"Well, folks. Here we go. Before we do anything else, I'm going to read Dane's letter. 'I know a woman like the one Eve described. Someone completely unselfish, giving, and loving. Over the last year, she's helped me and my son through the darkest period in our lives. She's kind and comforting. Always listens and knows what we need without asking. I would be honored to be part of this special night. Maybe I can't ask my special lady out, but in some small way this evening will help me honor the woman who has been so good to me and my son.' "

Dane felt his insides knot and he looked away. That letter expressed so much of what he felt for and about Ashleigh. *Who knows so much about my private life?* he wondered, stroking his chin.

"How's that, folks? Wasn't it beautiful? So, Dane, tell me, is Ashleigh that woman?"

"Maybe."

"Mmm. Playing coy. I've got another question for you. Dane, why would you want to go out with a woman who has a child?"

"Because I have a son. She'll understand the problems that arise with a kid. How your time is not always your own and all the problems that evolve."

"Mmm. It sounds good to me. How about this, what part or parts of Ashleigh's letter appealed to you and compelled you to write to us?"

Eve's letter was a complete mystery to Dane. He felt confident he could bluff his way through this. He cleared his throat and readjusted his tie before speaking. "Who she is shined through the words on the page."

"Oh really?" Alonzo Clark returned. "Give me an example."

"I mean, not just her physical beauty, although she is a beautiful woman." Dane's gaze slid over her. "But the beauty that comes from inside. No amount of makeup or expensive clothes can hide that. Her ability to care for and about others was so apparent in Eve's letter and I wanted to meet and get to know this woman."

"That sounds great." Alonzo paused, then asked on the end of a chuckle, "Be honest. How long have you been rehearsing that speech?"

"There's no need to practice. This is the way I feel and it's what I felt when I heard Eve's letter for the first time. Now, looking at Ashleigh, it all makes sense. What I was feeling stems from the fact that I understand and knew her."

"What do you say, folks? Do we need to be quiet and let Dane continue?"

"Ashleigh's been very good to me and my son. Whatever we've needed, she's given without hesitation." Dane held Ashleigh's gaze with his own, willing her to understand and forgive. "Not many people give so completely of themselves the way she does. It's beautiful. And I'm proud to be here to share her evening."

"That's the truth," Alonzo agreed. "Okay, so you wrote this letter about a woman who gives of herself. Is that the only thing that appealed to you?"

"No. I loved the fact that Eve felt her mother works so hard for others that she deserved to enjoy herself, take time out for herself. I wanted to be the person who helped her have a great evening. I want her to have a night to remember."

"I like what I'm hearing. Can you keep it going?"

Dane raised a finger and spoke in that deep, husky voice that Ashleigh loved. "There's one more thing I'd like to add."

"Go for it."

"When Ashleigh stepped off the elevator, she looked beautiful. I mean absolutely stunning."

Ashleigh flushed under her coffee-brown skin.

"Whoa!" Alonzo cheered. "I think it's time to talk with our lady here. It's your turn, Ashleigh. You've been quiet through all of this. What do you think about the things Dane said about you?"

A nervous breath gushed from her lungs as her hand snaked around a glass of water. "I'm flabbergasted. I didn't think Dane had noticed those things. It's quite overwhelming."

Alonzo complimented, "Yeah, but you're really loving this, aren't you?"

"It's certainly wonderful to have the attention of such a powerful and attractive man. And to be perfectly honest, I'm enjoying every word."

Ashleigh turned to Dane. The expression in his eyes made her melt like ice cream in the sun. All the emotions she had felt that afternoon at Scott's baseball game rushed back to her. They were in tune with each other, once more.

"So, Ashleigh, tell us how you feel about going out with Dane."

She stretched her lips into something resembling a smile and said, "A little shocked by the event." That was an understatement if she'd ever made one. "But, I have to admit there's a part of me that's excited and looking forward to our evening."

Discreetly assessing Dane from head to toe, Ashleigh silently admitted the navy suit and pastel tie made him look sexier than she'd ever seen him. But, what was he thinking?

If she thought back to their last encounter, he'd made it clear that he didn't want her anywhere near him or his son, demanded that she should stay in her place as educator and leave the parenting to him. That encounter had strengthened her resolve to steer clear of Mr. Dane Harris at every turn and until tonight she'd been able to stick to that promise.

Alonzo's next question brought her attention back to the situation at hand. "Okay, that's all well and good. But what do you think of Dane?"

"He's a wonderful Mother's Day present," popped out of Ashleigh's mouth before she realized it. She slapped her hand over her mouth. *Oh Lord, what was I thinking?*

"I'm not going to touch that one," Alonzo said and a hardy chuckle came through the headsets. "Now, it's your turn, Dane. What was your first reaction when you found Ashleigh was your date?"

Dane ran an eye over Ashleigh and decided to tell the truth. If he wanted her to forgive him, he needed to turn up the charm a notch and mean it. "I would have followed her anywhere. She was the most beautiful thing I'd ever seen."

Her pulse accelerated when she found genuine sincerity gleaming back at her from his brown eyes.

"Whoa! I like a man who says what he means and means what he says. Have you swept her off her feet yet? Ashleigh, what's your take on a statement like that?"

What indeed. She knew she looked good, but how true were Dane's words? She'd like to get to know him better and have that chance at a real relationship. Her tongue slid across her lips. Everything in her wanted to believe his words.

Dane's stomach clenched into a tight knot while he watched her pink tongue moisten her lips. *Look away, man. Look away.* But he couldn't. Every gesture, every movement drew him closer to her. Torture. Ashleigh was sweet torture.

Drawing in a deep breath, she plunged ahead, "What can I say? I'm just waiting for more."

"So are we," Alonzo's deep voice boomed through the headsets. "So are we. Dane, Ashleigh, thanks for the fun interview. We look forward to hearing how your evening goes. Okay, folks, you've heard from our winners. Now, we're going to let you see them. Check out our Web site tomorrow for photos of Dane and Ashleigh and their night out."

After the interview, Dane and Ashleigh found themselves back in the lobby, waiting for the limo. She couldn't hold her question in.

"Did you mean all of that? Or was that just for show?"

He reached across the coffee table and took her hand. His touch felt warm and reassuring. "I meant every word. Ashleigh," he began, then drew his tongue across his dry lips. "Some heated words—"

"Nina, come over here, will you?" called Bree Evans, who moved between the pair. "I want to introduce you."

A tiny redhead sashayed across the lobby and stopped next to Bree. "This is Nina Fitzgerald. She's our publicity person and she and Gary Willis will be accompanying you for a part of your evening."

Damn, Dane wanted to yell as he got to his feet. *I'm going to strangle this woman if she interrupts me one more time.*

Eight

*A*re *these people going to be with us through the whole evening?* Ashleigh wondered, strolling across the Rattlesnake Club Restaurant. Dane followed, with the photographer and reporter on his heels.

The maître d' stopped at a table for four, seated Ashleigh and Nina, then waited while the men sat down. With a formal bow, he quietly disappeared.

Immediately, the photographer began to snap photos. Dane gazed at Ashleigh, turned to Gary with an arched brow, and asked, "I hope you're going to stop long enough for us to eat our dinner."

Gary lowered the camera. "Oh yeah," he muttered, red creeping up the side of his neck. "We need a few more before you settle down for your meal. You won't notice that we're here."

"That should be interesting to see, considering you light up this section of the restaurant each time you take a picture."

On that note, the fast-talking redhead pounced. "Ms. Davis, how does it feel to be out with someone who felt moved by a letter about you?"

"I'm not sure yet." Ashleigh settled her evening bag on the edge of the table. "Everything seems surreal right now."

The photographer stood. "Smile," he muttered, snapping several additional shots of the pair. "Dane, can you stand behind Ashleigh's chair?"

He complied without a word.

"Put your hands on her shoulders. Good, that's it. Smile." Several more flashes blinded her. Ashleigh blinked repeatedly and a tear or two slid down her cheek.

The men returned to their seats while the explosion of flashes drew the curious gazes of several restaurant patrons. After a moment of silent perusal, they returned their attention to their meals.

"Can we have a few minutes before you take any more pictures?" Dane asked, offering Ashleigh his handkerchief.

"Thank you," Ashleigh said, shaking out the cloth and dabbing at her eyes. The cotton fabric felt warm.

"Yeah. Sure," the photographer agreed, returning to his chair to reload his camera.

A tuxedo-clad waiter approached their table. "Good evening." He whipped the linen napkin from the water glass and laid it across Ashleigh's lap, repeating this gesture for Nina. "May I get you something from the bar?"

Dane smiled at Ashleigh and the warmth of it made her feel giddy. "We'd like champagne. After all, we're celebrating."

"An anniversary?" the waiter inquired, gazing at the pair.

"No," Dane uttered in a husky bass voice as he held her gaze with his own. "A wonderful new beginning."

Her mouth dropped open and her heart raced. Was Dane saying what she hoped he was saying? *Ashleigh, calm yourself,* she thought. *That's not a declaration of marriage, only a slick statement that could be interpreted any number of ways. Enjoy the evening and see what develops.*

"Ashleigh," Nina called, breaking the mood. "What about your daughter? How old is she? What's her take on this?"

"Eve is six. And she is ecstatic about my going out and having a good time."

"How did you react when you learned that you had been selected for the night out?" the redhead shot at Ashleigh.

"Disbelief pretty much summed it up," Ashleigh answered, pulling her eyes away from Dane. "I didn't believe Eve had enough knowledge or skill to write a letter that would catch the attention of the judges."

"Obviously, she did. Because not only did she catch the judges' attention"—the redhead nodded toward Dane—"she caught Mr. Harris's attention as well."

The waiter arrived with the champagne and filled each person's glass. Dane lifted his. "To the wonderful evening ahead," he saluted, touching his glass to Ashleigh's.

The photographer jumped up and snapped more pictures. "Wait," he yelped, "do that again. I want to get a shot."

Ashleigh complied, but her visions of a wonderful, romantic evening were quickly flying out the front door of the Rattlesnake Club.

Nina rose, pulled a chair from an empty table, and planted herself firmly between Ashleigh and Dane. Her gaze slid from Dane to Ashleigh and then returned to Dane. Within seconds she began to fire question after question, hardly giving him time to answer before shooting another his way. "Mr. Harris, was it a complete surprise to find your date is someone you knew?"

"Yes." Dane's tilted his head to the left, studying Ashleigh. "Quite a surprise."

"What appealed to you about Eve's letter? Is this the first time you've ever done anything like this?"

Dane smiled indulgently. "Yes, it is. Normally, I'm very reserved. But Eve's letter highlighted Ashleigh's gentleness and concern for others. Her ability to put everyone before her own needs."

"Well," the redhead began, "that's high praise indeed. Ms. Davis, how do you feel about Mr. Harris's compliments?"

This is getting old, Ashleigh thought as she formed a reply. "How does one react? These are beautiful words."

The redhead opened her mouth to say something, but stopped. She turned to the photographer. "Is that your alarm?"

"Damn. I bet the valet tried to move my van and the alarm went off." He stood, placed his camera on his chair, and said, "I'll be right back."

Watching Gary rush from the restaurant, Nina leaned in for the kill. "While he's gone, I'm going to keep going and try to finish up my questions."

Five minutes later, Gary returned, a crazed, confused expression in his eyes. "I can't stop the alarm. Even when I use the remote the horn keeps up a bunch of noise. The valet told me that if I don't shut it off the neighbors will call the police and I'll get a three-hundred-dollar ticket. I can't afford that, guys, so I'm going to call it a night." He loaded the camera and his equipment into his bag and tossed it over his left shoulder. "I think I have enough shots for the station. Enjoy your evening."

Surprised, Ashleigh muttered, "Thank you."

"Nina, you comin'?" Gary asked.

She shook her head. "Nah. I've got a couple more questions, I'll catch a cab. You go right ahead. I'm fine." Turning to Ashleigh, Nina flipped to a clean page of her notebook.

Oh, I wish she would go away, Ashleigh thought. *I want to enjoy the evening, not play five hundred questions.*

From another table Ashleigh caught the tail end of a question from a young girl, "Hey, Mom, what's that gold light? How come our food didn't have one?"

Ashleigh turned to check out what the child was referring to, and pandemonium hit with the blink of an eye. The whole thing happened like a scene from a Laurel and Hardy comedy.

A passing waiter stumbled and a tray loaded with food landed in Nina's lap. She gasped, jumped to her feet, and brushed at the burgundy goop, ice cream, and chocolate cake, running down her apricot pantsuit.

The waiter picked at the remains of cherries flambé from her clothes. The liquid oozed down the front of her suit while the cherries dotted her jacket.

"I'm so sorry. Sorry. So sorry," he chanted, dropping cherries onto the tray. "Of course, we'll pay for your suit. Please forgive me. I don't know what happened. The tray flew from my hands. Oh, I'm so, so, sorry."

Taking a deep breath, Nina seemed to muster all the dignity within her power. "It's okay. It was nothing more than an accident." She restrained his busy hands as he tried to clear up the mess. "Dane, Ashleigh, I'm afraid we're going to have to cut our interview short. I've got to get out of these clothes. I'm sorry. Thank you for your time. If Gary is still outside, I'm going to catch a ride with him." Grabbing her purse and notepad, she hurried from the main dining room.

Ashleigh looked at Dane and they both laughed. "It looks as if our interview and photo shoot are over."

He watched the redhead for an additional beat, then turned his deep, penetrating gaze on Ashleigh. Her body hummed in response. "You may be right. That's fine with me. The questions and photos were getting a bit tedious."

"Amen to that."

The maître d' coughed discreetly and said, "We have set up a new table for you. If you'll follow me I'll seat you."

Dane rounded the table and helped Ashleigh from her chair. With his hand at her elbow they followed the maître d' to a table overlooking the Detroit River. The setting sun reflected off the water as the sky filled with an array of red, blue, and orange colors. The scenery was breathtaking.

"Now, isn't this better?" the maître d' questioned, refilling their champagne glasses.

"Much." Ashleigh smiled her thanks.

Dane lifted his champagne glass and saluted her. "Let's enjoy our evening, now that the press has left the building."

He cleared his throat, repositioned the napkin in his lap, and looked at Ashleigh. "Before anything else is said, I want to apologize for my actions a couple of weeks ago. I know you were only trying to offer me a heads-up on what was going on with Scott. I took it way out of proportion and snapped at you for doing your job. Please forgive me."

She sat, quietly watching him.

"Please," he begged.

The minutes ticked by and still she made no comment.

"Please," he asked again.

Without comment, she placed her purse on the edge of the table and studied him.

"Since my wife died, all this responsibility has fallen on me, and I'm really afraid I'll screw up with Scott." He looked away and confessed, "Sometimes it scares the hell out of me."

That got her attention. Dane noticed the softening of her expression.

"As long as you understand that my concern was for Scott, apology accepted," Ashleigh offered with a smile. "Let's not talk about work or family problems. We both need to unwind with an evening out with no strings. Well, our strings have left for the night."

"Thank goodness," Dane responded.

By the time they left the Rattlesnake Club, Gary, Nina, and their mishaps had been forgotten.

~

Sultry jazz greeted Ashleigh and Dane when they entered Baker's Keyboard Lounge. The intimate crowd was mellow as they crossed the room and slipped into a big, soft leather booth. Ashleigh glanced around the room, checking out the crowd. A winding bar painted in the shape of a piano keyboard dominated the room, and contemporary jazz flowed freely as her head bopped to the electric keyboard.

Dane cleared his throat before asking, "Was Baker's your choice?"

She gave him a big, affirming grin. "What gives you that idea?"

Dane nodded forward the table and her fingers. "You haven't stopped popping your fingers or swaying to the music since we stepped through the doors."

Ashleigh giggled. "Guilty." Her smiled dropped. "Is Baker's okay with you? I didn't know who my date was so I thought this would be a great place to visit."

"And you're right. It is," he confirmed, unbuttoning his jacket and leaning heavily into the booth's cushioned seat.

"Since we're here, let's talk jazz." Ashleigh brushed her hair over her shoulder. "Do you have any favorites?"

"Yeah. I can go classic or contemporary. I love Cab Calloway, Ray Charles, or Dizzy Gillespie. But, I wouldn't turn down a night with Najee."

"Oh, I'm with you on that. I love jazz sax players."

"I noticed a dance floor." Dane nodded toward the center of the room. "How about trying it out? I promise I won't step on your feet."

Ashleigh's gaze slid over Dane, assessing him. "My instincts tell me that won't be a problem. For some reason, I believe you are pretty good on your feet."

His eyebrows lifted in a questioning manner and he challenged, "The only way you're going to find out is to come and dance with me."

Dane helped her from the booth. They moved toward the dance floor hand in hand. Ashleigh moved into his arms. Holding on tight to each other, they swayed back and forth until the music ended.

I'm liking this. She inhaled, enjoying his clean, fresh scent. This was what she'd dreamed up, spending uninterrupted time with him while they got to know each other.

They stayed on the dance floor through a series of jazz tunes, enjoying dance after dance, until the pace of the music picked up and they returned to the table. Dane and Ashleigh sat quiet, absorbing the club's ambience. A waiter replaced their drinks and they relaxed, watching the milling crowd.

Dane's hand inched across the small table and captured Ashleigh's. She looked up and saw the glimmer of what she felt reflected in his eyes. Smiling, she linked her fingers with his.

Silently sipping her drink, Ashleigh studied the lounge's crowd. The ringing of a phone disturbed their comfortable silence. Turning to Dane with a question on her lips, she watched him remove his cell phone from his pocket and answer the call.

Why didn't he get someone else to pick up his calls tonight? she wondered, watching him as he drew a small spiral notepad from his breast pocket and scribbled some notes. *I thought he wanted to be here with me.*

Couldn't he have taken the night off? Made their night special by focusing completely on her?

Dane snapped the phone shut and returned it to his pocket, a look of regret on his face. Retrieving his drink, he took a long swallow. "I'm sorry. That was a client, and I need to leave. I don't want to cut your evening short. Stay. Take the limo. I'll get a cab."

"Isn't that sweet of you," Ashleigh answered. "You're just too considerate."

"Look, I'm sorry." Dane removed his wallet from his back pocket, tossed several bills on the table, and glanced at Ashleigh, then looked away. "I'm sorry. This can't be helped. My client needs me and that's where I'm going to be. Maybe we can pick this up on another occasion."

"And when anyone else needs you? Where are you then?"

"You're talking in riddles. I have no idea what you're trying to say."

"What if Scott needed you and a client called? Would you leave him with the limo driver and go about your business?"

"We've had this discussion before. I'm not going to remind you of the obvious. Now, do you plan to leave when I do or are you going to stick around?"

"When we go out the next time, what happens when your phone rings again? Will you put me back on the shelf until you have a free moment? Does everyone come second to your job? Including Scott? No wonder he's talking and playing with imaginary friends. There's no one in his home who has a minute for him."

"Leave my son out of this." Dane's tone turned frosty. "I told you before, stick to teaching."

Ashleigh's head snapped back as if she'd struck her. With hurt and disappointment, her emotions were out of control. "Not this time, buddy. You're going to listen to me. I care about Scott and I'm going to say my piece for his benefit," she said with more determination than she'd ever displayed. "Scott needs you. Now. Not when you have a free moment. Not when you're finished with clients. He needs you now. The minutes you offer him between your busy schedule are not enough. Give him what he needs and do it now." She released Dane's hand.

"Are you finished?"

"No. You need to reevaluate what's important to you and then put your son ahead of everything." Ashleigh leaned back in her chair. "Now, I'm finished."

Nine

"*Does everyone come second to your job? Including Scott?*" echoed over and over inside Dane's head as he loaded the dishwasher. The haunting image of Ashleigh's hurt and disappointed face filled his mind. For the umpteenth time, guilt made him feel very small.

Shaking his head, he tried to expel Ashleigh's continuous presence from his thoughts. *I've got to get this woman out of my mind. She doesn't know what she's talking about.*

Or does she? Dane's conscience whispered.

He closed and locked the door on the dishwasher, did a final check of the kitchen, and switched off the light before heading out the door. Standing in the family room doorway, he observed Scott on the sofa all into the television. Uneasiness gnawed at Dane's insides.

Granted, he and Scott didn't talk much. That didn't mean they weren't close, right? Had he deliberately pushed Scott away after Helen died? Focused on his career to ease the pain of losing the woman he loved?

How many days had Scott sat watching television or playing alone, while he went into his study and worked? Even before Helen's death, how much time had he truly spent with his son? Had he taken the easy way out and let his wife handle everything related to the household, including raising their son?

What about the most important question? Did Ashleigh's accusations have any merit? Had he been ignoring his son's needs in favor of his career? If so, he'd been a fool, and there was no excuse for that.

No more, Dane decided, stiffening his back, ready to compete with the wonderful graphic images on the television. No more of this. There was still time to gain his son's trust and build a relationship.

I'm not going to be a second-class dad in my child's eyes. Oh no. Dane didn't plan to substitute expensive gifts and toys for quality time with Scott. He wanted to make a major contribution in his child's life.

Dropping onto the sofa next to Scott, he watched the Tiger baseball game with his son in silence for several minutes. At the close of the sixth inning, Dane drew in a deep breath and made his first attempt to communicate. "How's school going?"

"Fine," Scott answered without taking his eyes from the Playstation 2 commercial.

"Anything new going on?"

"No."

Again, Dane observed Scott silently. *This is my son and we have nothing to talk about. I've got to change this.*

"Turn off the television, son. I want to talk to you."

Scott pulled his gaze away from the television and studied his father. His eyes were large with surprise. Dane heard the question loud and clear, although no words were spoken.

"You're not in trouble. This is more about me," Dane explained, softening his voice to reassure his son.

Silence and tension threatened to explode once Scott hit the off button on the remote. He faced his father and waited. After a few minutes, Scott asked, "What's wrong, Dad?"

Subtlety wasn't his strong suit, so Dane took the direct approach and asked the question that topped his list. "Son, do you have a friend that you talk to? Someone who isn't a real person? Maybe an invisible friend?"

Scott's lips moved, but no words came out. His eyes were guarded.

"Tell me the truth. I need to know."

"Yeah," Scott whispered in an embarrassed tone.

"You know that I love you?" Dane stated in a gentle tone. "There's nothing I wouldn't do for you, right?"

Looking away, Scott nodded, plucking at the sofa cushion.

Okay, I've made the big, passionate declaration. What do I do now? he wondered, stroking his chin.

"Do you talk to your friend because you're lonely? Because I wasn't around when you needed to talk?"

Scott shrugged. Eyes focused on the floor, he answered, "Sometimes."

"It's okay." Dane gave his son a pat on the knee and added in a soothing tone, "I haven't been a very good dad lately. If I'm honest, I haven't been a very nice person these past several months. And I hope you'll forgive me. I've done a lousy job as your father. You should have been able to come to me and talk. And I should have been available to listen. I'm sorry, son. My only excuse is sometime after your mom died, I got lost. I've found my way back and things are going to be better."

He watched Dane with those huge, soulful eyes. "Did Miss Davis help you find your way?"

"Partly," Dane answered. "How do you know that?"

"I think she likes you, Dad."

"Do you now?"

"Yeah."

"I've got a question for you. Did you send the letter to the Alonzo Clark show?"

Guilt was written all over Scott's face. His eyes darted away, and he refused to look at Dane.

"I'm not upset, just curious. How did you know all those things about me? How did you know to write all of that? And where did you get my signature?"

"Off your computer. I watched you when you were with Miss Davis. You clear your throat, like a hundred times, and you try to hide how you look at her." A big self-satisfied smile spread across Scott's face.

"Don't smile too much. Things didn't go real well for us."

"Ahhh!"

"That's okay, son. She taught me a few things along the way."

"Like what?"

"That I had to stop hiding and get on with my life. Spend time with you and move on."

Shaking his head, Scott said, "I don't understand."

"Son, losing your mother was the worst thing I ever felt. The only way I knew how to cope was to work. Stay busy so that I wouldn't have time to feel anything. It kept me from feeling sad or good. Unfortunately, that didn't help us."

Chewing on his bottom lip, Scott glanced at his father, then hastily looked away, "You were always busy," came his softly muttered admonishment.

He felt Scott's pain as keenly as if someone had plunged a knife straight into his heart. There it was, confirmation that he hadn't done his job as a parent. Now, it was up to him to fix things.

"You're right. I was too busy. That part is done. I'm not going to be too busy anymore. I'll prove it to you right now. Put on your Reeboks. Let's go in the backyard and practice for your next game."

Scott's eyes grew large and his tone held a mixture of disbelief and hope. "Really?"

"Really." Dane searched the floor for his Nikes. "If you don't move off this couch, I'm first at bat."

Excited, Scott jumped from the sofa and raced around the room, grabbing his shoes off the floor. He shoved his feet inside his shoes, grabbed his baseball mitt from the coffee table and his bat on his way out the door. He stopped inside the doorway to call to his father, "Dad, thanks."

"No thanks needed. I want to do this." Dane held Scott's gaze so that he'd recognize his sincerity.

Scott yelled, "Hurry up."

"I'm coming," he returned.

Rising, Dane glanced out the window overlooking the backyard and a moment of uncertainty gripped him. He wasn't positive he could pull this off, put things right between himself and Scott. But he planned to give it all that was in him. His son deserved the best. And he planned to give it to him.

Several hours later, Dane pushed open the back door. They dropped their gear on the kitchen floor and headed for the refrigerator.

Tossing a strawberry-kiwi juice box at Scott, Dane suggested, "Next time let's get a couple of your teammates and have practice. What do you think? You up for it?"

"Yeah! Thanks, Dad." Scott caught the yellow box, inserted the straw from the side into the juice box, and drank heartily.

"No problem." He removed the lid from his bottle and chug-a-lugged the cold water.

"If Mom was here, she'd get you for drinking from the bottle."

Dane waited for the pain to hit him that always followed when someone mentioned Helen. He felt a dull ache of regret for what might have been. Maybe he was finally doing what Joyce suggested, moving on. "She sure would."

"I miss her," Scott admitted softly.

"So do I. She'd want us to get on with things. To help each other do right. And that's what we're going to do." Dane glanced around the kitchen that Helen had filled with so much love and life. An idea struck him as he watched Scott finish off the juice box.

"Talk to your buddies and see if they want to come by and practice. Try to set it up for this Friday. And if you want, they can sleep over. Let's make a night of it."

"That's tight."

Dane chuckled, pleased by Scott's enthusiasm. "You know, when I did Little League, we practiced together, even without the coach."

Slurping the final drops of juice, Scott stopped and examined his father. "You played Little League?"

"Mmm-hmm," Dane answered with a slow nod of his head. "I was the pitcher. And I was good too."

Eyes round with surprise, Scott muttered, "Wow!"

"Don't act so surprised." Dane leaned against the kitchen counter and folded his arms across his chest. "When I turned eleven we made it to the finals."

"Really?"

"Really." He glanced at his watch. "I'll tell you what, if you hurry and take your shower, I'll dig out my old photo album and I'll show you my Little League stuff."

Scott shot across the room, yelling back at his father, "I'll see you in my room, okay?"

"Okay." Dane strolled from the room, smiling. Things were looking better. Scott was responding to his tentative gestures. In time, they would get back on track. For now, he'd better find that photo album.

~

"All right, are you ready?" Dane asked from the doorway, a photo album tucked under his arm.

Grinning, Scott threw back the covers, tossed his legs over the side of the bed, and patted the space next to him. "I'm ready."

Dane strolled into the room and sat down next to his son. He kicked off his shoes and placed the faded gray photo album in his lap. "Okay, remember, this is really old. So be careful with the pictures."

"Okay."

Opening the book, Dane pointed at a brown-edged shot. "This is the whole team. I was taller than a lot of the kids, so the coach always stuck me in the back." He pointed at a fuzzy face in the last row. "That's me."

Scott leaned closer, frowning over the small shot. "Your face is fuzzy."

He waved away Scott's comment, turned the page, and explained, "There are other shots. You'll be able to recognize me. Here's Clyde. We were best friends. He was the catcher of my pitches. Nobody could beat us."

"Where is he now, Dad?"

"That's a good question." He ran a hand over his hair and made a mental note to call Clyde. "Last time I talked to him, he was practicing medicine in Atlanta."

"That's tight."

"It was."

Scott leaned closer and pointed a finger at a particular face. "Dad, who's this?"

Dane looked a bit closer at the photo and grinned. "That's me."

Scott stared at the picture. Shock and confusion were etched like stone on his face.

"What's wrong?"

Scott's forehead was crinkled, and he bit his lip as if he were trying to figure out a particularly difficult puzzle. "You . . . look . . . just . . . like . . . Tony."

"Tony? Who's Tony?" He'd never heard that name before. Wait a minute, when Scott first started acting odd, he mentioned a Tony was in his room.

A little embarrassed, Scott muttered, "My friend."

"Friend?"

"The friend I talk to when you're not around."

"Your imaginary friend."

Scott nodded solemnly.

Tiptoeing his way through this unfamiliar territory, Dane suggested, "Maybe you just kind of made your friend look like me because what you truly wanted was for me to be with you? Could that be it?"

"I've never seen pictures of you when you were little," Scott answered straightforwardly. "How did I make up your face?"

"Calm down, son. It's just a coincidence. Nothing more. Why are you letting this upset you so?"

"He looked just like you, Dad. Just like you."

"Whatever was going on, you don't need an invisible friend. I'm here for you. Come and talk to me when you need anything. Deal?"

Slowly nodding his head, Scott glanced down at the picture. "Yeah."

"We've had enough excitement for one evening. Time for bed."

～

Securing the blanket over Scott, Dane leaned down and hugged him, noting the look of concern on his face. "Are you all right?"

"Yeah."

"Are you sure?"

"I'm okay, Dad. Really."

Reassuring Scott was his priority. But he wasn't convinced that he'd succeeded. Scott was really upset. Could an imaginary friend look like someone you'd never met but later recognized?

Dane relaxed next to him. "I'll stay until you fall asleep. Okay?"

Scott wrapped his arm around Dane's middle and burrowed his face into his pillow. "Night, Dad."

"Good night, son."

He stayed with Scott until he felt his son's body relax. Dane rose from the bed, crossed the room, and shut off the light. Moving down the hallway, he couldn't shake the sensation that there was more to this invisible friend thing, something that he was missing. Something important.

$\mathcal{T}en$

"Well, folks," Alonzo Clark intoned from the car radio. "We're back with some interesting news. It's been more than three weeks since our Mother's Day winners had their evening out."

Thank goodness, I'm done with you, Dane thought, reaching for the black button on the dashboard console. Scott sat in the front passenger seat, listening intently. Dane returned his hand to the steering wheel; maybe he should let Scott listen to what interested him.

"Here's a little background info for you, folks. After our Mother's Day event, we put photos and a story about the winners' evening out, plus a questionnaire, on the station's Web site. We asked our listening audience to choose the couple they'd most like to see have a second date. And guess what? Ashleigh and Dane received the largest number of votes. Since our listeners find this pairing so interesting, the station and I decided to help this budding romance along. We're going to provide them with a second opportunity to learn more about each other."

Joy bubbled inside Dane as he considered what this chance could do for his relationship with Ashleigh.

"Dad." Scott's smile widened in approval and he repeated with quiet wonder, "You and Ms. Davis got a second date."

Dane's heart lunged with hope; then reality gripped him in its painful vise. He took a deep breath and tried to relax. *That won't happen after the way*

I acted, he thought, maneuvering the car through the quiet suburban neighborhood and onto Telegraph Road's morning traffic.

Ashleigh looked ready to do bodily harm when I left her at Baker's. And I deserved it. He stroked his chin. *Boy, did I act like an ass.*

"Yes, indeed," Alonzo explained. "We're offering our couple a second date. The locale is up to them. We'll pay for the evening, supply the limo, and buy them dinner."

"Dad." Scott called for his father's attention. There was a slight tinge of hope in his voice. "Do you think Ms. Davis will go out with you again?"

Doubtful, Dane thought. When he remembered the unforgiving gleam in Ashleigh's eyes, he felt as if he couldn't breathe. But he recognized how much his son liked Ashleigh, and Scott required an explanation.

Running a finger across his chin, he pretended to consider the question. "Well, son"—he cleared his voice—"to be perfectly honest, my date with your teacher didn't go too well."

Scott's eyebrows set in a straight line over confused eyes and he asked in a soothing but probing voice, "How come? What happened?"

"It's complicated," Dane muttered, hoping to cut off Scott's stream of questions.

"Why?"

Dane drew in a deep breath and answered in a voice that lacked his normal commanding tone, "Your dad did a dumb thing. And I don't think Ms. Davis will forgive me for it."

"Yes, she will." Scott nodded, patting Dane's hand like a little old man dispensing advice. "Ms. Davis always talks to my class about understanding and forgiveness. She says you have to understand what makes people do what they do. If you apologize, maybe buy her some flowers and ask her real nice, I bet she'll listen. She's a good listener, Dad."

Dane drummed his fingers against the steering wheel and confessed another detail. "We had kind of a blowup." That was enough information for Scott. This was adult business.

"Do you like her, Dad?" Scott tilted his head in curiosity and asked in a soft but insistent tone, "Would you like to go out with her again?"

Yeah, he liked her. He liked her more than he cared to admit. Each time they met, he fought the feelings burrowing their way into his heart.

His heart rate increased when he thought of the special way she had of listening to him. It made him feel as if her attention was focused squarely on him. And her eyes, those soft, expressive eyes that filled with a curious empathy, always got to him.

He had felt so in tune with her that day at Scott's game. Not since his wife died had he felt anything like this. Yes, he would like to see Ashleigh again and tell her how her redress forced him to rethink his relationship with Scott and make things right between them. He wanted to thank her for giving him back his son.

"Yeah. I like her." Dane's quiet response revealed more than he wanted. "It would be great to go out again."

"Then why don't you? Call her, Dad," Scott suggested eagerly. "Let her know that you're sorry and that you want to try again."

Could he make Ashleigh understand how vulnerable he felt, how afraid he truly was of losing another person he cared for? How the emotions churning inside him had made him act real stupid. His emotions made him run away from the best thing to happen to him since Helen died.

Would Ashleigh listen to him? Or slam the phone on him?

On cue, Scott added, gazing at his father through clear, intelligent eyes, "You always told me anyone can make a mistake, but you have to be man enough to admit it and be ready to fix it, remember? You got to fix things, Dad. I know you can do it. Just try."

Maybe I can, Dane thought, a surge of confidence boosting him. "You may be right," he answered, nodding. "I'll give her a call after dinner tonight."

"Yes." Scott balled his hand into a fist and jerked down on it. "That's tight."

Hopefully, things would smooth out, Dane thought, switching on his turn signal before making a left into the school parking lot.

～

"Guess what, Ma?" Eve said, smiling at her mother.

"What?"

"Scotty told me you got another date for Mother's Day with Scotty's dad." Eve dug into her plate of spaghetti and meatballs. "Can we go too?"

Oh God, Ashleigh thought, dropping her folk onto her plate. *What have I done in life to deserve this punishment? I thought I was through with all of this contest stuff when Dane Harris walked out on me at Baker's.* "Don't worry about that, just eat your dinner."

"Can we, Ma?" Eve asked a second time.

"I haven't decided anything yet," Ashleigh answered, using her firm teacher's voice to dodge Eve's question.

Eve's bottom lip hung low as she pouted. Ashleigh watched her for a beat, then turned away. This time Eve's emotional blackmail wouldn't change her mind.

She'd had enough of Mr. Dane Harris. He was out of their lives for good. Oh boy, it would be just perfect if she had the power to stick it to Dane in a way he'd never forget, make him feel like a fool the way she felt when he'd left her at Baker's. *That's not the way to think,* she chastened herself. That incident was over, she needed to forget it and move on.

Glancing at her daughter's near empty glass, Ashleigh asked, "Eve, want some more milk?"

"Yes, please," she answered, twirling her noodles around her fork.

Ashleigh rose as the telephone began to ring. She removed the milk from the refrigerator before picking up the cordless phone. "Hello?" she said, filling Eve's glass, then returning the carton to the refrigerator.

"Umm, Ashleigh?" queried the husky, bass voice.

The sound of his voice made her shiver. Shocked, her eyebrows furrowed up and she drew the phone away from her ear, examining it. Was that Dane Harris on the other end of the telephone? Had her thoughts conjured him up?

"Yes," Ashleigh answered in a crisp impersonal tone.

"This is Dane Harris."

"Yes."

He cleared his throat again and asked in a tone that lacked his normal confidence, "Is this a bad time? If so, I can try you later this evening."

"No," Ashleigh answered, feeling a frisson of excitement surging through her. She gathered all her strength to combat her swirling mess of emotions. "I can talk now." She didn't want him calling again. Better to get whatever he wanted to say out of the way and be done with him. He probably wanted to offer her another meaningless apology.

"Let me start with an apology."

I knew it. She sighed, weary of him and his apologies. She felt drained and far too tired for another bout with him.

"I'm sorry for leaving you at Baker's that night. You were right. I was rude, and it was arrogant of me to think that it was okay, especially when it was supposed to be your special evening. I'm sorry."

Ashleigh sank into her chair and pushed her plate of food toward the center of the table. He was sorry. Well, that was nice. He still had walked off and left her. But what difference did it make now?

"Ashleigh?"

"Yes, I'm here."

He cleared his throat again. "Did you hear me?"

"Yes."

"Do you have anything to add?"

"No."

"I got scared," he confessed. "Things were going so good, too good actually, and I used the call from work to run away before I let my feelings get too involved."

For a moment her resolve wavered; then she hardened her heart against his explanation. She understood being afraid to open your heart to someone new. She tightened her grip on the telephone, determined not to give in.

"Can you understand what I'm saying?" Dane asked.

Her lips twisted into an expression of distaste. "No. I can't." Although that wasn't completely true.

"I suppose you've heard about the second date."

"Yes," Ashleigh answered in an empty voice.

"How about it?" His voice dropped a persuasive octave. "Do you think we can make it through another date?"

"We didn't make it through the first," she reminded him, fidgeting with her fork.

"True. But, I really want to try. Would you give us another chance? I know I asked for forgiveness before and screwed up royally but this time will be different. I promise."

Ashleigh smiled. Oh, things were going to end differently, all right. She didn't plan to go anywhere with him.

"Do you understand what I'm trying to say?"

"Actually, no. I don't understand any of this," she answered, trying to control the hand shaking in her lap. "You made yourself pretty clear the last time we were together. Why are you on the other end of my phone? What do you think you'll gain from this conversation?"

"That's just it. I didn't say the right things, do anything right. What I want to know is, what do I have to do to make things up to you?"

"Been there, done that, don't want to do it again, Mr. Harris. That was the second time you went off on me. I don't plan to put myself in harm's way again. The school year will be over in less than six weeks. Then we'll be done with each other. You can't do anything for me, except don't call my house again. Good night." Ashleigh reached for the off button.

"Wait. Wait," shot through the phone from Dane's end of the telephone. The urgency in Dane's voice reached inside her and her hand stilted.

"Please, Ms. Davis, please. Please listen to me before you hang up. My son says that you are the most forgiving person he knows. He told me that you always tell his class to try and understand what the person is going through when they say or do something that you don't like." His voice turned challenging. "Are you telling me that my son was wrong and that you don't listen to explanations?"

"This is low. You're using Scott to make me listen to you."

"No. What my son told me gave me the strength to call you," Dane corrected. "I want us to try to get through a date together. Until I acted like a jackass, things were fun and light. We had so much potential. Please, don't let my stupid stunt end what could be something special for us both."

The memories of those special moments they had shared were pure and clear. Ashleigh had to admit she had enjoyed being with him until he turned evil. She sighed, gnawing on her bottom lip. "Mr. Harris, what do you want me to say?"

"I want you to give me another chance, give us another chance."

"I don't think so."

"Please, just think about it. We had a good time until I screwed up."

The silence that followed stretched, lasting way too long. Ashleigh disliked how Dane believed all he had to do was say he was sorry, turn up the charm, and everything would be magically put right between them. Oh, she wished she could turn the tables on him and teach him a thing or three about tossing out the words *I'm sorry* so capriciously.

As she examined her kitchen, Ashleigh's eyes settled on the clock radio mounted under her cabinet as an idea stuck her. She smiled, plotting Mr. Dane Harris's demise. *I'm going to get my revenge,* she decided.

"Okay. I'll go," Ashleigh answered before she chickened out.

"You will?" Dane asked in stunned wonder.

"Yes. Understand this, I'll do one date. No more."

"Great," he stated in that bass voice. "Thank you."

"Oh. I have one request for you."

"What's that? Just tell me, and I'll do it."

Her expression turned sour at this attempt to win her. "I want to choose the place."

"It's yours."

"Thank you."

"I'll call the station and get everything organized," Dane stated with a return of his usual arrogance.

"No," Ashleigh vetoed hurriedly. Lowering her voice, she said, "Let me. Since I'm going to decide on the place, I should be the one to talk to them."

"Good point. Are you going to give me a hint of what you're planning?"

"No. That would be telling, wouldn't it? It's a surprise."

"What should I wear? Dockers or a suit? Keep in mind, I owe you an evening and I want you to have it with all the extras."

"Mmm. Then dress similar to that night."

"Will do."

After several awkward moments of silence, Dane said, "Ashleigh?"

"Hmm?"

"Thanks for giving me a second chance. I'm going to make everything right between us. You'll see."

No. You'll see, Ashleigh thought. Dropping the telephone in its cradle, she mumbled, "Oh, I've got a little something for you."

"What did you say, Ma?" Eve asked.

"Nothing. Don't worry about a thing."

I'll teach him to use kids to get what he wants, Ashleigh promised, smiling as her plan kicked into high gear. *Oh yeah, I'll teach him.*

Eleven

"You know, we could have watched the game in the station's air-conditioned booth." Dane moved through the bleachers, removing his olive double-breasted suit jacket and loosening his tie. The sun beat down hot against his skin as the first drops of moisture formed under his armpits. "It would be much more comfortable."

Ashleigh looked beautiful and comfortable in a cranberry short-sleeve T-shirt and tan safari shorts. "Oh, but you'd miss the feel of the game. The roar of the crowd." She waved her arm around the massive ballpark. In the other arm, she carried a plush cushion that she tossed on the bench and sank gracefully onto. "It's not a game without hot dogs and beer. We're in the right place."

We're in the right place, if you want to fry under the hot sun or keep everything and everyone at a distance. Dane sat on the end of the bleacher and felt pain shoot through his butt. *This is your payback for treating her so shabbily. She's got you, old boy,* he admitted, examining his surroundings.

When she said she'd give him another chance, he had every intention of wining and dining her, using all of his charm and wit to persuade her to forgive him completely. How in the hell was he supposed to do that on a bleacher in the center of Comerica Park surrounded by a crowd of beer-guzzling baseball fans? Dane gazed at Ashleigh's still features, pondering how long she planned to keep up this particular brand of punishment. Didn't matter, until Ashleigh got tired of dishing it, he planned to keep taking it.

"Oh, look, there's the hot dog vendor." She pointed at the man laboring down the steps with a portable unit and asked sweetly, "Please catch him. I'd like a beer."

"Sure." He signaled the man with a raised hand, ordered two beers and hot dogs. Offering her the food and drink, he caught the slight glimmer of a smirk in her eyes. *Oh yeah, old boy, she's got you and she knows it. All you can do is hang on for the ride and hope you can pull this one out of the fire.*

He polished off his hot dog and rose to sing the National Anthem. The first ball was tossed after the last note was sung and the game began. The White Sox batter came to the plate and hit a line drive that put a man on second.

He shifted on the bench, feeling pain shoot up his leg and settle in his rear end. The game provided an excellent diversion from the agony of sitting on the wooden bleachers.

Dane took off his tie, opened the neck of his shirt, and rolled up his sleeves. They sat silently side by side until the top of the third inning. He tried small talk, but received little or no response until he hit on the topic that was dearest to her heart.

"Is there some rivalry between the teams?" Dane asked, waving a finger at the playing field.

"Oh yeah. It's been that way all season. I love it when the White Sox come to town," she explained, turning to face him as she warmed to the subject. "The games are always high drama to the very end. This is the first time I've had a chance to catch them live." She pointed a finger at home plate. "Oh, look, here comes the next batter."

Watching her closely, he enjoyed her animated features.

"No!" Ashleigh yelled, as a base hit shot past second and the shortstop, putting the White Sox ahead of the Tigers by one.

Amused, Dane hid his smile from her. *She truly is a baseball fan.*

Ashleigh massaged her temples and waited for the next batter. She chewed on her nails, leaning toward the stadium while twisting on the accordion band of her wristwatch.

The bat connected with the ball and the Tigers landed their first solid hit of the game. Unfortunately, the batters weren't able to score a run.

Dane felt the tension knotting inside her. His hand hovered over hers for half a second as he debated whether he should attempt to calm and comfort her. He lowered it and patted her hand reassuringly. "It's still early. Don't let things get you down. It ain't over till it's over."

"I know. I get a little excited when I'm at a game." She giggled, turning to Dane with the first tentative smile he'd received since arriving on her doorstep. "Sorry."

His heart raced and he smiled back at her. "No problem. I love your enthusiasm. I'm predicting that the Tigers will win this game. You'll see." As soon as those words left his lips he realized he'd just put himself in deep trouble. That was stupid. What if the Tigers lost the game? He'd look like a fool and that wouldn't endear him to her at all.

Dane leaned close to her ear and whispered, "Ashleigh?"

"Yes?" Without warning, she turned in his direction and his lips scraped across her cheek. Immediately, she pulled away, blushing bright red. "Sorry," she muttered, eyes darkening with embarrassment.

"That's okay. I-I-I didn't realize I was so close. My mistake," he stammered an apology.

"What did you want?" she asked.

"Nothing. I wanted to ask something about the game." He waved away his question. "But, I forgot what it was."

She nodded and returned her attention to the game.

For the next two hours, the score flip-flopped between the Tigers and the White Sox and back again. At the bottom of the eighth inning, the White Sox were ahead by two and the Tigers were up to bat. Dane could feel the tension in the stadium, zipping back and forth around the ballpark. Ashleigh chewed on her nails, eyes glued to the batter.

A wild pitch and walk put two Tiger men on bases, giving the Tigers a chance to even the score.

The White Sox manager called time out, strolled to the mound with a hand in his pocket, and gave the sign for a new pitcher.

Ashleigh looked at Dane. A worried frown marred her features. "Oh, man, a fresh pitcher will take the Tigers down one after the other."

Dane patted her hand. "Don't worry. I told you the Tigers are going to win."

The White Sox's pitcher struck out the next batter.

"Oh, man," Ashleigh cried.

"The Tigers are going to win."

She studied the scoreboard, shaking her head with a dubious expression on her face. "I wish I had your confidence."

George Lombard stepped up to the plate and took a few practice swings.

She jumped to her feet, cupped her hands around her mouth, and yelled, "Home run. We need a home run."

Lombard took a swing.

The umpire's hand rose. "Strike one."

"Ahh, man," Ashleigh muttered, shaking her head.

"Strike two" came swiftly after the first.

With two batters on plate and two strikes against him, Lombard swung and hit a home run out of the stadium. The statues of Tigers, perched on top of the scoreboard, roared, and the fountain in center field shot water in the air as Lombard rounded third and headed to home plate.

Dane's mouth dropped open and he jumped to his feet. Ashleigh did the same and turned to him with a smile of surprise and happiness on her fuchsia-painted lips. Without taking the time to think about what he was doing, Dane swept her, weightless, into his arms.

For a second, she stiffened, then relaxed, sank into his cushioned embrace, and buried her face against the corded muscles of his neck. Dane felt her uneven breathing against his throat as he held her.

Ashleigh stood so close he could feel the heat from her body. He swallowed hard and his heart thumped erratically against his chest, enjoying the feeling of having her in his arms.

Reluctantly, she stepped from his embrace.

He didn't want to let her go, but he allowed a few inches of space between them and maintained a grip on her arms.

Red color rose from her neck and stained her cheeks. "They're going to win," she declared. "You were right. They're going to win."

"Yes, they are," he whispered.

Her breath felt warm against his face.

Just as I'm going to win you, he promised silently, holding her hand for a moment longer.

∼

Ashleigh sat quietly in the rear of the limo, watching the scenery as they inched their way through the after-game traffic. She glanced at Dane as a knot rose in her throat. How had she ended up in his arms? Granted she had been caught up in the moment, but there was no way she could deny how much she'd enjoyed the moments spent in his arms.

"Ashleigh," Dane began. "Please look at me. Again, I'm sorry about everything. You believe me, don't you?"

Drawn by an invisible string, she faced him. All of the emotions in his heart were open for her to see, breaking down the barriers that she planned to keep her heart safe.

Each time he said her name, unwanted sensations shot through her, wrapping around her like a warm blanket. And she wanted to believe, truly believe, what Dane was saying to her. "Mmm-hmm," she muttered, trying to cover her own confusion without committing to anything.

Sliding across the leather seat, he spoke in a hurried whisper. "I know I've been like a bear for the last several months. I'm sorry. Helen's death hit me hard and I had a lot of anger in me with no way to release it," he confessed. "I'm a man. I'm supposed to be able to handle it all. I had no way to express it."

Ashleigh studied his lean dark-skinned face as compassion for him and his plight surged through her, securing a place in her heart. No matter how much she wanted to dislike him, she couldn't.

Dane cleared his throat and tossed his jacket and tie on the opposite seat, moving closer. "That's another thing I have to apologize to you about. Please forgive me."

She lifted a hand to brush her hair away from her eyes. Spilling his guts wasn't going to make her forget how he left her sitting in Baker's, Ashleigh thought.

"It's been a rough year for me and Scott. I haven't been the parent I should be. You made me realize that. My son deserves the kind of relationship where he can come to me about anything. I don't want him to ever be afraid to talk to me."

She clenched her fists, determined that he would not sway her. Dane couldn't move her with his confessions. Or could he?

"You are the first woman I've had any interest in since my wife died, and it frightened me." The intensity of his deep bass voice refused to be ignored. Dane rubbed a finger back and forth across his chin. "I fought it with everything in me. I wasn't ready to care about anyone again. Although I believe Helen would be happy if I found someone new, I felt as if I was betraying her and her memory. No matter how much I tried to deny my feelings for you, they wouldn't go away. Please say you understand. Do you understand?"

She did, but she'd never admit it to him. *Wait a minute, stop. Ashleigh, you're letting him get to you. Stop it.*

"You've made such a difference in my life. Our lives, mine and Scott's. With your help I realized that I was turning away from my son," he admitted with his deep bass voice. "I don't want to fight anymore and I'm not going to deny that I have strong feelings for you."

Her chest felt as if it would burst and she knew it was time to get everything out. All the pain and embarrassment overwhelmed her, egging her to express her feelings. "Why should I?" she demanded, tossing her hair across her shoulders in a gesture of defiance.

"You must understand—"

"Really?" Ashleigh plunged on carelessly, "Must I? Give me one good reason why I should. You've gone off on me twice, once in private and once in a very public place." She lifted her chin, meeting his gaze straight on. "Each time I forgave you and things got worse. Each time I give you another chance, you disappoint me." Triumph flooded through her when Dane winced at her words. Good. He needed to know how his actions hurt and embarrassed her.

Dane held out his hands, offering an apology. "I'm sorry."

Ashleigh frowned, studying Dane with frustrated eyes. "That's what you don't understand. Sorry isn't enough. You think that saying the words makes everything okay. Well, it doesn't. I don't trust you."

"If it's not enough, what would be? How can I make you trust me again?"

She raised her hands and let them down in her lap. "Honestly, I don't know. Too many things have happened. I'm not sure trust is possible between us."

"Of course it is."

"How? Tell me how when you've promised me this wonderful evening and then you let me down. When I tried to approach you with information about your son, my comments were met with scorn. Have you done anything that would count as positive? What do you think would motivate me to allow you in my life again?"

"I admit that I've done some unpleasant things and that you have every right to feel that I don't deserve a second chance. But something in me tells me that we need to explore the attraction between us." Dane's hand came down over hers possessively. With his thumb, he stroked the back of her hand. "That it might lead to something more, something that we're both looking for. And I'm not going to give up without trying to find out."

His nearness rekindled feelings that Ashleigh was trying to fight. She closed her eyes at the feel of his hand on hers, powerless to resist. A brief shiver rippled through her as she felt her skin prickle pleasantly.

The limo stopped. Ashleigh gazed out the window surprised to find that they had arrived at her house. She withdrew her hand quickly, gathered her belongings, and said, "Good night, Dane."

"Is that it?" He placed a restraining hand on her arm, disbelief in his voice. "You're going to walk away without considering what I've said? Walk away from what we might have one day?"

Ashleigh sighed, tired of going over the same conversation. "There's nothing more to be said."

Shaking off his hand, she pulled the handle and the door flew open. "We blew our chance," she explained, stepping from the limo and heading up the walkway.

Dane followed and stopped her on her porch. "I don't know what else to say that would convince you. But I can tell you this. If you give me this chance, I promise you'll never regret it. There's something going on between us and I've got to—" He shook his head. "No, we've got to explore it. Because I believe if we let this opportunity pass without doing so, we'll never be happy again."

"Are you saying you love me?"

His brown eyes gleamed back at her, clear and true. She turned away, embarrassed by the compelling honesty gazing back at her. "No. I like you, and I think you like me. That's what I'm sure of. Maybe it wasn't our time before. In my heart I believe it is now. And something deep within me tells me if we don't seize this opportunity we'll regret it for the rest of our lives."

Was she being a fool? Letting him persuade her to give him another chance. Would she end up with her feelings hurt and her heart broken? The truth of the matter was, only time would tell the truth.

Dane pulled her close and continued, "Regardless of what came before, I want us to go out with or without our kids and see where our feelings take us. That's as honest as I can be to you."

She looked into Dane's clear, honest eyes and everything that came before lost its importance. Maybe it hadn't been the right time for them. That was obvious because of the way things ended.

Yes, she liked Dane. Always had. She liked him as the concerned father of one of her students. And there had been times when she liked the man, although he always screwed that up. Was she willing to give him one more chance?

"All right. Let's try again."

"I'm saying I want to get to know you and find out if love is possible. Now, what do you want?"

"I want someone in my life I can depend on. Who'll care about me and my daughter. I want to be loved."

"If it's meant to be, then I'm here and I'll be that person for you. But, you've got to open up one more time. Give me this chance and I promise, you'll never, never regret it."

Dane gathered her into his arms and Ashleigh inhaled sharply at the contact. Her soft curves molded to the hard contours of his lean body while his hands explored the hollows of her back. He whispered, "Let's see where this leads."

His lips covered hers. His kiss was slow and exploratory, learning her taste. Raising his mouth from hers, he gazed into her eyes. "You'll never regret giving me this chance."

Twelve

Scott rose from the bed, yawned, and stretched, taking in the tantalizing aroma of frying bacon. Inhaling deeply, he caught the slightest hint of cocoa in the air. "That's tight," he muttered. Dad made hot chocolate.

Tony popped in next to the dresser and said, "Hey."

"Hey." Scott curved his hand into a short wave.

Tony picked up his baseball mitt, shoved it under his arm, and wandered around Scott's bedroom, picking up the framed photo of Scott's mother. "Dawg, we're done," he announced with grim determination. "We've done everything we can." He caressed the frame for several minutes before returning to the dresser. "It's up to your dad and Ms. Davis now."

"Do you think it's enough?" Scott asked. "Will they get together?"

He shrugged. "I don't know."

A worried scowl covered Scott's face. He touched Tony on the arm and asked, "What about you? Are you going to stick around to see what happens?"

Tony shook his head. "Can't. It's time for me to go back."

Shock flew through Scott. "No! We just got to be friends. You need to be here to see how things turn out," he cried, feeling his body stiffen. "You can't leave me."

"I don't want to go," Tony admitted with a catch in his throat. "But, dawg, it's time for me to go back."

"You mean to heaven?"

Tony nodded.

Scott's thoughts filtered back to Tony's sudden appearance in his life. It looked as if Tony would have a sudden departure as well. "What's it like?" he asked, stepping closer, eager to put all the pieces together. "To be in heaven, I mean."

"It's beautiful. It's whatever you want it to be." His brown face lit up as he spoke. "It's warm and has all kinds of people. Everyone likes each other and we laugh together. Nobody ever gets mad or says bad things about each other. It's a good place. I like it. It's my home."

"Is my mom there?" Scott asked quietly.

Tony nodded.

"When you go back—" Scott stopped, chewed on his lip. "Would you tell her I miss her and that I love her?"

"Okay."

"Thanks." Tears welled in Scott's eyes, and he turned away trying to hide them.

"What's wrong, dawg?"

"I'm going to miss you."

"Me too. Me too."

"Why does everyone I like leave me?"

Placing a hand on his shoulder, Tony assured him, "Dawg, nobody's left you."

"My mom did."

"You're wrong." He turned Scott to face him and looked straight into his eyes. "She's in your heart. And that means she's never gone. Remember that."

"Can she come and see me like you did?"

A look of remorse crossed Tony's face. "I'm sorry." He placed a hand on Scott's shoulder and shook it a little. "She can't come back."

"You did."

"That was different. You made a wish and I was sent to help you."

"I won't see you anymore?"

"Not like this. But one day, we'll get together again."

Scott turned away. He didn't want Tony to leave. They had so much fun together. Even though he and his dad were doing better, he'd miss Tony.

"Is there any way you can stay?"

"No."

Resigned, Scott turned to Tony and said, "Don't forget me, okay?"

"I can't. You're like my brother or something."

Grinning, Scott gave Tony a quick, hard hug. "We had fun, didn't we?"

"Yeah. We did."

"So when do you go?" Scott asked in a tiny voice.

"Now."

"Oh, but—"

"Morning, son," his dad called from the doorway, dressed in his bathrobe and slippers. "Breakfast is ready. I thought we might go on a picnic with Ms. Davis and Eve. What do you say?"

Turning to his father, Scott grinned. "That's tight. Let me wash my face and brush my teeth and I'll be right down."

"Okay. I made waffles and hot chocolate, so don't be too long," Dad explained, moving down the hallway.

Scott whirled around and called, "Tony?"

But there was no answer. A sense of emptiness filled Scott as he glanced around the empty room. *I'll miss you,* he thought.

～

Two years later

The sun was bright and the sky clear as Tony raced through Mr. George's vegetable garden.

A bronze and wrinkled face peeked from between the tall stalks of corn. "Hey, little man," Mr. George greeted with a wave, moving into the clearing. "What's going on? You're running around here like you've got some place to be."

"Hi, Mr. George." Tony stopped, grinned broadly, and confessed, "I do. This is the day."

George brushed the dirt from his knees and stared back at Tony. "You mean *the* day?"

Tony nodded solemnly and answered with a touch of reverence in his voice, "Yes."

"Well!" The man drew in a deep breath and scratched the side of his head. "Well! Good for you. I'd say things are going to be truly quiet around here without you."

"Ahh. Come on, Mr. George."

"You know, little man, I'm going to miss you," George muttered, a trace of loneliness in his voice. "I like having you in the garden with me. You've turned into quite a gardener."

"Thanks, Mr. George. I'm going to miss you too," Tony admitted. "But I'm going today. It finally happened."

"I wish you all the best and love." Opening his arms, he instructed, "Give old Mr. George a good-bye hug."

Tony rushed into his arms, wrapped his arms around George's waist, and squeezed him tight. Mr. George was a good guy. He let him help in his garden and he never got upset when Tony made a mistake. Maybe he could start a garden with his brother and sister. Then they could work on it to-gether.

"I'm gonna miss you. But, I'll have a brother and sister." He practically jumped up and down with delight. "I've got a family, Mr. George. I can't wait."

"When you leavin'?"

"Real soon. Maybe today. Maybe even in a few minutes. So, I've got to go. I need to say good-bye to some of my friends."

"Well, good luck." Mr. George held out his hand. "You deserve it. Think about old George every once in a while."

"I will." With a wide happy grin, Tony took George's hand and shook it. "Thanks." He scurried along the edge of the vegetable garden, across the lawn, and on to the house.

Entering through the white iron gates, he paused, taking in everything for what could be the last time. Tears sprang to his eyes. "I'm going to miss everybody," he whispered to himself, feeling the loss of everything that was familiar to him.

"Tony," called a soft, gentle voice.

He turned, saw the figure moving closer, and waited.

"I heard your good news," she said, taking his hand between both of hers. "Congratulations."

"Thank you."

"Are you excited?"

He nodded. "Yeah."

For a moment, she was silent, studying his still face. "Little scared too?"

Tony nodded.

She drew him into her arms and kissed the top of his head, rocking back and forth. "Don't be afraid. You'll do just fine."

"I hope so."

"Trust me. I know." She drew away and looked into Tony's face. "Do me a favor."

"Sure." He tilted his head and asked, "What?"

"Watch over my boy for me. Help him stay out of trouble and make the correct choices."

"I will," Tony promised.

~

"Eve, Scotty, come and meet your new brother." Ashleigh waved them to the hospital bed with her free hand. The other hand held a blue bundle, whisks of dark hair peeping from the top of the blanket. Dane brought up the rear of the small group.

He leaned closer to Ashleigh and kissed her on the lips, then kissed the crown of the infant's head. Taking the seat next to the bed, he refocused on his wife. "How are you?" Dane asked in that bass voice she loved so well.

"Recovering," she answered in an exhausted but happy voice. She glanced at the bundle in her arms and love seemed to fill her for this new life they had created. "But, he was well worth the struggle."

"Does he look like me, Ma?" Eve asked, stretching her neck to see the baby.

Ashleigh considered the question, studying her baby boy. "A little. But, there's a little bit of Scotty too."

"Let me see," Eve demanded, pulling at the bedrails. Dane picked her up and placed her on his hip, leaning close to the bed so that she could see the baby.

"Don't I get a kiss?" Ashleigh asked. Eve leaned close and gave her mother a smack on the cheek. "Thank you, my dear. How about you, Scotty?"

He moved around the bed and leaned in to kiss Ashleigh.

"And thank you too."

Eve's face scrunched up. "Scotty, look at him. He's funny looking. When is he going to wake up?"

"Babies need a lot of rest," Ashleigh explained. "Give him a few months and you'll want him to go to sleep."

Surveying the addition to his family, Scott uttered his first words, "What's his name?"

"We haven't come up with one yet," Dane answered. "Do you have any ideas?"

Shrugging, Scott looked closer at the infant. "He sure is little."

"Yeah, he is. But, he'll get bigger soon enough." Lovingly watching the baby, Ashleigh said, "Sweetheart, what about Anthony for a first name? Then we can call him Tony."

"Anthony Harris. Tony Harris." His lips pursed as he considered Ashleigh's suggestion. "I like it. But what about a middle name?"

Ashleigh pondered Dane's question for a second. "How about Spencer? Anthony Spencer Harris."

Nodding, Dane said, "I like it."

The nurse approached the bed, dragging a portable blood-pressure monitor in one hand and a thermometer kit in the other. "Excuse me, Mrs. Harris. We need to take your vitals. Let me put the baby back in his crib." She took the baby from Ashleigh. The baby let out a yelp of protest at being removed from his mother's arms.

"I'll take him," Dane volunteered, holding out his arms for the baby.

The nurse coddled him close and gazed at the infant. "He is gorgeous. I've never seen a newborn with such beautiful coloring. His skin seems to glow."

The nurse placed the blue bundle in Dane's arm.

Dane gazed at his new son with pride. "He is perfect." His eyes found and held Ashleigh's over the children's head. He mouthed the words "I love you."

"Me too," she muttered back.